d

D0612712

LP
F   Seifert, Elizabeth
Sei   Pay the doctor

          c1990 $15.95
              0002200015275 BE

CASS COUNTY PUBLIC LIBRARY   12-14-90
400 E. MECHANIC
HARRISONVILLE, MO 64701

PAY THE DOCTOR

Also by Elizabeth Seifert
in Thorndike Large Print

So Young, So Fair
The Doctor Takes a Wife
The Doctor Disagrees
A Doctor in the Family
The Doctor Makes a Choice
Katie's Young Doctor
Doctor with a Mission
Bachelor Doctor
Doctor's Destiny
The Doctor's Second Wife
Doctor in Judgment
The Rival Doctors

This Large Print Book carries the
Seal of Approval of N.A.V.H.

PAY THE DOCTOR

Elizabeth Seifert

Thorndike Press • Thorndike, Maine

CASS COUNTY PUBLIC LIBRARY
400 E. MECHANIC
HARRISONVILLE, MO 64701

0 0022 0001527 5

BE

Library of Congress Cataloging in Publication Data:

Seifert, Elizabeth, 1897–
  Pay the doctor / Elizabeth Seifert.
    p. cm.
    ISBN 1-56054-062-1 (alk. paper : lg. print)
    1. Large type books. I. Title.
[PS3537.E352P39   1990]   90-45017
813'.52--dc20   CIP

Copyright © 1966 by Elizabeth Seifert.
All rights reserved.

Thorndike Press Large Print edition published in 1990
by arrangement with Spectrum Literary Agency.

Cover design by James B. Murray.

The tree indicium is a trademark of Thorndike Press.

CASS COUNTY PUBLIC LIBRARY
400 E. MECHANIC
HARRISONVILLE, MO 64701

This book is printed on acid-free, high opacity paper. ∞

*For Dan and Catherine Forney,
good friends for a long time*

CHAPTER 1

"Dr. Battle. Dr. *Battle!*" The enunciator droned persistently. "Dr. Aaron Battle."

"Answer the thing, will you, Battle?" the nurse asked plaintively. "I'd like to hear some other name."

"So would I," muttered Aaron. He glanced at the med student. "Carry on, will you?" he asked courteously.

He pushed through the curtains to the corridor and the house phone fastened there to the gleaming tile wall. "First place," he growled to himself, "I'm a doctor in name only. Second place, since I'm already doing E.R. duty, what can they possibly want?"

"Battle here," he said briskly into the phone.

He came back to the cubicle and the med student — it was the poor guy's first night on Emergency. Aaron, just about to finish his intern duty, could easily, and vividly, remember when he had been in this chap's shoes and embarked upon what the hospital called the "confidence course."

Well, a confidence course might work for the army . . .

Their patient with the head wound was struggling into consciousness. Both the senior med and the nurse were looking inquiringly at the "experienced doctor," there to supervise the student.

"Oh yes!" said Aaron. "It was Medicine. I'm supposed to be on the floor there, you know? An attending is sending a girl in with migraine; he wants to put her into traction — see if it will help." He examined the patient's eyes, bending close.

"Do you have to go upstairs?" asked the nurse.

"Will traction help migraine?" asked the student.

Aaron smiled at them both. "If an attending physician, after a history of fifteen years of migraine, thinks traction will help his patient, who am I to question? It won't hurt her, that's for sure. As for going upstairs, Miss Polley — Dr. Pasco is due in here any minute now. I am assigned now to E.R., so obviously I cannot be on Medicine as well. I've handled that problem. Dr. Pasco will be coming in to cover for me here for a few hours."

"But you're not going up to Medicine."

Aaron smiled. *"That's* right!"

"You've got a date," said the nurse.

"Tag this fellow and send him upstairs. I think a night's sleep and six stitches will fix him up fine. What's next?"

"Take your pick, Doctor — another crash injury, a third-degree burn, a heart attack — "

"Yeah, yeah," said Dr. Battle. "And a baby about to precipitate. Let's get the lead out, shall we?"

The injured man was taken away. The next patient came in — an old, old woman, disoriented, found wandering on the street, and brought to the Emergency Room of the hospital. Dr. Battle talked swiftly to the woman and to his med student. He even managed to say a word about his "date" to the nurse. All the time he was watching the patient; he checked on the student's reading of pulse and pressure . . .

Promptly at seven Dr. Pasco strolled in. Aaron said he had timed things nicely; they were just between patients. . . .

"And he'll do something nice for you sometime," contributed the nurse.

"I already have," Aaron called over his shoulder. "Or he'd not be here."

He disappeared, and the nurse fetched an orderly to take their patient to a ward for observation. "Battle's O.K." she offered. "I'm dubious about interns marrying — "

9

"That why you're free and single?" asked Dr. Pasco. He was a bold one.

Miss Polley straightened. She was forty and had "raised" many an intern. "I've only found one intern as smart as Battle," she said quietly. "And he's spoken for. Get your next patient, Doctor?"

The intern looked ruefully at the student and then at the nurse. "I'll get him," he said meekly.

Freed of his duty in the Emergency Room, Aaron Battle sprinted for the interns' dormitory and his own particular cubby there. This was a corner in the large room, where he had a bed, a locker, a small desk with drawers. At the time there were three other men in the room. One was trying to sleep; the other two lounged in the chairs afforded, one to each man, their feet and legs propped on the beds.

"Date, Battle?" asked one of these chaps, a small, dark man. He wore a T shirt and ducks; a fresh jumper was on a hanger hooked to the foot of his bed. He was on call.

"Date," Aaron agreed. He checked his watch with the clock on the wall. "I have to meet Laurie's brother and his wife — at the airport — in forty-five minutes."

"You'll not make that."

"Yes, I will. Tommy's lent me his car."

"Pasco said he was covering for you."

"He is." Aaron pulled a shirt from a drawer and took his suit from his locker.

The second man got up and selected a tie for him — one of three. Aaron pulled up his trousers, sat down to put on his shoes and tie the strings.

"They're coming for the wedding," he said a little breathlessly. Spots of bright color burned in his cheeks.

"Whose wedding?" asked the small dark man, Leon Boccardi.

"Mine," Aaron obliged him, fumbling with the button of his right cuff. "And Laurie's," he added, his eyes smiling.

"She know what line of work you're in?"

"Lay off, Boccardi," urged the second man.

"Laurie's known me for a year," said Aaron quietly, tucking in his shirttails. But his mind, his heart, his nerves were not quiet. When he thought of Laurie — the pretty littleness of her, her shining yellow hair, the color that lay below her white skin, her blue eyes . . .

"And she knows you're an intern," Boccardi persisted.

Aaron took a deep breath and attacked his dark hair with vigorous swipes of his brushes. "Ever date a girl more than once and not tell her you're an intern?" he asked mildly. "Sure she knows — that I've been one. But by the end of this week — by the time of the wedding — I'll not be an intern any more."

"Shakes you just to think of it." drawled Boccardi.

It did. "To stop being an intern?" asked Aaron innocently. "Of course that shakes me."

"Aaagh," growled Boccardi.

Aaron's eyes twinkled. "I waited until I was through the thing before I took on marriage," he pointed out.

"But you didn't have the guts to take on a residency," Boccardi persisted.

"I haven't the *money* to take that on," he corrected.

"Someone," spoke up Joe Calloway, who had listened to the interchange, again tipped back in his chair, his eyes on the ceiling, "somebody told me you were recruited your third year at med."

Aaron had been. In his junior year at medical school, on the promise of his grades and performance, he had been assured of a residency along with an offer of internship. That had been too early to judge if he had any real competence with patients, but —

"I was recruited," he admitted. "But I still can't afford a residency."

"Because of a girl," said Boccardi disgustedly.

Aaron checked his pockets — wallet, keys,

12

handkerchief. "Because of a *girl!*" he agreed. He couldn't be happier, unless it would be to see Tommy Dreiserward show up with the keys to his car.

He started for the door. "I suppose you're going to spend your honeymoon," drawled Boccardi, "studying for your licensure exams?"

In spite of himself Aaron's step slowed a very little.

"He'll pass 'em," said Tommy from the doorway. Thank Pete, he'd shown up. "Battle never flunked an exam in his life."

"But this could be the first time," Aaron assured him soberly.

The two men started along the hall, toward the tunnel to the parking lot. Intern and assistant resident, their pace was one acquired and used habitually in the hospital. A fast walk, steady — long-legged, ground-covering.

"You know?" Aaron said to the blond man who was his friend. "All of a sudden I'm panicky about those exams."

"You shouldn't let Boccardi get to you."

"It isn't hard. He uses a long needle. But the exams — "

"You'll pass them," said Tommy, pushing through a glass door.

"Not without some heavy study, I'm afraid. I've been away from the books for a year,

Tommy. I hope Laurie won't be too upset if I do some swatting on the honeymoon."

They greeted a staff attending who came toward them and passed them. "I wouldn't even bother to take the books to that affair," said Tommy. "How long will you be gone?"

"Just the weekend. You know — no money, less time."

"Then *don't* take them!"

"But — "

"Study before and after — if you think you must. And don't worry any time about the exams. You have made good grades; your record as an intern is good — "

"So?"

"Well, medical schools base their teaching, and hospitals their doctor training, on what the state board wants from the medics it licenses. Isn't that true?"

"You're licensed. I'm not and wouldn't know."

"I have to be licensed to be a resident. You have to be licensed to practice — and your diploma, your successful completion of your internship, should do the trick. Certainly your unfitness could have been certified by now. Which it hasn't been."

"But I still have to take the exams. *And* pass."

"Things could be tougher. You might have

14

been foreign-born."

Aaron grinned. "Little ray of sunshine, you are. And I think I will take an armful of those books on our honeymoon."

"Have you anticipated how Laurie is going to react to her first three days of married bliss spent among all those thick volumes and bulging notebooks?"

"*You* think she won't like it."

"Judging from my bride, she won't like it violently. But then Carol hates — repeat, *hates* — everything about medicine."

"That must make it nice for you." Aaron knew it did not make it nice for Tommy. The swell guy had a tough time with such a wife.

"There's one theory," said Tommy, slowing as they approached the outer door. He fished for his keys. "It is that I am a resident surgeon in order to get away from home and — quote — do things on my own." His heavy-lashed eyes lifted to Aaron's face.

Aaron chuckled. "Your feet have the calluses to prove it, too" he said "Thanks, Tommy. I'll be careful of your car, and I will admit that I'm a little worried about Laurie's feelings over the study — but not much. Not about Laurie."

Tommy clapped his hand on Aaron's shoulder, then watched him cross the parking lot to the old T-bird which was the resident's pride

15

and joy. Aaron would take care of it — Aaron would pass his licensures in a breeze — Aaron should not be giving up his hospital training. Especially not if Laurie was the "understanding sort." She was, Tommy knew, a very nice girl. And maybe she was understanding.

By midnight, of course, interns' obligations being what they were, Aaron was back at the hospital, on call, but trying to get some sleep before he was due up on the medical floor the next morning. Tommy's car was safely back in the parking lot and the keys returned to his hand.

"Get some sleep," the resident told his friend.

"I will do."

"Are you going to be in o.r. tomorrow?"

Aaron shrugged. "Duty on Medicine doesn't afford many goodies like that."

"Weren't you the one to find the lesion in that old man's chest?"

"I saw it. Others did too. Barr found the tumor."

"And tomorrow he will take it out."

"Yes — and return us an uncontrolled diabetic with all the post-operative trimmings."

Tommy laughed. "Go to bed. And be bright and bushy-tailed in case you are invited up to surgery."

16

Aaron did not expect any such invitation. But at three, when he was called upstairs to give a pain pill, he stifled his routine irritation at the head nurse and looked in on the diabetic. The old duck was a true character; he had entered the hospital in acute acidosis and was most recalcitrant about taking his insulin or eating — or both. The lesion having been found, his chest surgery was necessary and would be interesting. Aaron wished he could observe. Because he still hoped, one distant day, to be a surgeon. During the past year he had particularly enjoyed his weeks on surgery.

"Go to sleep and don't dream," he admonished himself when he came downstairs again and fell into bed.

But the next morning . . . Had Tommy — *could* Tommy have — pulled wires? In any case, Dr. Battle was instructed to go to Surgical and observe the surgery on old Mr. Clatto. "He's your baby," the head told the intern. She grinned at Aaron.

Baby or no, Aaron was glad to have any reason to go up to surgery. He checked on his jumper — clean! — and took off. If the great and wonderful Barr were operating . . .

He was. The schedule said so. Aaron checked in with the nurse at the desk; he threaded his way down the corridor between carts, doctors, nurses, and gear. He took a gown and mask and eased his way into the small amphitheater.

There were a dozen other observers in the gallery. Scrubbed and ready, Dr. Miller was looking things over. He was to be the second surgeon. Sam Miller, fellowship resident, and as first-class as doctors come.

Marshall, the surgical supervisor, came in, but she was not going to work. She cast an eye — a bright and pretty eye! — over everything in the room. The anesthetist was already at work — and what a nice job he must be having! What with diabetes, chronic bronchitis, the man's sixty-three years ....

A half dozen students came in and found seats; down on the floor Barr had entered, two more nurses, and Tommy Dreiserward. Aaron leaned forward; he had never seen Tommy work. Of course, on this he would be only — what he was — second assistant surgical resident. But he was down there, scrubbed, and a member of the team. Aaron stared hard at the capped, masked, gowned, and booted figure of his friend. It was so easy to picture himself in those wrinkled, loose garments. Only a frustrated surgeon would ever call them beautiful, but to Aaron Battle, days away from leaving the hospital scene, Tommy was garbed in the best of Saville Row.

18

The surgery proceeded. Sam Miller opened the chest, Tommy retracted — the tumor was located. Dr. Barr removed it and explored the entire pleural cavity.

There was some talk on the floor but no lecture. However, Aaron could hear enough to be sure that the eminent chest surgeon was pleased both with the diagnosis and its confirmation by surgery.

Finished, and stepping back to let Dr. Miller close up, the Chief of Thoracic Surgery glanced up at the students in the gallery.

"I would advise a close perusal of this man's history and chart," he said crisply, "including the record of the surgery done. And if Dr. Battle is present, I would like to see him in my office as soon as convenient."

Aaron was too stunned to be absolutely sure that Tommy did nod his head. But how had the guy known? Did Dr. Barr talk these things over with his most junior resident?

Well, *as soon as convenient* meant right away! So Aaron scrambled to his feet and was out of the place *instanter*, a word his father had used, but which Aaron had not come to understand completely until he was an intern. He moved fast!

Dr. Barr's office would be on Thoracic, but Aaron had to ask the nurse where to locate it.

"You're to wait," the young woman said.

"This was all set up, wasn't it?"

She smiled at him.

"I suppose everything will be all right on my own floor?"

"You could check." She indicated the phone.

Aaron shook his head. "I'll wait." he decided. He went down the hall to the indicated door. He liked the smells on Surgical better than he did those on Medical. Glory to Patsy, yes! And the sights and the sounds too.

Of all his intern duties, Aaron had liked Surgical best, though he had never been assigned to Thoracic. That's why he didn't know where Barr's office was.

Now! Did he go right in? Or find a place to wait in the corridor?

"Go in and pretend you're Chief," said the floor head, passing him. She was a cute one. Young. Her skirts fanned her knees in the prettiest way!

Aaron turned the knob of the flat brown door and went into the Chief's office. It was a corner room, with wide windows that looked, one way, across the city and, the other, down at the park, green with summer and flower-bed bright. The doctor's big desk sat between the windows. Around the room there were shelves, packed with books. An X-ray scanner — a comfortable couch — two paintings on the wall, one of a ship, the other of a sunlit hill.

Aaron chose the chair which faced the desk and wondered what the great, the wonderful Dr. Barr could want of him. The only possibility was a word of commendation for a lucky diagnosis. Which would be nice, but would scarcely justify all this time away from his duties. Still . . .

Aaron leaned back in the chair — if it had a high back, he'd go to sleep! — and thought about Laurie, counting again the days, and the hours, until their wedding. She'd been cute last night — all fluttery over her brother's arrival. The man, Robert, was ten years older than Laurie and inclined to be — well . . .

So he *was* doing well as an engineer! So he had been able to take a job right out of college. So . . .

Aaron lifted his shoulders and told himself not to start his marriage with an even unspoken row with his in-laws. He —

Behind him, the door opened, and Dr. Barr came in. He was wearing a lab coat over his dark-blue trousers and vest, and he greeted Aaron cordially, telling the intern that he was Dr. Barr.

"Yes, sir, I know."

"You do, eh?" Dr. Barr went around his

21

desk, sat down, and studied a memo on the blotter. He picked up the phone and spoke to someone named Mary. "Hold the calls for a little, will you?" he asked.

Then he looked at Dr. Battle. The Chief of Thoracic Surgery was a large man with a square-cut brush of iron — gray hair, a smoothly tanned skin, steady eyes behind dark-rimmed glasses, a straight-lipped mouth. "Where did you do your surgical intern work, Battle?" he asked.

Aaron told him, adding, "I like surgery."

"You do, eh? Didn't get to chest, though."

"No, sir. I've observed, of course. Both as a student and as intern."

"Dr. Gage?"

"Yes, sir. As classes, we watched heart surgery. And of course I have observed you, and you've lectured. I observed this morning." Aaron's cheeks warmed. Dr. Barr knew *that!*

"I was pleased to learn that an intern had detected that man's lesion."

"I was lucky."

"Maybe. And observant." The doctor leaned back in his chair and studied the young man across the desk from him.

Aaron Battle had a pleasant face, not excessively handsome. His hair was dark brown, and his eyes were gray; they looked light behind his heavy, dark lashes. His teeth were good and his shoulders broad.

Dr. Barr nodded at what he saw. "Being observant is just about the best quality a doctor can have," he commented. "You're an intern now. What are your future plans, Doctor?"

Aaron was well aware that he was talking to a *big shot.* They didn't come any bigger than Daniel Barr. And Aaron was about as impressed as a man on the first rung of his professional ladder could be. That he should be sitting here, the center of interest to such a man . . .

He lifted his chin. And he spoke staunchly. "I am going into private practice, sir."

Now he was looking into doctor eyes. Intent, alert, impersonal. "Are you going to practice surgery?" Dr. Barr asked politely.

Aaron smiled. A little. "No, sir," he said quietly. "I'll be doing general practice. G.P."

"I see. Can you afford private practice?"

"No, sir," said Aaron again. He felt on firmer ground, having explained all this several times to his friends and to himself. "Not if you mean equipping an office and the rest of it. I have no money at all. My plan is to work several hours a day as a physician in an industrial plant — I already have that job. Contingent upon my licensure, of course." He smiled at Dr. Barr who nodded, unsmiling.

"Then," Aaron continued, "I'll fill in at an office with three other doctors. Do work-ups for them, leg work — and I hope, gradually, to acquire my own list of patients."

"Yes," said Dr. Barr. "But can you do this, Battle? I mean, is it what you want?"

Aaron was familiar with that question too. So the answer came readily and firmly. "I have to earn my way, sir. It is entirely a matter of money."

Dr. Barr nodded. "With your record and your powers of observation — you say you like surgery — I would think that you should now be doing some residencies in surgery. Isn't *that* what you want to do?"

"It's what I want to do, all right," Aaron conceded. This part of the argument still was not firmly in hand. "Rather, it's what I'd very much like to do. But the thing is, I cannot live on a resident's pay. My family has helped me through medical school. I've just barely managed this last year. Now I can't ask them for any more help and they can't give me any more, because they need a chance to help my younger brother. I'm afraid this must be a familiar story to you, sir. To me, of course, it is as significant as if no other medic had ever had to trim down his dreams to fit what can be accomplished."

"It is a familiar story," Dr. Barr agreed.

"Too familiar. But the facts of medicine are these, Dr. Battle; there is too much to learn — Don't you want to specialize?"

"Yes, of course I do."

"As a surgeon?"

"Yes, sir."

"Your record has been excellent, Doctor. And as an intern you were very good."

Aaron shook his head. "I mostly remember the too-tight bandages, the mistaken diagnoses, the excessive sedation — "

Now Dr. Barr laughed. "You know? That's what I remember of my rotating internship too."

"I'm just surprised that any good word about me got put down on paper."

"It did. In fact, Battle — in talking over your case — You see, we knew you had not applied for any residency. The Chief of Staff told me that we should try to get your course straightened out."

"Well, I appreciate that, sir, but — "

"I don't believe I'll overinflate your ego, Battle — I wouldn't risk it with some of the other interns, but then, I'd not have occasion to say to *them* what I'll say to you. Your evaluation reports say you have a good relationship with the patients, that you are both thoughtful of them and conscientious. This leads us to think that you seem to have not only medical ability but what many, what most, doctor-candidates seem to lack — a fine sense of social responsibility."

Now this was praise indeed. How had Barr . . . ? The lesion discovery, of course. When it came up, Barr had asked a question and been answered. Favorably. Though that lack of responsibility had struck Aaron too. He had first marveled at it when a senior med. He couldn't understand why such men ever wanted to study medicine. Gradually he had come to suspect why, but —

"The Chief and I," Dr. Barr was saying, "think that dedication and mercy are the very hardest things there are to teach you young men. You seem to have it, Battle. Perhaps it was in your genes. Though I would like to think that our faculty taught some of it to you."

Aaron swallowed the hard spot in his throat. Here was a man he could die for! "The faculty here is very good, sir," he said politely. "But — though I am sorry to disappoint you — I still think, at this time, that I must work in private practice."

"One doctor in a hundred," mused Dr. Barr sadly.

"I plan to do my residencies later," Aaron hastened to say.

"You won't do it," said Dr. Barr. His

mouth was a grim line.

"I hope that I will, sir," protested Aaron.

"If you have any thought, or hope, or dream, of ever being a surgeon, you should go on right now as a resident. With your internship just completed, now is the time to complete your training."

Aaron knew that Dr. Barr was right. But . . . "One year's residency, as second assistant, wouldn't do much good."

"The first step you took as a baby didn't exactly qualify you to run a race," said Dr. Barr crisply. "But it was a start and a first year as resident would be a start to better things. Now I will grant there are faults in our system of training future doctors. When Flexner cleaned our house he didn't quite go far enough. Our medical schools are attached to universities, who should know about teaching and training in every field they embrace. But at this time the universities stop short when they give a diploma to certify graduation from medical school. The intern training, the resident training, is not the university's responsibility, and it should be.

"But the fact remains, Battle, that a diploma from medical school does not qualify you, in most states, even to take your licensure exams. Your one year as rotating intern — ten minutes ago you said that you had no firsthand knowledge of chest surgery. So — what do you have? Three months of Medicine, three months in Pediatrics? Did you do any Orthopedics? Were you in the Psychiatric wards? How about Neurosurgery?

"No! Though you did learn some medicine. You know more now about diagnosis and treatment than you did a year ago. But, since the universities don't take, or have, the responsibility of saying when a medic is trained, we teachers, we staff men, have to do what we can, Battle, to persuade promising doctors to go on and train themselves, at least in one line of medicine. I so urge you. I would fail my profession if I did not do this.

"I know money is an item with you. It is with most starting medics. What with the shortage of doctors, this situation could be greatly improved. Grants should be made for you beginners. But the foundations say a medic must do research and write some papers to qualify for their assistance. That's all very fine, except who feeds him while he does his research and while he writes his papers?

"It's a fouled-up system, and I wish, right here and now, we could straighten it out. Maybe sometime we shall. But that won't solve your problem, will it?" He brushed his hand across his jaw, took off his glasses, and shook them at Aaron. "I do run on, don't I?"

he asked in a fatherly tone.

"It's a big problem, sir."

"Yes, it is. And it isn't an easy one to solve, it hasn't been. Do you, perhaps, know a resident on my service, a man named Sam Miller?"

"Oh yes, sir," said Aaron, his face brightening. "I know him and like him. He has been a great help to me this past year."

"Yes, he's a fine boy. And an excellent doctor. But do you know, Battle? I can remember when Miller was in exactly the spot you are in now; he talked the same as you do — he could not afford to do his residencies, he said; he must practice for a time . . .

"But now he has a fellowship, and he is assured of a fine Staff position here or in any medical center where he might choose to work."

"Yes, but there still were those years of residency. One, two, three of them — "

"Six," said Dr. Barr.

"And *then* he got a fellowship on which a man can live."

Dr. Barr nodded and shrugged. "If you were interested in research, Battle, the thing might go more quickly for you. I mean, the money would come in sooner."

"But not during my first year or two, would it, sir?"

"No. But after — say — three years, if you

29

did some good work — "

"I wouldn't. Now, research is fine. I know all its good points. But it just isn't for me, Dr. Barr. And, anyway, I couldn't manage those first three years."

For a minute Dr. Barr sat silent, tapping his folded glasses on the back of his left hand. Then he snapped them back in place and leaned toward Aaron.

"Tell me," he said. "Is there a girl in all this?"

Aaron took a deep breath. He had hoped they could continue their discussion on a solely professional basis. "Yes, sir," he said quietly. "There is a girl."

He was twenty-seven years old, and he had every right to have a girl in his life, to want one. He would not let even this great doctor tell him that he didn't have such a right.

"What about her?" Dr. Barr was asking. "How does she feel about your career?"

"I don't know, sir. I mean — we haven't talked very much about it in your sense. Of course she knows that I've been an intern this past year, and we've made our plans together — for my job and the office work, you know. We are going to be married next week."

"I see. But she doesn't know what you are giving up?"

"A residency, you mean?"

30

"I do mean that. Because it's too bad, you know. To make that sacrifice."

"I suppose you're right, sir."

"I think I am. I wish you would do some thinking about it too."

Aaron stood up. He was being dismissed.

"I wish you would talk to Dr. Miller. Will you?"

"Yes, sir. Of course."

"You do that. And thank you for stopping in, Battle."

Aaron smiled uncertainly and went out into the corridor.

Miller was a fine example to set before any beginning doctor. Aaron would like very much to be like Sam. He'd even like to try — except that with Miller there wasn't any wife, such as Aaron would have in a week. His finger shook a little as he reached for the elevator button. So deeply in thought, he was completly unaware of all that was going on in the corridor where he stood. A cart came down the hall with an orderly carrying the glucose bottle. Two post-operatives walked gingerly — a nurse hurried . . .

And Dr. Miller himself, still in his o.r. scrub suit, went into one of the wards. Miller was a swell guy and a fine doctor. They didn't come any better! But —

Aaron stepped into the elevator. Of course

he would talk to Miller. Though it couldn't change things. He wished — almost wished — he had not found the lesion in that old man's lung. Someone else would have seen it — surely.

And then Dr. Barr would not have talked to Aaron in such a disturbing way as to make him feel that he was failing the whole medical profession, wasting his years of study. Or would he, perhaps, have talked to him anyway? He or some surgeon would have.

Aaron had liked such surgery as he had done during his internship. And he had had a few lucky breaks. A few others down in emergency surgery . . . He had, from the first, always opted for surgery on any questionnaire. . . .

So the staff would have been watching for him and noticing that he was not applying for a residency.

On Medical, Aaron checked with his resident, said, yes, old Mr. Clatto had survived the surgery. Mhmmm, they'd found a tumor. Oh, not too big — he'd be back with them, griping and raising hell within a too short time.

"We've three new admissions," said the resident. "Work them up, will you?"

Aaron went to the desk for the charts, thinking how differently he felt in these last days of his internship from the way he had sweated out his first ones. Then three admissions on a busy morning would have put him into a flap. Here he had a diabetic, a probable endocrine disturbance; the third was referred by a specialist in hematology. . . .

Calmly Aaron went to work.

The diabetic was a talkative woman; she told Aaron she was borderline, which he doubted, and he managed to get the chart going and her tests ordered without hearing too much of all she said about her four pregnancies.

He paid close attention to what he was doing, but he still was conscious of the clouds which his talk with Barr had blown up on his horizon.

Barr.

That morning in surgery, his hands graceful, strong, and quick. The red gloves stretched thin and shining upon them as he held a scalpel poised. Aaron stole a glance at his own hands, scrubbed clean, with square-cut nails. His fingers, too, were long and spatulate. Automatically, as he thought, he flexed them the way he had seen Miller and other surgeons do habitually. As a pianist does, or a violinist . . .

Aaron completed the diabetic's history, and on his way to lunch he stopped to look at the hysterical patient they were keeping in a deep sleep. She was in good shape. Probably by tomorrow evening she could come out of it, quieted, rested, ready to handle such problems as she might have.

He went down to the cafeteria and ordered a sandwich and a glass of milk. He sat at the counter and answered those who spoke to him — all the time continuing to think.

He had to disagree with Barr. No, not *disagree*. For one thing, Barr was dead right in all he said. But — the thing was —

"Hear you were up on the well-worn carpet this morning," said the intern who took the stool next to him.

"Me?" asked Aaron in exaggerated surprise.

"I hear you got called out of o.r. for sneezing."

Aaron laughed. "Dr. Barr wanted my advice on something."

"I'll bet."

Aaron cut his sandwich and picked up a section of it. The ham could have been thicker. "He was riding me for not applying for a residency," he admitted.

"So?" said Harry Berkel. "You surely know you should have applied."

"Well — "

"Look, Battle. Who are you to disagree with Barr?"

Aaron shook his head. "I've been asking myself the same thing, Berkel, but the facts don't change."

Joe Calloway slid on the stool beyond Berkel's and had to be told what the discussion was about. Berkel told him dramatically. "Battle thinks he can't afford a residency," he concluded.

"We can't any of us afford 'em," said Calloway. "But it's still something we have to do."

"I don't agree," said Aaron stubbornly.

"If you don't agree, you'll end up in some small-town practice," Dr. Calloway predicted. "You'd better do some, Battle."

Aaron stubbornly said nothing.

"Look," Berkel attempted. "Aren't you pals with Tommy Dreiserward?"

"Yes." Tommy was going to be Aaron's best man. Next week.

"Well, then! He's managing this year's residency, and he's going to manage next year's — "

"I'm not Tommy," said Aaron shortly.

"Damn right you're not. For one thing, you're a better doctor than he is."

"Agggh!" said Aaron, draining his milk glass.

"Ask anybody. Ask Tommy. And besides — Tommy, has a bitch of a wife."

Aaron tried to think of something to say. But Tommy's wife was just what Berkel said she was. She worked. She freely went on dates while Tommy worked. She made her own money and spent it as she pleased. She —

"If Tommy can make it, you should be able to."

"There are times when Tommy doubts if he will make it," said Aaron. "A wife against a man's work makes it harder than it should be."

The other two interns nodded. "He'll make it in spite of Carol," decided Calloway. "Anyway, more will depend on the staffs he gets. They come good and bad, I understand. He'll have to take the sheep with the goats."

Aaron stepped down from the stool. "Me, too," he pointed out.

"Yes, you will," agreed Berkel.

"Yes, I *would*," said Aaron softly as he walked away.

He spent the afternoon admitting new patients. At four he went off duty, but he was due back at twelve, so he must sleep part of the time. He thought about seeing Laurie, but she had planned an evening with her family; she had not seen her brother in four years. And at best Aaron could not have given more than an hour.

So he went down to the library to read up a little on endocrinology. He played two fast games of ping-pong with Tommy Dreiserward who, a little breathlessly, asked him what Barr had had to say. Aaron told him. "And you know what I answered," he added, in a way to shut Tommy up, though the man's blue eyes studied his friend.

Tommy got called, and as Aaron started for the cafeteria and his dinner, Sam Miller caught up with him. Not to Aaron's surprise.

But he liked Miller and readily agreed to eat with him. They filled their trays with pork chops and mashed potatoes and broccoli and took them to a small table. Sam smiled at Aaron, who faced him, not smiling.

Dr. Miller was not a handsome man; in fact, he was homely, though in a pleasant sort of way. His skin had the pallor of one who spends his days in the operating room or on the surgical wards. He had a large mouth, but one which laughed easily. There were pouches under his eyes, but those eyes were keen and ready to smile. People trusted Sam on sight. Aaron trusted him.

They spoke first of old Mr. Clatto, who was responding quickly and well to his surgery, Sam told Aaron. "But, geez, does he have a disposition!"

Aaron laughed and told some of the things which Clatto had done on Medicine. He lied about taking his medication; he hid his food in the slops can. "And no coke machine is safe from him, dime or no!"

"I sometimes wonder why we work so damn hard to save guys like that," Miller mused. "While on the other hand — we had two cases this afternoon — this was with Gage. A husband and wife, Battle. Sixty-seven and sixty-five. Both with narrowed heart arteries. They decided to have surgery together — and they did have it. Both did fine, though even Gage felt the pressure lest one do well and the other — not."

Aaron could understand that pressure. "You're going to specialize in heart surgery, aren't you, Sam?" he asked.

Sam nodded. "I can go in with Gage, though I'll never be the surgeon he is."

"You'll do," Aaron assured him. "I'll never forget the tips you gave me when I was on surgical duty."

Miller grinned. "Mainly how to talk back to the head nurse who would call you out of bed to give sedation she herself had orders to give."

Aaron nodded. "That and other things. I — this morning Barr spent some valuable time urging me to get myself a residency in surgery. Of course he didn't specify *where* I would get one, at this particular time."

"But he meant whatever he said to you, Aaron."

"I am sure he did. Though you understand

my problem — there just isn't any money."

"I do understand. But then I can see Barr's side too. Which, I'm afraid, would have to be my side as well."

"Sure. It would be."

Dr. Miller got up to refill his coffee cup. He came back to say, "You probably could swing it if there weren't a girl . . . "

"Which isn't much of an argument. Because there is a girl."

"I know there is, Aaron. But — "

Aaron leaned across the table toward the older man. "A man my age *wants* a girl, Sam!"

Sam nodded. "Yes," he said quietly, "he does."

"Dr. Barr talked about you this morning."

"Oh?"

"Yes, he cited you as a shining example of what an ambitious young surgeon should be. And do."

Sam chuckled.

"And he pointed out that you hadn't let any girl change things for you."

"Well — "

"But how did you *manage*, Miller? I mean, *has* your work been enough?"

"At times, frankly, no, Battle, it hasn't been. I am, and have been, what is called normal. And during these past years — even when I was interning — there was a girl or two. Probably not the cute little blonde I've seen you with — but there were girls. I didn't marry any of them, of course."

"Didn't you want to?"

Sam leaned back and squinted up at the ceiling lights. His face was as mobile as a rubber mask. "I guess I didn't want to strongly enough," he decided. "Of course with me, too, there was money. I couldn't afford to marry. A resident's pay — " He threw out his hands expressively.

"Yeah," said Aaron glumly.

"But an even more potent force with me," Dr. Miller continued, "was the fact that, from my internship on, Gage has been my idol. Certainly from the first decision to specialize in heart surgery I have tried to pattern myself on him. And you know that he has never married."

Aaron thought of the elegant, the clever, heart specialist, the prestige which Dr. Gage had in the center, his real ability in o.r. — his fine car in the parking lot, his perfectly cut dark-blue suits, the time or two Aaron had seen him in a dinner coat, coming or going to some evening affair, and —

"There's Linda Marshall, too," he said aloud to Sam. The whole hospital complex knew of the affair the chief surgical nurse had been having with Dr. Gage for the past couple of years.

40

"Yes," said Sam Miller, tight-lipped. "Yes, there is."

Laurie Toole, whom Aaron loved so dearly, and for whom he was ready to sacrifice so much, was a very pretty girl. She was twenty-four, though she looked scarcely more than eighteen, and often she became irritated that people would not take her seriously and treat her like a grown woman. One with a little sense!

Aaron did treat her so, and that was one of the qualities which she loved in him. Loved him so dearly, if truth were told, that he could have treated her any way — caveman's bride, or spoiled idiot — and she still would have liked it.

Laurie appeared fragile and young, but she was a capable businesswoman. She had, in fact, been working for more than three years as secretary to a municipal official. A small-town girl, she had come to the city to take a business course — her parents were dead, and college was not possible. She had stayed on to work in the city, living in a woman's hotel. A year ago Aaron Battle had met her when she was doing volunteer work in the Children's Hospital of his big complex. She was a small girl, with blond hair that swung free, or which she lacquered into a silver-gilt cap against her head. She was a pert little thing, cute as a button, and no fool.

On this particular evening she was fizzing with excitement. Her wedding was now only three days away, and just to think of the dwindling hours could put bubbles into her blood, a shine in her blue eyes, and a tremor into her voice.

"You'd better simmer down," said her roommate, "or you'll be in orbit by midnight."

"But this was my last working day, Nancy!" cried Laurie breathlessly. "And I come home to all these packages — "

Nancy glanced at the welter of wrapping paper and string on the two beds. "Yeah," she drawled. "Candlesticks, goblets — and a blanket, twin-bed size."

Laurie giggled. "I can exchange it. Aunt Lou just doesn't notice such things. She may never have heard of twin beds even."

"D'you keep her in a museum?"

"No, but we could. She's the one that wrote me and said to be sure Aaron wore good shoes to the wedding. She says a hole in a shoe sole shows up pretty plainly at such times."

"Mhmmm."

"I picked up my blouse this afternoon, too," said Laurie. "I was so afraid it wouldn't get here in time. Now, Nancy" — her eyes rounded prettily — "I'm all ready. New clothes! I think

I'll give away all my smart, working-girl suits and basic dresses. Not to mention the pearls."

"Don't look at me," said tall and rangy Nancy Parks. "Even the pearls wouldn't fit."

"And you wouldn't want them anyway. They are about worn out. I haven't bought anything new since last Christmas. Except my trousseau." She performed a pirouette in the middle of the floor. "Isn't that an exciting word!"

"Yeah. Like rice and . . ."

Laurie smiled at her tenderly. "You are happy for me," she said.

"Well, of course I am, kid. Jealous, of course, but, yes, you could say happy."

"Mhmmmn. The office gave me a gift, too," Laurie told her, scrabbling among the paper and string. "Here. See this?" She produced a large, flat box.

"Good heavens!" cried Nancy. "What's in it?"

"An electric skillet," said Laurie impressively.

"Must be a whopping big one."

"Well it is, rather. But Nancy, I can cook whole dinners in it. I suppose they took up a collection and this fitted the amount they got. But it is lovely."

"You'll need to have six kids to make it pay off."

Laurie blushed, which always tickled Nancy Parks. She was enough older than Laurie — she was thirty — that she often indulged in maternal feelings toward the younger girl. Then scolded herself for prematurely placing herself in such a category.

"They had ice-cream cups and petits fours, too," Laurie told her. "At the office, you know. It was really like a wedding reception."

"All among the tax bills and the subpoenas," chuckled Nancy.

"Oh, you!" Laurie grinned. "They were nice," she said softly.

"And you're sorry to leave them?"

"Well, not really. I mean — while I like the job, and the office — the people, generally, were swell. But, you know, ever since Christmas, Nancy, I've just been marking time until Aaron could get through his internship." She began to gather up the paper and string.

"Shake it out," Nancy advised. "You don't want to throw out any diamond brooches or stuff."

Laurie looked across at the table where she had stacked her wedding gifts. "I know each thing," she said, crooning.

"You could have married the guy sooner, you know, and stayed working — supported yourself," Nancy pointed out.

"Yes, I could have done that," Laurie

agreed. "And I would have done it, too, if Aaron had ever asked me."

"Now you're not going to work at all."

Laurie turned on the light at the mirror and did things to her hair. She wore a gray linen dress with a white collar. "Is this fresh enough?" she asked Nancy, touching the collar.

"Are you eating dinner with Aaron?"

"No. I'd like to. But — I'm eating with Bob and Diane. They're at the hotel, you know. They — they want to see the apartment we've rented, and — "

"They won't think it's good enough for you."

"It's as good as they had when they first married!" said Laurie spunkily. "And it's going to *be* good enough! It's all we can afford on what we know Aaron's income will be. Because, no, I'm not going to work. I would, if he asked me to, or if I thought it was needed. Later — it may turn out that I should help. I certainly would do it. I don't mean to let my shorthand or typing get rusty. Though I fully expect him to make good as things are planned. He'll work up to a full place in the office and get his own patients. A lot of them. Then — "

She clapped a skull cap of black straw on her head, picked up her purse and gloves. "I'll be home by nine," she told Nancy. "And

I'll take an armful of that paper to the incinerator chute as I go."

A half hour later, seated with her brother and sister-in-law at a table in the dining room of the hotel where they were staying, she told them much the same things. No, she did not plan to work; perhaps she would do volunteer work of some sort once she got used to being a housewife. But Aaron thought things were in such shape that their income would be adequate.

She told about the job at the industrial plant and the hours he would spend in the office. "He's going to make good and build up a practice. He's a very good doctor."

"Did he tell you so?" asked Bob.

Laurie flushed, then laughed. "Of course not. But his friends have told me. And he's won a prize or two. He took his degree with honors."

"What does he specialize in?" asked Diane.

"Oh," cried Laurie, "a first-year intern moves from one thing to another. They call it rotating. Two months, or something like that, in one department, then to another. Aaron likes surgery best, but he's learned to do all kinds of doctoring."

"But don't these men," asked Bob hesitantly, "usually do more than one year of intern service? It seems to me — "

"Yes," said Laurie wisely, "They do. Either a second-year internship in some special field, or they get a residency. That's for licensed doctors, you know, who want to have more training. Aaron says that they should have it, that they need it. And he plans to do some residencies later."

"Later," said Diane dryly. "Later there will be reasons not to do it. Reasons like babies, bills, and a house to pay for. Because you aren't going to want to stay in that little apartment near the hospital. And why near the hospital, Laurie, if he's through working there?"

"Oh, that's understandable," said Laurie quickly. "Aaron thinks he can do some work at the clinic and attend classes — seminars, he calls them. He will save time by living close. His friends will be near us — "

"Is it near his work?"

"It's near the office where he'll work from three to six. But, no — it's not near the plant. That's out in the county."

"Then he'll have to have a car."

"No, there is bus service."

"He'll still want a car," said her brother firmly. He was ten years older than Laurie.

"And he'll want a boat, too!" said Diane slyly, lifting her eyes to Bob's face.

"Lay off, will you?" cried Bob, his face flushing. "As hard as I work, I need my recreation. What's the use of living in Chicago if we don't make use of the lake?"

"There must be an answer to that," murmured Diane.

Unhappily Laurie looked from one to the other. "We've decided to get along without a car for a while," she said. "At first. You see, we have an over-all plan for how we'll manage such things."

Bob laughed and shook his head. "Lots of luck, little sister," he said, not unkindly.

"I'll take your luck," she agreed. "But we do have a plan. And I am sure it will work out."

CHAPTER 2

Aaron and Laurie were married on Thursday evening, a pretty wedding in the chapel, with champagne and cake afterward at Bob's hotel. Nancy wept joyously, and Tommy Dreiserward was ample competition for the groom when it came to being kissed by the girls from Laurie's office.

Tommy's gift to the bride and groom was the use of his car for their trip down to the lake, where they spent a blissful honeymoon, returning to the city late on Sunday night, happy, replete, and a little tired. Aaron carried their three bags and his heavy sack of thick medical books up the three flights of stairs. It took two trips, and he was puffing hard when he dumped the bag of books inside the door, spilling them out across the floor.

"Be careful," said Laurie, who was hanging her coat in the tiny closet.

"Yeah," gasped Aaron. "I mustn't ruin the parquetry."

"The — what?"

He grinned at her. "I was making a joke at the expense of our unvarnished floor," he said wryly.

"Oh, now, Aaron . . . " She turned full circle to look at their apartment. It could be surveyed at a glance. It was really only one long room, with the farthest end of it partitioned off into a tiny bath and a kitchen not much larger. One part of the partition contained the clothes closet, the other concealed the retractable bed. "This isn't so bad," Laurie told Aaron.

"Except that it really is, you know," he assured her.

"We'll make do."

"Sure we will, honey. But — meantime — let's face it. Our castle is a rather chinchy thing." He came over to her and kissed her.

She clung to him.

"Not sorry?" he asked.

"Oh, not!" She sighed. "Oh no! Except — "

"Here it comes!"

"Well . . . " Her eyes shone. "I did think it a little odd that you found all those dull books at least as interesting as me on our honeymoon."

"Odd, maybe," he agreed, picking up the books and stacking them on the small desk-table. It wobbled under their weight. "But studying them, oh, beautiful wife of a still unlicensed doctor, was very, very necessary."

"You'll be licensed," said Laurie confidently.

"Who told you?"

"Well, you just will. You have to be, don't you, in order to be a doctor?"

"Yes, Ma'am, I do."

"Then!"

He chuckled. "I wish I had your confidence. To me those exams next month look as big — as *big!*"

"But you've studied those books; you know what is in them."

"Mhmmm."

"Don't you?"

"I just hope you're right. I am remembering that I studied those books in years past. Then I remember that for the past eleven months I've been frittering away my time in the hospital doing scut work and trying to make it seem that I could function as a doctor."

"Aaron, when you tease me about these things, I get a little frightened for fear you might be serious."

He put his arms around her. "I am serious, my darling. Medicine is a big and complex profession, and I'm only now beginning to realize how big it is. But don't you ever be frightened."

"If I just knew more about it . . . ."

He kissed the top of her head. "If you knew more about it, you wouldn't be Laurie. And you know? I'm crazy about that girl!"

"Oh, Aaron . . ."

He pushed her away from him. "We have to get ourselves unpacked," he said sternly. "Else we can't go to bed. And if we don't go to bed, how can I ever get up at the crack of dawn and sprint it over to the hospital by seven A.M.?"

"You tell me," she said demurely.

He lifted one of the suitcases to the couch and opened it. Immediately they found that there was almost no place to put things. They had one closet, already two-thirds filled by the clothes which Laurie had brought to the apartment before the wedding. Their wedding gifts crowded the cupboards of the kitchen and every available counter and table top.

Laurie looked around her in dismay. The furnished apartment really was not very nice. She had done what she could with the gift candlesticks and her pretty towels in the kitchen and bath. The living room was sizable — they could stack things in a corner of it for a time. There was the couch — not really good. An armchair, and a second chair that did not promise any comfort. There was one large window that looked out across a court to the other wing of the apartment building and from which one could see the street.

There was a second window in their kitchen, above the sink. There also was a narrow stove and a small refrigerator. A wall filled with cabinets and shelves. There was a small table and two chairs. The bath had a narrow linen closet; here Laurie had already arranged her trousseau linens. There was the closet.

"I'll figure things out tomorrow," she promised Aaron. "Now we'll go to bed."

Aaron puzzled out how to drop the bed, and he helped Laurie make it up with pink sheets and a new blanket. He had some jokes to make about sleeping between pink sheets — and he left her as rosy as they were when he went to take his shower and shave. She had watched him, wide-eyed, set out his white clothes against the morning's dash.

"Hey, Laurie," he called back to her, "there isn't any tub in here."

"I know."

He stuck his head around the door. "You're in trouble," he teased. "For a girl that likes to put perfumed oil into her bath water and then scrub with deodorant soap — "

"Aaron Battle!" she cried, starting toward him. "Are you going to *keep* on teasing me about that?"

"Sure am," he said. "I mean to keep up a

lot of things I started on our honeymoon." He turned on the water, and Laurie went over to close the window draperies.

"I'm so happy," she whispered. "So — *happy!*"

The next morning Aaron left his bride. Previously he had, and many times, explained that, as an intern, he must leave her, that he could not return to her each night, as a proper husband would do, and as he, surely, would want to do. No, when on duty he must stay in the hospital, either on the "floor" or getting his rest down in the interns' dormitory. He would, he said, work two days, be off eighteen hours, work three days, then be off for thirty-six hours. He hoped.

"But the three-day tours are stiff, and after them I am always tired."

"I know," said Laurie wisely. Thinking that she did know from the limitations which had been put upon his courtship of her.

But of course she didn't know, Aaron told himself as he walked fast along the early-morning city street. The air was fresh — the apartment would probably get as hot as the hinges in the summer. He must manage something better for Laurie . . .

Just about then he remembered Tommy's car, and he must sprint back to pick it up from where he had parked it and drive it to the hospital. Really, he had lost little time. . . .

Time. He must, these next two weeks, find plenty of time to study. The licensure exams were before him; he had spent the past year doing clinical medicine. Now he must endeavor to brush up on theory. Biochemistry — and his notes on pathology lectures — the exams would last four days, and they would be grim.

If he failed those exams, he must wait six months to take them a second time. And he could fail! He most certainly could!

"Lo, the merry bridegroom," said Tommy, when Aaron brought him his car keys. "With a scowl one could scrape off with a hoe."

Aaron blinked. "I didn't know I was scowling."

"You were."

"It's those blasted exams. I'm scared blue about them."

"I know. They can tie me in knots too."

Aaron stared at the blond man. "But you've passed them!"

Tommy smiled sweetly. "I'm scared I'll forget to renew that license each year. I'd never pass 'em again. The farther I get from the books — "

Aaron nodded. "Thanks for the car. I've got to run."

"That makes two of us. I'll run along with you."

Two tall men in white, they hurried along the corridor — and thus Aaron's day went, made up of corridors, hurrying feet, too much to do in too little time.

It was noon before he could examine the registry and see what patients were under his care. An early-morning admission had had to be cared for, a history started — there were two deaths which he was called upon to pronounce — but by noon he was back into step, concerned with potassium loss, dehydration, and, by then, not having to tell too often "how the honeymoon had gone," or "how it feels to be an old married man." Of course, he had not yet thought of a really adequate answer to either question.

Their morning admission had been an old woman in coma, probably from a stroke, and about the time Aaron was thinking longingly of lunch, the resident asked him to take the patient up to heart-and-chest on nine. "They may pass the buck to Neurosurgical, but we'll see if we can start her on vascular. Stay with it, Battle, but not too long. You took her history —"

"Ha!" said Aaron. "She's dead out of this world, and her granddaughter guesses the old lady hasn't been any more sick than the aver-

56

age. O'course she had eight kids."

"History enough." The resident laughed. "Get going."

Tall, and efficient-looking in his white jumper and ducks, Aaron got an orderly to help him and the nurse transfer their old woman to a cart. "I'll manage now," he said, starting down the hall.

He secured an elevator and, juggling the chart board, he steered the recalcitrant cart into the thing. His patient was moaning, but he doubted if that meant any imminent return to consciousness. On nine he managed to get out into the corridor again and looked questioningly down the hall toward the chart desk.

The nurse pointed to the left, then she got up and came toward him. "If it's the new admission," she said, "take her into Suspect. We're getting some respiratory goodies in here lately, and we don't exactly appreciate them. That ward's at the end of East. Aren't you the intern that got married this weekend?"

"I did," Aaron agreed, turning the cart.

"Lucky girl!" said the nurse.

"On my income?" Aaron asked her as he started away.

She flipped her hand at him and, grinning, he went on. He wished they had nurses like that on Medicine.

He was still grinning and wishing when he brought the cart to the doors of the Suspect ward, a room where newly admitted patients could be held in quarantine until it was determined if some viral infection might have come in with them.

It was not the easiest thing in the world, alone, to push a cart and patient in through ward doors, so Aaron was preoccupied with what he was doing and almost into the room before he saw that its only other occupants were a doctor and a nurse. They stood against the windows. . . .

The doctor was Sam Miller; the nurse was Linda Marshall. And so absorbed were they in each other that they had not heard the row which Aaron must have made pushing the door open and banging the end of the cart through.

Sam held Linda's two hands in his, and he was bending over her, talking earnestly. She was looking up into his face, and her eyes were troubled. Could she have been weeping? Even as he stood there like a lump, Aaron saw Sam take tissue and wipe her eyes, the gesture so tender, so compassionate, so loving . . .

Wow!

Slowly, carefully, Aaron drew the cart back into the hall and stood, gasping a little. Had he ever . . . ?

Just last week he had said something smart to Miller about Linda's being Dr. Gage's girl. And the hospital talk said that she *was!* But those two in there — the evidence said Aaron had put his foot largely into his mouth! Because if he was any judge of such matters, those two in that empty ward were really in love with each other.

And what did Aaron do now? Well, he must go into the ward with his cart, but this time he would really announce himself. He only hoped his face would not give him away. For a year he had been trying to learn to conceal his feelings. Right now it would seem that he must pass an examination on that!

It was only minutes before two when Aaron was free enough to go down for some lunch. Of course he found others in the cafeteria. The hospital personnel ate all day long. A whole surgical team was there, with Tommy one of them. Aaron brought his egg sandwich and milk over to the table where the men sat, bracing himself for the greeting he would get, and which he did get, as a bridegroom.

These chaps got a little rough, which he had best take quietly. He ate his sandwich and said what had to be said.

"He married a rich girl," said the surgical resident, Lamczyk. "Next month he's going into private practice."

"Hey!" cried Gunn, the resident in anesthesia. "He can't just skip right over and not do any residencies. Can he, Tommy?"

Tommy Dreiserward had been sitting back in his watchful, half-smiling way. "Aaron can, if anybody," he said softly.

"Yeah, but I thought — Oh, Battle, you're not really going to do it! Are you?"

"He's smart," said Lamczyk. "He could get a residency."

"He isn't smart if he tries practicing without one," said Gunn flatly. "What gives, Battle?"

Aaron shrugged. "Ever hear of money? I don't have any."

"Oh, but look!"

And they were off, telling him in all the old familiar ways that he should do a residency, that he had to do a residency — and for pete's sake, where had he got the idea that it took money?

"Tommy," pleaded Gunn, "have you talked to this guy?"

Tommy smiled. "I've talked to him," he said. "And of course I've had to admit to him that doing a residency, and being married on that resident's pay, is hard . . ."

"I am not going to ask Laurie to starve!" said Aaron stubbornly.

60

"That's the hard part," said Tommy. "I know. But I am still persuaded — and I've told Battle this, too — that resident training is a definite and necessary part of any successful doctor's advance in his profession."

"You just don't get anywhere without it," said Sam Miller, coming up to their table. The men made room for him. "Battle will find that out. I only wish he could find it out earlier than late."

"Why hasn't somebody *talked* to the guy?"

"They have talked to him, Gunn. He was recruited in med school — weren't you, Battle?"

"Yes, but I've had to welsh on that agreement. And I wish you chaps would lay off. I just can't do it now."

Sam suspiciously inspected the interior of his sandwich.

"We'll find a way to get you to do it." He spoke confidently.

Aaron turned in his chair to look directly at the older man. "I've explained to you, Sam, I can't possibly — "

"If you read your Norman Vincent, Battle — in your free time, that is" — the homely face folded itself into a grin — "you would know that there is no such word as 'can't.' "

"Well, I must be wasting all that there free time, because I know that there is a word like

61

that. To begin with — and you know it! — I have made no application for a residency."

"It's never too late to rectify a mistake."

"The words you know!" said Aaron in disgust. The other men chuckled. Sam, too.

"Somewhat frequently there are openings — "

"*Somewhat*," Aaron repeated. "You know as well as I do that applications for first-year residencies exceed the supply of places. How could I expect to be able to change my mind now and still get selected for a spot I'd want?"

"Sam will give you his place," said someone.

Aaron glared at the man.

"I wish you would be able to find a way to do it," said Sam.

"Forget it. I made this decision months ago. Now — I wouldn't know of one place to apply."

"There should be a matching service for residents," said Gunn, "like the one there is for interns. And of course it's harder to get in as assistant resident than it is for the fellows in the upper years."

Sam nodded in agreement. "While it still isn't required to do a residency," he said, "it has become commonplace enough to justify some sort of service. The thing is routine in all specialized fields. And, Battle, I'd still urge you, if you could find a spot, almost any spot, to take your residency."

Aaron stood up. "And I still say I can't do it."

He went over to the coffee machine and filled his cup, half hoping that the bunch would think of some other subject to talk about while he was gone. He knew better than any one of them that he should continue his training. He wouldn't so much mind all this talk if anyone could find a solution to his problem. But no one did. Gunn and Lamczyk were single — and Sam Miller. Tommy's troubles with his wife offered no good argument in that direction.

"If you really were recruited," Gunn had ready for Aaron when he returned, "I don't see how you can escape serving."

It had not been easy. Only the most promising medical students were "recruited." It involved special interest from the teaching staff, a promise on Aaron's part to train in some specialized field — but last January he had begun to explain why that training must be deferred.

"All that's water over the dam," he now said coldly.

"It's not any such thing," cried the anesthesia resident. "It's water backing up to drown you, Battle. And you're just plain crazy to let it happen!"

Aaron put sugar into his coffee. "That could be," he agreed. "But I still must feed myself and the wife I've just acquired. I knew what I was doing then too."

"The Directory," offered Gunn, in a delicate tone and diction, "says that of the residencies offered this next year, the average beginning salary is thirty-five hundred dollars."

All of the men laughed.

"And it also said," Aaron agreed, "that eleven fellowships were available at *ten* thousand." He glanced at Sam Miller. "Are you getting that, Miller?"

"Not me," said Sam good-naturedly. "But I am being paid something now. However, when I started, I sure as hell didn't get thirty-five hundred. But then, I wanted to work under Gage, and this center doesn't pay anything like that salary. Not that Battle could really support a wife on thirty-five hundred."

"I'd come closer to trying on such pay," Aaron said. "But a ten-thousand fellowship! I suspect that sort of thing is offered only to men of extraordinary experience, performance, and —"

"Pull," suggested Tommy softly.

"Could be," Aaron agreed. "But I'd say, for the most part, residents are poorly paid, long suffering, and utterly, devoted to patient care."

64

"Here, here!" cried Sam.

"I appreciate you guys," Aaron told him. "And I still can dream about joining you. But not vividly enough to take Laurie along with me."

"It seems really too bad," said Tommy, tipping his chair back, "that money should make the difference between a good man's becoming the best possible surgeon or just an average g.p."

"I'll be a surgeon one day," Aaron promised him.

Tommy shrugged. "Not on the road you've chosen," he said definitely.

"Even if I'm as good as you fellows have been saying? For the sake of argument, of course."

"No," said Sam. "Because you are going to travel a dead-end street, Battle. If money is your only, your best, argument in this thing — "

Aaron stood up. "By God," he cried angrily, "it *has* to be my argument! I can't ask Laurie to live on seventy-five dollars a month!"

The smiles around the table were polite and unconvinced.

"There must be some way," said Dr. Gunn. "How about your family, Battle? Wouldn't they help? I mean — Laurie could live with them — or something."

"Yes, she could," Aaron agreed. He did not sit down again. "But I would not ask that of her or my mother. My family would probably help in other ways, but they should not. They've helped me long enough — most of pre-med, all of med — and even this past year. The cost has been terrific. They are not rich people."

"But what about that bride of yours? Laurie? Pretty name."

"Pretty girl," said Sam.

"Well, what I mean — a lot of girls hold jobs while their men — "

"Yes, they do," said Aaron. "And there again, she probably would do it. But — "

"But," said Tommy, "you don't want to get into *that* rat race, do you, my friend?" He stood up. "And it is one. I speak from experience!"

CHAPTER 3

In mid-July the exams were over, and Aaron joined as often as he dared the interns who came over to look at the bulletin board where, that day, the results would be posted. His number was 103; he would get an official notice through the mail. But of course he wanted the suspense over as soon as possible. He had promised to phone Laurie . . .

That hot day he had been assigned to outpatient clinic, and it wasn't easy to get away. Tommy said he would bring him word, but Tommy was busy upstairs.

At noon, on his break, Aaron detoured past the board — and there the notice was! With a solid phalanx of white coats before it. Heck! They didn't need to *stand* there — once they'd seen the thing!

But Aaron, although he could spot his number from ten feet back, still must shoulder his way to the front.

"D'you make it, Battle?" asked Leon Boccardi, stepping aside for him.

"Yes but I still don't believe it."

"If it ain't true and your number's up, you can sue."

Aaron laughed.

"You going to apply for that residency?"

Aaron winced. Not that again!

"You ought to, Battle," said one of the interns. "It isn't often such an opening comes up at this time of the year. Even if you've had another offer — "

"What are you talking about?" Aaron asked, beginning to back out of the crowd. He needed his lunch — he was needed back in the clinic. The place had been stacked all morning.

Not waiting for whatever was shouted after him, he went on to the cafeteria and found the place buzzing — about those who had passed the licensures and the two who had not. And about the unexpected opening, right here at University, for a second-assistant surgical resident.

Aaron heard about it three times before the fact registered with him that such an opening had presented itself overnight. What happened? asked the man behind him in line.

Aaron put two slices of bread on his tray, butter — and listened for the answer.

Some guys, he heard it explained, made several applications. This chap had — and he was accepted in two places. He couldn't fill them both — though he must be pretty good at that! And — well, he notified the staff here, and —

Aaron gulped. He asked for sliced roast beef — his hand was shaking.

An opening! Right here in his own hospital. Second assistant meant rotating, and that was the way a surgeon should properly start. He must know the whole field. . . .

Aaron decided against pickles, but he took a glass of milk, a cup of ice cream, and went to a table. He looked at his food, suddenly not hungry. He actually had a pain — a griping pain it was — of wanting to *snatch* at that opening. He could, this minute, run out of this smelly, noisy dining room; he could find someone — the chief in charge of resident service, he guessed — and tell him —

He sighed and put the roast beef on one of his slices of bread. He buttered the other slice as if the task were a wearying one. Well, he was weary. This was his last week of intern duty. Next week he would not be eating in the cafeteria. . . .

He had passed his exams, and he should be glad. Instead, he felt let down, disappointed — and very sorry for himself. At what he was giving up, at what he was losing. At what could be snatched at and which must be let go by.

He straightened in his chair, cut his sandwich, and began to eat. He had better forget all about that vacancy!

An hour ago he had thought he only needed to know that he had passed the exams to be content. Now, well . . .

A man passed his table, and the raincoat which he carried over his arm caught Aaron's milk glass, tipped it, spilled it.

"Oh, I am terribly sorry," said the man. He was not personnel.

Aaron dabbed at the stream of white which threatencd his trousers. "It's all right," he muttered.

"Look — I'll get you another one."

"Don't bother," said Aaron.

The man hesitated, then walked away. Aaron looked after him. No, he was not personnel, or he would know that an intern could not afford to lose the price of a glass of milk. But then, Aaron should not have refused to let him replace that same milk. He needed it, and he couldn't afford to spend another dime.

Now he *was* sorry for himself and gruff with Tommy Dreiserward when he came to the clinic to be sure Aaron knew that he had passed — and ask if he knew about the opening as surgical resident.

"I know — both things," said Aaron shortly. "Glad about the exams — don't care about the residency."

"Oh, now, look," said Tommy.

"You need a haircut," Aaron told him, walking out on his friend, who did need a haircut. Tommy wore his yellow hair entirely too long; it was always falling over his eyes, and it positively rippled if he moved fast! Besides, Tommy could just jolly well attend to his own affairs.

An hour later Aaron remembered his promise to call Laurie, which he did, though he told her he hadn't time, really, to talk. He was on clinic duty and busy. And he went back to giving shots to the kids.

The clinic closed at three, and Aaron went upstairs to check the medicine cart and, if he had time, to get the history on a new admission. He would go off duty at five.

At four he was in the diet kitchen drinking coffee and, gratefully, eating a Danish when Sam Miller came hunting him.

Somehow Aaron had expected Sam to show up. The man, he decided, had the face of a basset hound. Not the ears, of course, but —

Sam found a cup and filled it. Aaron waved at the tray of sweet rolls. "Some good fairy left them."

Sam selected one. "I wanted to talk to you, Battle," he said.

"All right."

Word of the Danish had got around, and traffic was getting heavy in the narrow room. "Can we go some place?" asked Sam.

"The station must be deserted," drawled Aaron.

Sam grinned. "Well, we can't eat out there. So I'll say here what I came to say."

"I know what you came to say."

"I expect you do. But — I have been authorized to tell you that the position is yours, Battle, if you'll take it."

There was that stabbing pain again. Aaron set his jaw. "I can't take it, Miller."

"Don't you want it?"

"Sure I want it. But nothing has changed in my position on taking a residency just now."

"There will be a dozen applications for this; you know that."

Aaron nodded gloomily. He did know that.

"I wish you would give this whole matter a quick review."

Aaron frowned.

"Have you ever talked to your wife about it?" Sam persisted.

"She doesn't understand these things, Sam."

"Maybe you could make her understand."

"And sound crybaby."

"No need for that."

"I married her to support her and take care of her."

"Of course you did. But if she knew what a valuable investment in your future this training would be — "

"I still mean to take my residencies later."

"This opportunity is now, Aaron."

"I know . . ." And the interest of the staff was his too. Now.

Sam, however, could only elicit from him a promise to think the thing over — not to refuse the offer until he had carefully reviewed it again. And with Laurie, if possible.

"You owe that to her, Battle."

Aaron supposed he did. Should Laurie hear of it later, when it was too late, she would reproach him. So . . .

Wanting desperately to accept the thing and be done with all this talk, Aaron thanked Sam as cordially as he could for his interest. In his gratitude he had a wild minute of thinking he should apologize to him for what he had said about Linda Marshall — but he did not speak of that.

And Sam went back to surgery, Aaron out on the floor where he tried to get some sort of work-up done on the new patient, a woman with intractable nausea. He began to despair of getting off on time, but at a quarter to five the resident came and said he would "finish up."

Aaron looked at the man in amazement.

This sort of consideration had never happened to him before. When he spoke of it downstairs where he went to change, one of the interns predicted that the hospital would exact its pound of flesh. Aaron frowned. *Was* the machinery working so intricately that word had been passed to Medicine to see that he got home that evening with time to talk to his wife? To make up his mind, by morning, to take the residency? Oh, nonsense! As a doctor, he wasn't all that good!

He had made few enemies during his studies and intern service, but there must be a dozen men as able as he was, and at least eleven of them must really want that blasted residency. Which he did not.

Well — *want* was perhaps not the word. . . .

He checked out and started home, his feet dragging. He recognized his pace for what it was. Reluctance to go home and face Laurie. Which was a fine thing! Married only a month, he usually ran the whole way! But tonight — he had promised to talk to her about the residency, and she was going to think that he was regretting the circumstances. Well, of course he was not sorry that he had married her! She knew that, she must know that! He wished he had not promised Sam to tell her.

He would break that promise in a wink,

too, except that Sam was right. Some day Laurie would find out about it, and she would wish he had told her.

So, yes, he must talk to her about it and explain both sides, fairly, but —

Even dragging his feet, he finally reached the big apartment house. He signaled to Laurie from the lobby and took the then-working elevator up to the third floor. She was waiting at the door, clean, fresh, and pretty in blue-checked gingham.

He kissed her and agreed that it was a hot day.

"You could have a shower . . . "

"I showered when I changed. I was a mess."

"I like to see you boys walking around the streets here in your white clothes."

Aaron grinned. "You must have a crush on some doctor."

In a month Laurie had done wonders for the "chinchy" apartment. She had scrubbed and waxed and polished; she had washed the curtains and rearranged things. They still had a stack of boxes in one corner, but it was a tidy stack. Aaron could not have listed exactly all that she had done — maybe the little pots of growing green things, maybe just the cleaning. Anyway, the place looked much better. Probably because such a pretty girl as Laurie lived there.

Aaron sat down on the couch and wanted her to sit beside him. "I should get supper," she protested.

"That can wait a little while. Do you know how long it's been since — "

"I know," she told him demurely, cuddling up beside him. A little breeze blew the curtains of the window behind them.

"All right. So tell me what you've been doing."

"Oh, Aaron, you don't want to know about my going to market and washing sheets."

"Yes, I do."

So she told him, while he held her small hand in his and rubbed his thumb over the wedding ring which he had put on her finger. And he tried to think of a way to tell her about the residency.

"Now," she said, "tell me what you've been doing." Aaron glanced at her, and she giggled. "Oh, not all of it," she agreed. "But things must have happened. For one, you passed your exams."

"Yes, I did."

"Of course I knew you would."

"If you had only told me."

"I did tell you." She had too.

"I thought you didn't know what you were talking about."

"I know more than you think about your

being a doctor, Aaron."

Aaron devoutly hoped that she did. Because —

"Do you remember," he asked idly, trying to make it *sound* idly, "my ever talking about a man named Sam Miller?"

Laurie pursed her pretty lips and drew her brows together. "A doctor?"

"I never talk about anyone else, do I?"

"Oh — now and then. What about this Dr. Miller?"

"He came to see me today during coffee break. He had a matter he wanted to discuss with me. I hope you'll meet Sam sometime, Laurie. He's a really grand guy."

"An intern?"

"Oh no. He's a senior resident in heart surgery. He has a fellowship; he's doing some research in new and better sutures for cardiac surgery."

"Goodness! He must be older."

"Well, he is, a little. Six years maybe. That doesn't make him ancient."

"Isn't that what Tommy wants to specialize in?"

"Well, yes. Chest surgery, at least. But Tommy will only start in that this next year."

"I know. Have you seen Tommy lately?"

Aaron laughed. This was the way any talk about the hospital always went with Laurie.

She hunted for familiar things. "I see Tommy every day," he told her gently.

"He's sweet."

All the girls thought Tommy was sweet. His almost pretty face, his soft yellow hair, and his quiet way of gazing at a girl with his large blue eyes — they should hear the man cuss sometime!

"That's enough of Tommy," said Aaron definitely.

Laurie laughed. "All right, tell me about the other one. Sam. Is he good-looking?"

"Oh no. He looks like a basset hound."

"Aaron, nobody — "

"Sam does. His face sort of folds — and his eyes are prominent. But he's a really nice guy and a bang-up surgeon. I'm glad he even knows I'm alive. He was really kind to me when I did my surgical. He's a fine teacher — "

"Do residents teach?"

"They teach. They're learning, of course, training, but they teach men who are below them on the scale. Students and interns — nurses — by the time you get where Miller is, you know an awful lot to teach the young ones."

"I see. Is this Sam married? I thought maybe you could invite him and his wife — sometime — "

"No, he isn't married. And that's quite a

situation, Laurie. Because I just happen to know — oh, I guess others know it, too — but Sam is in love with Miss Marshall, the supervisor of surgical nursing."

"Oh, how nice."

Aaron's fist scrubbed the back of his head. "Not exactly *nice*, honey."

"Why? Is she already married? I know you said *Miss*, but — "

"No she isn't married. And yes, she's pretty. Well, handsome would be the word, I guess. She's a nice person. She has sort of red hair and striking blue eyes, a fair, clear skin, and a friendly way about her. When she laughs, she shows a deep dimple — "

"That gets a man every time!"

Aaron chuckled. "I guess it does. Because Sam is hot in love with her, and for about two years, the hospital scuttle butt has it, *she* has been loved by, and been — well — the companion, or girl friend, if you like — to Dr. Gage."

"Who's he?"

Aaron took a deep breath. "He's just about the most famous man we have at the center — a heart surgeon at that."

"But then your friend Sam — "

"Mhmmmn."

"Is Dr. Gage married?"

"No. And because I see you are about to

ask, I don't know why he hasn't married Marshall by now. I suppose they could, but they just haven't. Ever since I was in med school, I've been aware that those two were a thing."

"And now Dr. Miller is stepping in." Laurie looked excited.

"Oh, I don't know about anyone's stepping in. But I do think he and Marshall have fallen in love with each other."

"She, too?"

"From what I've seen, yes."

"But — *Aaron!*"

"Mhmmmn. It's going to be interesting to see what will happen."

"Yes, it will," said Laurie happily. "It hardly ever is safe to fall in love with the boss's girl." She stood up. "I'll fix dinner."

She went out into the kitchen. "It's only salmon salad and biscuits," she called back to Aaron.

"Sounds good to me. Can I help?"

"In this kitchen? Your mother brought some magazines yesterday." She chattered about his mother and the things she had brought — some plums and the magazines. "She thinks we should have an air conditioner."

"Who?" Aaron was looking at a magazine.

"Your mother."

"Then why doesn't she bring one of those?"

Laurie came to the doorway. "Oh, Aaron!" she reproved.

"I just want to have her happy."

Laurie smiled and went back to her work. When Aaron could smell the biscuits baking, he got up and strolled toward the kitchen.

"What did Sam Miller come to discuss with you?" Laurie asked over her shoulder. She had a pretty shoulder, and her bare arms were round . . .

"Aaron?" she prodded him.

"Oh," he said. "Why, he wanted to tell me that there was an opening as a second-assistant surgical resident."

Laurie put the plates of salad on the table. They looked pretty, the lettuce a crisp ruffle of green around the pink fish. "That doesn't sound too important," she said. "*Second* assistant."

"A man has to step on the first rung of the ladder to climb."

"Meaning *you* would have to?" Laurie was looking at him.

Aaron shrugged. "Any man," he said.

Laurie got the biscuits out of the oven and put them into a little basket which she covered with a cloth. "Sit down," she said, "and tell me about this whole thing, Aaron."

He gazed at her. She was so young, so pretty — so dear. Her hair was like silver-gilt feathers, and her face . . . He sighed. "Let me eat my dinner."

"You can eat and talk. This is important to you, I can tell. So explain it to me."

"Well, do you even know what a residency is?"

"It's hospital training — it comes after internship, and it's what Tommy is. Carol says it's slave labor."

Aaron laughed. "Carol could be right, Laurie. Because it does mean hard work, and it pays very little. Our medical center pays somewhat less than some others, but — "

"Why?"

"Why what?"

"Why does the center pay less?"

"Well, there are various reasons. University is an exceedingly good teaching hospital and has no trouble getting residents at what they do pay."

"That's where the slave trade comes in."

"No, not really. Because, you see, the patients have to pay for the doctors such a center trains. And in order to get a wide spectrum of cases, the center has to admit many, many free patients. Also, the paying ones can't be asked to pay too much! One way to effect both things is to pay the residents less."

"How much?"

"Well, it isn't enough, of course. Some hospitals pay — oh, thirty-five hundred a year, but — "

"How much does Tommy get?"

"Any first-year resident gets seventy-five a month."

Laurie's mouth fell open.

"Second year he gets a hundred, one hundred and twenty-five the third year, and two hundred in his fourth year when he becomes a senior resident."

"But — *Aaron!* No wonder Carol doesn't think much of what Tommy is doing."

"He's learning to be a surgeon, Laurie. He has to have this training!"

Laurie studied her husband's intent face. "I guess," she said thoughtfully, "you would need a lot of training to be a surgeon. It isn't something you can learn by experimenting . . . "

"No medicine can be learned that way, honey, without somebody being hurt."

"No. I guess not. Put some preserves on your biscuit, Aaron. It's the only dessert."

He obliged her, and she smiled. "Tell me again about who pays these residents that work and teach and all."

Aaron took a deep breath. "They get their monthly checks from the hospital organization, Laurie. But the money comes from those patients who pay for their care."

"In the pavilion."

"No. We're tearing down the pavilion, for one thing." He grinned. "And putting in some apartment-like suites for rich patients. But, no, Laurie — I don't mean the rich patients. They pay, of course. But so do working people, professional people — a businessman with high blood pressure — anybody who has hospitalization or who can pay. This money is used to run the hospital, and part of the expense of doing that is the pay of interns and residents."

"Seventy-five dollars a month."

"Yes."

"But how do they get anybody?"

"Tommy has borrowed five thousand dollars to see himself through, and he thinks it's worth it."

"Could you do that?"

"I wouldn't want to."

"No, I'd worry if we were in debt. Maybe that's what Tommy and Carol fight about. Couldn't the paying patients pay more?"

"I don't think they'll be asked."

"I see. But these residencies are so important that a lot of doctors want them."

"That's it. I'll do some later. We'll save our money toward that."

Laurie nodded. That she knew about. "A medical education," she said softly, "requires a lot from a man, doesn't it?"

84

Aaron nodded soberly. "Yes, it does, honey. More time, more extended and intensive training, more skills — developed skills — and maybe more sincere devotion than any other field of study."

"Is being a resident the end of a doctor's training?"

"Yes. After next year Dr. Miller will be a staff doctor and on his own. It will be a very good *own* too."

"It should be, to take seven years."

"Some do it in three or four. They don't learn as much as Miller has, but enough for their purposes."

"Could you?"

"It would depend on what specialty I'd choose. And — well, I'm planning to practice without any residency. So of course I could work, and a little better, with one year — two — or four. You see? It's a degree of training."

"Would you work as hard as you've been doing as an intern?"

"Maybe harder. Because there would be more responsibility. I — or any resident — am usually badly overworked."

"And underpaid."

Aaron chuckled. "And underpaid. Often, you know, he isn't considered a doctor at all. By the patients."

85

"I can't see why any man would want to be a resident."

"It probably is because he wants to be a doctor. Resident training has to be a part of it, and a man keeps that in his mind."

"You talked about this Sam coming to tell you about the residency as if this offer was something special. And I can see it is, with you. But if it means such hard work, and so little pay, I cannot for the life of me see why."

"I know you can't, honey."

"But it *is* special?"

"Yes. There will be a dozen applications for the job."

"Why?"

"Because it offers some ex-intern a chance to work in the best possible medical center, under the best possible surgeons. To learn, Laurie! To learn what is a very difficult profession. Why, do you remember, when I was doing surgical duty as an intern, how I practiced tying knots?"

"Yes, you and Tommy both did. I thought you were pretty good."

Aaron snorted. "I'm not good at it at all."

Laurie took and buttered a biscuit, her face troubled. "Is this the only surgical residency open this year?"

"Oh no!" cried Aaron. "Our center this year, had openings for twelve assistant residents. But those were offered and filled several months ago, Laurie. That this one is offered now amounts to a miracle."

"How does it happen. . . ?"

"Oh, some man was chosen to fill it, and he can't do it. For his own reasons."

"Who was it?"

"I don't know."

"So it was offered to you."

"Yes. Miller knew about it, and he thought he could persuade me. In a way an offer like this is better than if I had applied and been selected along with the other assistants. I mean, some special interest is being shown — "

Laurie opened her mouth to ask if he had accepted, but before she could speak, the door buzzer sounded, and Aaron went to answer. Then immediately she found herself in such a flurry of shoving their dishes out of sight into the oven, smoothing her hair, taking off her apron, that she forgot remote things like residencies and surgical training in the necessity to go out and greet the group of Aaron's friends who had dropped in to see them.

There were three men — Tommy was one of them. And two women. A tall, good-looking one with red hair, and a cute little dark one named Ruth.

Aaron greeted these people cordially and told them to come in, come in! To what did he owe this honor? All the time he was calling "Laurie! *Laurie!*"

"Oh, there you are," he said. "Look what we have. Company!"

"You hate surprises, don't you, Laurie?" said the tall redhead, smiling at her.

"No, I'm glad you came." She smiled at the one familiar face. "Hello, Tommy," she said softly.

He stooped to kiss her cheek.

"Where's Carol?" she asked.

Naïvely, she supposed, because everyone else laughed loudly. "*He* brought Linda!" said one of the men boisterously. "How's that for living dangerously on Chest Surgery?"

"I've been in love with Linda since my third year in med," said Tommy softly.

"Which took doing," Aaron pointed out, "what with your going to med school in California."

"I did," Tommy agreed. "But I knew all the time that Linda was out there somewhere."

"That's our Tommy," said the stunning redhead. She wore a simply perfect dress of green linen, tiny gold earrings, a single gold bracelet. "I'm Linda Marshall, Laurie," she said, "since no one else seems to have manners enough to make introductions."

Laurie smiled. "I've heard about you," she said eagerly.

Aaron moved fast then to make the other introductions. The dark girl was Ruth Campbell. The two strange men were doctors.

Chairs were brought in from the kitchen. Laurie said she'd make a fresh pot of coffee. Her mother-in-law had brought cookies . . . Within a few minutes everyone was seated, Aaron on the wide arm of the chair where Laurie sat. For some reason everyone had agreed that she should sit there. In the best chair.

"The couch has lumps" she apologized.

"We came on business" the dark-haired nurse said. "Lumps won't matter."

Aaron's hand tightened on Laurie's shoulder, and she looked up at him. She was wishing that her pretty china was not packed in the lowest box of the corner stack. But she thought she could muster five cups — six — seven —

"We came," Tommy was saying, "to get you on our side, Laurie."

She looked up at him questioningly. "What?" she asked stupidly.

"Pay attention," he said. "This is important."

She folded her hands in the lap of her blue gingham skirt. "Yes, sir," she said obediently.

Tommy grinned. "We came," he said impressively, leaning toward her, his hair falling across one eye, "to get you to persuade, or coax, or urge — use any method you can — to make Aaron take the residency that has just opened up in surgery."

Laurie glanced up at Aaron. He was looking stern. "I'd thank you, Dr. Dreiserward," he said coldly, "to shut up! Things are all set — our plans are all made . . ."

"You don't let your wife think for herself?" asked the dark young doctor with the Italian name.

Laurie jumped to her feet. "The coffee is done," she said. Her cheeks were pink. "Aaron has told me all about that residency," she added. "But he makes the doctoring decisions around here." She started toward the kitchen, her blue gingham skirt flipping, her blue slippers twinkling.

Linda Marshall followed her. "Can I help?"

Laurie smiled at her. There were tears in her eyes. "If you can find seven clean cups . . ." she gasped.

Linda opened the cupboard door. "This is a very important decision for Aaron," she said softly.

"I know." Laurie put oatmeal cookies on a plate. And milk into a cream pitcher. "But Aaron still has to be the one — "

"He'd need your help."

"Well, my goodness, don't you think he'd get it?"

Linda nodded. "Yes. I do think he would."

"Well, then!" said Laurie, setting everything on a tray.

For the next ten minutes or so she was the excited, and somewhat frightened, hostess serving the first guests she had ever entertained in her home. She was very young and very pretty — her guests appreciated that. Aaron offered no help, but the place was somewhat crowded, and he was always being drawn into the talk that got pretty noisy and sometimes out of hand. There were bursts of loud laughter, interspersed with the sound of one voice being emphatic on a point or another telling some tale.

Laurie tried to listen intelligently to all that was being said; she was very proud of Aaron's poise with these clever people.

Finally one of the men — his name was Leon Boccardi; he was a doctor, she was pretty sure; anyway, he was a dark man in a black shirt and light-gray trousers — he caught at Laurie's hand as she passed and drew her down to a seat on the couch beside him.

"Let them get their own coffee," he suggested.

He put his arm behind her, along the back of the couch, and as she expected, that hand soon was resting on her shoulder. Well, she

91

had been cuddled before and knew what to do or say. The man sat too close — but that also was routine. She nibbled on a cookie and listened to Tommy arguing hotly — with heat that really surprised Laurie — about the surgeon's responsibility for the anesthesia given a patient.

"He'd better know what goes on!" he cried.

"Tommy Dreiserward is a good doctor," this Boccardi told Laurie. "He and Aaron are buddy-buddy."

"Yes, I know. He was best man at our wedding."

"Have you known Aaron long?"

"About a year. We've been married a month."

"You're going to tell him to take that residency, aren't you?"

Laurie frowned a little, and the man's finger stroked down along her cheek. "You've got a very big thing in Aaron," he said softly.

"Well, I know that!"

He shook his head. "I'm afraid you don't know him," he murmured. "Not as a doctor. So let me tell you — "

So — he did tell her. And the others joined in, repeating all the reasons why Aaron should jump at the residency offer.

"With Barr interested in you," said someone, "you've got it made, boy!"

92

But Aaron still would not commit himself, and after an hour the group left. Laurie started to clear things away, thinking that a lot of Aaron's precious free evening was already gone. He began to gather up cups and brush cookie crumbs off things. Laurie went into the kitchen and put her apron on again. She stacked the dishes and filled the sink with hot suds. Aaron came out to dry. Neither mentioned the residency.

Laurie talked about Linda Marshall, about how nice she was and how good-looking! She was a nurse?

"If I were sick, I'd love to have her my nurse."

Aaron chuckled. "Better not get sick. She's not done bedside for some time."

"Then what does she do?"

"She supervises the nursing services of the surgical department."

Laurie handed him a cup. "What does that mean?"

"Just about everything, honey. She supervises the nurses who do bedside on surgical, the ones who work in o.r. — operating room. That means for twelve o.r.'s. She schedules their duties, their hours — she is responsible for having a nurse where she is needed, when she is needed. She sometimes goes into the operating room herself. Oh, Marshall does a bang-up job."

"How old is she?"

Aaron shrugged. "Anything from thirty to thirty-five."

"She certainly is good-looking."

"Smashing."

"And she's nice, too, Aaron. She really is."

"Sure she is. Sam Miller's the same way. Smart, able — and yet humanly nice too."

"He didn't come tonight."

"No, but you'll meet him some day. And when you do, you'll meet a really fine doctor. He's going right straight to the top."

"Stack the cups as closely as you can, will you? Tomorrow I'm going to unpack some of our good china — in case we have company again."

"Did you bake the cookies?"

"Oh no. They take too much butter. And our budget . . . Your mother made them."

She wiped the stove and the table top. "Linda Marshall wants to marry Dr. Miller," she said decisively.

Aaron looked around at her. "Did she talk about it?"

"Of course not. But I know she wants to."

"Yes, I expect she does, but I suppose she knows, too, that it won't be easy to swing it."

Laurie glanced around so quickly that her hair flew up and away from her head. "Why not?" she asked.

Aaron shrugged.

"I thought you said he had one of those fellowship things."

"He does. And next year — not this one coming up, but the next one — he'll have full staff status."

"Won't he make money?"

"Money isn't the whole thing, Laurie."

"It is for us."

Aaron smiled and looked regretful too. "Yes, I know it is for us," he said, "and it would have been for Sam six years ago. But the thing for him now is that he has a fellowship under Gage — "

"Who's he?"

Aaron took a cookie and perched on the step stool. "Well . . . " he began. "If you knew very much about medicine, you would know who Dr. Ivan Gage is."

"I don't know very much about medicine," said Laurie cheerfully. "So let's go out in the other room while you tell me about him. Is he handsome?"

"Oh, Laurie . . . "

She smiled at him. "That's important. If Linda has to choose between him and Dr. Miller . . . "

Aaron nodded and sat down on the couch, putting his arm around the pretty girl and nuzzling her shoulder.

"You act just like Dr. Boccardi," Laurie told him.

Aaron chuckled. "I saw him making time."

"Mhmmmn. But now tell me about this Dr. Gage."

"I know — is he handsome? Sam isn't, by the way. But I think his chances are still pretty good. Gage — well, yes, he is handsome. In a well-groomed, lots-of-money way. His eyes seem a little cold — but he dresses elegantly, and he has a precise way of speaking. He's very famous as a heart specialist, Laurie. Great-vessel surgery is his precise field. Right along with Barr, he has made our center famous for its chest surgery."

"How old a man is he?"

"Forty-eight. I saw that in an article about him just this past week. The same article said he began his work when he was a resident — as Sam is now. Gage and another doctor figured out an operation for coarctation of the aorta."

"That's heart."

Aaron nodded. "That's heart. The big artery of the heart is the aorta. He's gone on to devise or invent all sorts of techniques and gadgets. Artificial heart valves — things like that. A new method for freezing homografts. He practiced for years on animals and cadavers

96

— dead bodies, honey."

Laurie made a face, and Aaron rubbed his hand across her lips. She smiled.

"Now," he continued, "he can make a total valve replacement in six minutes — his team can — which means life for a patient whose heart has been arrested by deep hypothermia. He constantly experiments with new ideas and makes his residents keep on their toes. His great hobby, medically, seems to be to make expert and expensive, care available to patients who need it and yet not sacrifice the quality of that care."

"Why, he sounds pretty good!"

"I told you — he is good."

"I mean as a man."

"I don't know much about him as a man. He lectures, almost always, on the necessity for a doctor — any doctor — to keep up with and apply new ideas. He says that any doctor who does not read his journals and attend educational activities can become obsolete in five years' time."

"I'll remember that," said Laurie, "and remind you."

"You do just that!" Aaron agreed.

Laurie cuddled her head against his shoulder. "Forty-eight," she murmured reflectively. "Sam is younger?"

"Of course. He is in his early thirties —

thirty-four perhaps. But there's a side to this man . . . "

"Gage?"

"Gage. He is very successful in his profession. That means, as a man, he probably expects to be successful in other things too. So, if Sam Miller should steal his girl, Gage not only wouldn't like it, he would be in a position to ruin his chief resident."

"Oh, but he wouldn't do that, Aaron, would he?" She lifted her head to look at him.

"I don't know, Laurie."

"But — can he?"

"Oh yes. Of course he can."

Laurie sat stunned. "But, Aaron," she cried at last, "that's not right! If Sam is a good doctor and does his work . . . "

"He is, and he does. And maybe it would not be right for Gage to take any steps — but just the same, Sam had better forget Linda Marshall. Which would be hard to do, since he sees her every day. Though she knows, too, that he had better forget her as anything but the surgical supe."

Laurie took a deep breath. "It all sounds too terrible, Aaron, and this wonderful, great doctor sounds much too grim. Doesn't he know that love is important?"

Aaron drew her into his arms. "Thank you for reminding me, sweetie. Here I've been wasting my free evening . . . " He kissed her, and she clung to him hungrily.

"I do miss you so," she gasped.

"Don't talk. . . . "

And she did not talk. For a time. But she was still in his arms when she whispered, "Aaron?"

"Hmmmn?"

"You are to take that residency."

The room was dark, lighted only with such radiance as came up from the street. But Aaron straightened and looked hard at her. "No!" he said harshly. "Now, don't you be-gin — "

She reached up and put her soft lips against his mouth to silence him. "Yes," she said then, sweetly firm. "I want you to do it. I want us both to do this together, Aaron. You must let me. We can climb that ladder together. You know? The one you said had to be started with the first rung. And we can climb it — "

"Can we, Laurie?" he asked anxiously. "Can we?" He was deeply moved that, know-ing so little really about his profession, she should be willing to strike out blindly and make the sacrifices . . .

"Of course we can do it!" she said confi-dently. "I'm not Tommy's wife."

He drew her again into his embrace. "And I am glad!" he assured her. "But do you have the least idea . . . ?"

He didn't have time to finish the question, nor could she answer, because the buzzer went off loudly.

Aaron must jump to turn on the lamps; Laurie must run to straighten her hair and check her lipstick. "Company night!" she called from the bathroom.

This time their company was Aaron's parents. They came into the apartment, talking gaily and laughing, their arms filled with bundles.

"How could you find anything more to bring?" Laurie asked her mother-in-law, taking the basket of tomatoes and the flat cold package that surely would be a frozen steak. "You brought so much yesterday."

Aaron's father was a slender man who spoke rapidly, whose eyes darted about the room as he talked. Mrs. Battle was a short, plump woman with red-brown, curled hair. She always was suffering from some ailment which her son, and her friends, had learned to hear about and not to be too concerned.

Laurie told her how the cookies had "saved my life." "We had a whole mob come in, and my good cups are still in that bottom box."

Margaret Battle glanced at the pile of cartons. "You should unpack them, dear," she said. "I'll come over and help you some day."

"Well, if you'll find a place to put things —
we just don't have any place! Do we, Aaron?"

"Not unless we throw something else out
the window."

"Couldn't you put a chest or china closet
against that wall?" asked his father, going
over to measure the expanse of wall space.

"If we had a chest or china closet, yes, we
could," agreed Aaron.

"But you — " began his mother. "Look,
Dad. What about that blanket chest down in
our basement? It has wide, deep drawers, Laurie. And you could keep all your linens there
and then put your china on the shelves — "

"In the bathroom!" cried Laurie ecstati-
cally. "Oh, that would be a great help!"

The two women beamed at each other.

"I'll send it over tomorrow," said Mrs. Battle. "You'll be free, Aaron?"

"No, I go back on duty at seven A.M."

"All right. We'll manage. And we aren't
going to stay long now. We knew you'd be at
home, and we wanted to know if you'd passed
your examinations."

Aaron looked contrite. "Oh, I meant to call
you! Then this company came in. But — yes,
I did pass."

"Where did you rate?" asked his father
briskly.

"I don't know. There was just a list of those

who had passed. It was posted this afternoon, and I would have called you."

"He did all right," said Laurie confidently. "He's been offered a surgical residency, and he is going to take it."

"But I thought —" said Aaron's father. His mother's eyes were wide and round.

"We haven't quite talked that thing out," Aaron explained.

"Did you get such an offer?"

"Well, yes. An opening has presented itself, and I could have it — but there are many details —"

"What about your job at the plant?" asked his father?

Aaron nodded. "That's one of the details."

"But we're going to get them all lined up," said Laurie confidently. She straightened the ruffle at the edge of her sleeve. "The job — and the matter of money. I'll get myself a job and be ready to help in every way I can."

"What ways are those?" asked Mr. Battle, not unkindly.

"Oh — being very economical, and not having children for a while — things like that. Because this is something Aaron really should do."

"My dear . . . " said Mrs. Battle, her eyes tear-washed. Laurie looked so young in her blue gingham and her blue hair bow. That child . . .

"A residency, eh?" said Mr. Battle. "That's what you've planned on since early in medical school, isn't it, Aaron? Wasn't there some sort of agreement . . . ?"

"Yes, sir, there was. But early in med school I didn't know that I would have other claims upon me. In four years I've grown up about the facts of life."

"You mean money."

"I definitely mean money, sir. That's something I still need to talk about to Laurie — "

"We'll manage," she said firmly.

"Won't you be paid anything, Aaron?" asked his mother.

"Yes. Sure I'll be paid. Seventy-five bucks a month, every month. That would just about cover my laundry bills."

"I'd think the hospital would pay for those things."

"Scrub suits, colored gowns, bed linen and towels in the residents' quarters — they pay for that. But anything else I have to pay for."

"The seventy-five will pay the rent on this apartment," said Laurie. "Figure it that way."

Her father-in-law laughed and shook his head. "It still sounds like slave labor to me," he said. "You'll be a licensed doctor, Aaron, and working, won't you?"

"I'll be — I *would* be — licensed. And, yes, I would work. But the main thing, Dad, is that I would be learning. There are so many things a surgeon has to learn."

"He'll teach, too," said Laurie proudly.

The parents were impressed. Though, "Then you should be paid for doing it!" cried his father, who knew less than nothing on the subject.

"Others taught me on the same basis," said Aaron tightly. "And I will do some teaching — med students and interns. But the main thing is, I'll be learning. Just as if I were in school. What extra it costs a man to live can be considered the tuition he pays for that learning."

"I wouldn't think such a school would have too big an enrollment," said Philip Battle sadly. "Seventy-five dollars a month — these days . . . " He shook his head in disbelief.

"The competition, Dad — believe it or not — is fierce for just such residencies at our center. This word broke today. If the place isn't filled immediately, there will be a hundred applicants. I've been given first whack at it . . . "

Why?" asked his father. He fancied himself as a good businessman.

"Because he's good," said Laurie, getting up to fetch the coffee which she had started on the parents' arrival.

Aaron laughed. "Because I'm known here," he corrected. "Because I hadn't applied for a residency, and the medical school here likes to have its graduates complete their training. I will say the offer has both surprised and flattered me, but — "

Laurie came back with the coffee cups on a tray. "He's going to accept it," she said firmly. "If I get a job, that will take care of everything except the rent."

"Clothes, food — " said his mother.

"I get fed free at the hospital," said Aaron.

"Fine. But Laurie will need food. Can you get your old job back, Laurie?"

"Oh no. That has been filled. And what with the office collection for my wedding gift and all . . . " She laughed. "But I can get one. I'm a pretty good secretary."

"You were at the courthouse, weren't you?" asked her father-in-law.

"Yes, sir."

"Why I ask — I know a lawyer. He belongs to the Athletic Club — where I go for handball and the baths. I heard him saying today that he was going to need a new secretary. He couldn't advance one of the other girls in his office, and his old one — well, I don't know what's happening to her. I don't think he's advertised yet. And since he's sort of a friend, I could mention you. If you'd like, Laurie."

Her eyes were shining. "Well, of course I'd like! Thanks a million, Dad."

"Yes, Dad," said Aaron gravely. "And I'll promise you, that's all the help we'll ask of you. With Ed coming along, it's his turn to lean on you."

"Oh, we'll take care of your brother," said Margaret. "But we'll help you two of course!"

"No," said Aaron firmly. "I'd rather — You should let us try to do this thing on our own. It won't be easy, but I think we can make it." He stopped and sat, considering — he was talking in a way that showed the matter was decided. Excitement began to fizz bubbles through his veins. The palms of his hands, suddenly, were wet, and his lips dry. . . .

His mother was still talking. "Of course," she said, "if an emergency should arise . . . And you should have a car, shouldn't you?"

"Not now," said Aaron, his voice trembling a little with exultation. "I'd have had to manage one to go out to the plant, but why would I need one now? I live close enough to the center to walk, and Laurie — Where is this lawyer's office, Dad?"

His father told him.

"Well, then! Laurie can get a good bus at this corner — it stops in front of that building. A car would be a pure nuisance."

Everyone laughed except his mother. She was still gazing into the future. "There will be things," she said. "You'll need little trips —

106

diversions. Clothes can be a big item."

Aaron frowned. Laurie, looking at him, knew that he was ready to be stubborn. And after all his parents had done . . .

"Yes!" she cried gaily, "of course you can help! With cookies, and blanket chests — and other things, too, from time to time, if we need other things. And whatever we think now, we probably *will* need those other things! You've always been wonderful to us!"

By then Aaron knew what she was doing, and he smiled at her. "That's right," he said. "Keep us on your list."

Within a short time the parents left, reminding each other that Aaron would need to get up early. Mr. Battle would speak to Mark Hulsey the next day . . .

"*The* Mark Hulsey?" asked Aaron.

"That's the one. Criminal lawyer, and a good one. Well . . . Good night, kids. Mamma will be around tomorrow, Laurie, with the blanket chest. Good night!"

They went downstairs and along the sidewalk to where they had parked their car. Mr. Battle had left it locked, but he prudently flashed a light into the back seat, with his usual mutterings about one's life not being safe . . .

"I'm glad," said Margaret, settling into her

seat, "that Aaron can go on with his training. I've felt guilty about his postponing it."

"Yes," said her husband, "so have I."

"They'll make it."

"Sure they will. Those are good kids. I'm glad we like Laurie."

"She is such a pretty girl."

"She is that, but — teach her to make coffee, will you, Mother? If you don't, we're going to *need* a doctor in the family!"

CHAPTER 4

Aaron could not settle down to go to bed — he was too excited at what now seemed to lie ahead for him. He sat talking and making plans until midnight. He wanted to telephone the hospital that night and tell Miller that he was going to accept. But Miller, if sleeping, would have his ears! And if not sleeping, he'd be on duty — or on a date. Anyway, Aaron could tell him first thing in the morning.

He talked about this to Laurie and made plans for contacting the plant where he would have worked and the doctors' office. His decision would put them in a crack, and he was sorry . . .

"Don't be," said Laurie. "This is what you should have planned all along. It's what you would have been doing, too, if you hadn't married me."

"Now what kind of odds are those?" Aaron asked her.

Finally they let down the bed, and Laurie took her bath, Aaron teasing her again about the difficulties of using bubble-bath oil in a shower.

"But you'll have a proper place to live before too very long," he promised her. "And this way probably sooner than if I'd delayed my residency. Now we can go straight through poverty to a living income."

She laughed. "You make it all sound so glamorous."

"It's going to be tough," he assured her, lying on his back, his hands folded behind his head.

"Just what will you do?" asked Laurie. "I mean, you'll specialize, won't you?"

"Not this year."

"But —"

"This year I'll be assistant in surgery. So I won't be on the medical wards or O.B. — things like that. But I will move around in surgery. Do, I think, about three months in four different surgical services, or departments."

"Why?"

"This is to see what I like and for the center to decide what I'm good at."

"Suppose —"

"That they aren't the same?" Aaron laughed. "I imagine," he mused, "that any particular aptitude, skill, or talent — even any interest — will be modified as I go along. Right now

I'm inclined to chest surgery, but it may prove that I'd be better doing orthopedics or — Well, we'll find out. Just so it's surgery, I'll be able to fit my ideas to what develops. I —" He slipped his hand under Laurie's shoulder. "I'll never be able to thank you, honey. But I should say now, and finally, that you are giving me a chance to do what I want to do more than anything else."

"It's going to be hard work, Aaron."

"Yes, it will be. For both of us. But so far as I'm concerned, if I can do the really rough stuff ahead of me, I know that I'll reach my goal."

"And what goal is that?"

"Why, to pass the American Board of Surgery, of course. And doing that is no field of daisies, either."

She giggled and patted his cheek. "You'd better get some sleep," she said. "Tomorrow's apt to be a busy day."

It was certainly a busy day. Aaron left the apartment before six-thirty, planning a dash up to surgery before needing to report in on his own floor. He was lucky. The first person he saw was Sam Miller, come down to fetch the open-heart case on which Gage's team would work that day.

"Can I have a word . . . ?" Aaron asked the man.

"If it's important."

"It is. Laurie and I decided last night that I should fill in that place as assistant in surgery."

Sam watched the cart turn out of the child's room. "Good for you!" he cried.

"And Laurie."

"You bet. Now look, Battle — I'll drop the word. Close the hole. But you go to see Barr as soon as you can today."

"Not Gage?"

"Oh no. Barr is the man you want."

"He did talk to me . . ."

"That's right." Sam hurried after the cart which was ready to roll on the elevator.

For an intern on Medicine to see the Chief of Chest Surgery required a lot of moves. He must find a minute to phone for an appointment with Barr. On his own floor he must ask to be excused and arrange to be covered. He must change to fresh whites and shave again — and try to swallow the tremors which threatened to engulf him as he went up to the Chief's office. He had no success with this last effort. When he knocked on Dr. Barr's door at one forty-five, he was shaking like a leaf.

At the call from within he went inside. "I'm Battle, sir."

Dr. Barr looked up. "Of course you are. Sit down."

Aaron sat, wondering what the Chief could be doing with a slide rule. He held one in his left hand.

"Dr. Miller tells me," said Dr. Barr briskly, "that you have agreed to fill the vacancy as assistant surgical resident."

"Yes, sir."

"Against your better judgment?"

The question startled Aaron. "Oh, not that, sir. Before I didn't see how I could manage it. But I *wanted* to do my residency."

"I see. And now things have arranged themselves . . . ?"

Aaron shook his head. "No, sir, they didn't. My wife arranged them."

"Hmmmn. I believe you are newly married?"

"Yes, sir. Just a month. And Laurie — well, she doesn't know very much about what it takes to train for medicine."

"But whatever it takes, she wants you to have."

"That's about it, sir."

"Young?"

"Twenty-four. But she's a smart girl."

Dr. Barr nodded, his keen eyes warming. "The kind of wife a man has, Battle, can make all the difference in the kind of doctor he will become."

Aaron nodded. When he thought of Tommy,

and other men in training — of Sam Miller and the wife *he* would like to have — and himself and Laurie . . .

"Yes, sir," he said firmly. "I can tell already that it does make a difference. As I told you, she was the one to arrange things so that I could take this opening. But it is not going to be easy for her."

"It won't be easy for you, either. You must know what a resident faces — the long hours and the hard work — the grinding fatigue. A surgeon must learn to stand on his feet for hours on end; even today my back can scream and the soles of my feet seem to come up through my skull. . . . As a resident — and you should explain all this to that bride of yours — you are a graduate doctor, and the work you will do will require much of you in the way of skill and a high level of medical knowledge, as well as responsibility for what you do and for what your subordinates do. We think you have these capabilities or we would not accept you for a residency. But the work is intense, and it requires of you men — especially in the first couple of years — most of the hours of most of the days of the entire year. Your wife — all of your personal life — will be closely involved with your work. In your first year you will work twelve hours a day and three nights a week — often more.

Emergencies, shortage of help — things like that — will put you on extra call. You get a two weeks' vacation each year, and every three weeks you will be off from noon on Saturday until early Monday morning. That is rugged duty."

"Yes, sir."

"Do you have a specialty preference, Battle?"

"I have an interest in chest surgery, sir. But in any case I do plan — hope — to be a surgeon."

"Yes. Well, as you know, this first year you'll move around, take in three or four services. We'll try to make chest one of them."

"Yes, sir."

"And the next year you — "

Aaron put up his hand. "Wait a minute, sir," he said urgently. "I have no thought of being able to manage a 'next year.' "

Dr. Barr continued to look at him, gravely and intently. "Why not?" he asked quietly.

"Well, sir — "

"You are agreeing to manage this year."

"In prospect, yes, sir. That seems possible."

"Well, suppose we prospect the rest of it too. A second year — a third, and a fourth, a fifth. At the end of that time, Battle, you will be an experienced doctor. If you have survived, you will be a good doctor, on the way perhaps to being a big one."

Aaron said nothing. Yes, he thought he would be experienced, and even big.

"One of the chosen," said Dr. Barr, quietly still. "I — and others — have seen great promise in you. Tell your wife that, Battle."

Aaron laughed and stood up. "I thought perhaps she had told you, sir."

Aaron finished his last week of internship and was ready — or as ready as he could get — to embark as a resident surgeon. There were many preparations for this change. Mentally, physically — he talked to Laurie about whites. He had bought some jackets, secondhand, from a third-year man who was going into the Navy. Some of these coats were worn; a couple were almost new. They would suffice, and they fitted. He had, in turn, been able to sell his intern jumpers. But he would need white shirts — quite a few of them. Black ties — at least two. A belt. White trousers and white shoes. It didn't make too much difference *what* Ben Casey wore. Aaron's hospital had its own regulations. These purchases would just about exhaust the money they had in the bank from wedding-gift checks.

"We were going to buy furniture," he mourned.

116

"We'll put it back. This is something we have to do."

He talked to Laurie a little about moving up out of the interns' dorm, down at the ambulance entrance, to residents' quarters on the floor where he would work.

He wouldn't have his own room, of course, as Sam Miller did. As any chief resident did. But even with other men in the room, he would have some semblance of privacy. His own bed, locker, desk — the rooms were really quite pleasant and comfortable. The beds good.

Laurie laughed at him. "You sound much more excited about that room than you ever did about this apartment."

He looked ashamed. "You won't be there!" He clutched at a way to redeem himself.

Then he laughed. "At least you'd better not be. Once a girl did go into the residents' quarters. Lordy, we thought the guys would never get her out! The supe suspected she was there, and did she ever watch!"

But at last the waiting was over, the doubts and the fears, the anticipation.

The day came when Aaron Battle was a resident surgeon! Second assistant, of course, but he would be the one to tell the intern what to do, he would attend residents' meetings, he

117

would scrub for surgery . . .

The first scrub, of course, he forgot to tie his mask before he scrubbed, and he had to do the whole bit again — "a thousand and one, a thousand and two . . . " Which was ridiculous! He had been scrubbing, and doing it properly, since he was a third-year medic. All this talk about special ability and being recruited! He was the dumbest of the dumb. His first assignment, to his disappointment, was to Emergency duty. He had hoped . . .

Of course, on E.R. he would certainly get plenty of experience. He worked with a wide spectrum of staff surgeons assigned, in turn, to Emergency. He did, and would do, a lot of work himself. He had his own room too. But, again, it was near the ambulance entrance, which was noisy.

Whenever a man from chest surgery was needed for consultation or help, it usually was Tommy Dreiserward who came down to Emergency. Tommy and Aaron became ever closer friends. They liked each other and got along well. Tommy had just enough previous experience to be able to understand Aaron's problems and to offer some solutions for them.

He felt, he said, responsible for Aaron's being in the hot seat. He was the one who had organized the delegation that had enlisted Laurie's help in getting Aaron to accept the residency. "The least I can do is to keep an eye on you," he told Aaron.

Tommy was a nice chap, Aaron thought and said. But his wife was a pure horror. How Tommy had ever married her . . .

Well, of course the women thought Tommy was a nice chap too. They immediately responded to his baby-pretty face, his pink cheeks and yellow hair, his heavy-lashed blue eyes, and they wanted to mother him. Carol probably had been one of the earliest of these willing dames, and Tommy had thought it necessary to marry her. People were always imposing on Tommy's good nature. Aaron himself did a little of that. But it was a big help to have him around.

There were plenty of difficulties, just as there was plenty of hard work. As a resident, Dr. Aaron Battle was a member of the house staff of the big hospital. As a first-year resident, he occasionally needed to remind himself, he already had five years of medical training behind him. So he should not feel as green as he sometimes did.

But the residency program was, at best, an exceedingly complex teaching, learning, training program. The head of each department of medicine and surgery, with the help of one or two — or more — assistants, directed the work within their departments or services. These men performed all major clinical work and taught as well. These department men were responsible for the formal teaching of interns and medical students, but their major teaching effort was with the men directly under them, the Fellows and residents. The latter, in turn, had a major responsibility for the day-to-day instruction of the interns and medical students.

Aaron Battle took this responsibility very seriously; he prepared the material for a class by extra hours of study on the subject. Besides his intern classes, he attended residents' meetings, staff conferences, clinics — and always, always, he must read up on things that came into his phase of work.

The cases that came into Emergency could be, and were, distributed throughout the center for intensive care as was indicated. But the doctor on duty — Aaron Battle for instance — must receive the patient, make the preliminary diagnosis, treat any emergency, and decide where to send the case and with what recommendations. A man could do a good job — he could make a holy ass of himself. Aaron found himself about equally good at both efforts.

The emergencies did vary so. Of course a broken leg, a cracked skull — those were easy.

But the girl who came down from the university with her cheek and eye swollen, a raging fever, probably from infection in the ear lobe which, over the weekend, her roommate had pierced with a darning needle. Could this be treated focally? Was there danger of brain infection — her eye in peril . . . ? What should the resident do? Besides mutter about fool girls following a fad to an extremity . . .

There was the man who came in with a high fever. He had had several teeth pulled; his white count was astounding — and dangerous. By then Aaron had memorized the routine questions.

Was the man on medication? He meant, was he taking medicine?

"Only for his heart."

What was he taking for his heart?

Digitalis? Nitroglycerin?

"Has he had a heart attack?"

"Oh yes, Doctor. Six months ago. A bad one."

All right. A coronary — anti-coagulants, which should have been stopped in the presence of infection — but at least Dr. Battle knew where to send the patient, who would probably die.

Under the responsibilities that were loaded upon him, Aaron could fairly feel himself shape up. Now he must make the decisions, and having to make them, he learned to do it. He supposed he was still frightened, but under pressure he had to learn to suppress his terror. He learned to speak firmly to the nurse, to the orderly, and the intern assisting him. He learned how not to take the — the distemper of some of the older nurses. Sure, he was young, and only second assistant, but rather than brain a nurse with a bone chisel, he did learn to say, and quietly, "Now, that will be enough!" Which silenced the older nurse, who certainly had more experience than he did, but who had no ethical right to jaw at the doctor.

The center provided two operating-room suites on Emergency, with stand-by surgical teams on around-the-clock alert for the resident. There was a medical resident on duty; he also was a second assistant, and newly come to the center; he frequently asked Dr. Battle for advice. This was flattering, though Aaron, too, didn't know if the particular patient was in insulin shock, diabetic coma, or heart failure. She *was* a diabetic, and her heart *was* fibrillating . . .

The work could be rugged, cases coming in thick and fast — car crashes, gunshot wounds, a battered child. Or it could be deadly dull, with a surgical resident scarcely needed.

In these lulls Aaron missed Laurie and

hoped she would not get bored. She could, and did, eat dinner with him any evening, but sometimes he was delayed or called away. Still — they could see each other and talk.

About Tommy and the trouble he had with his wife. One evening Carol had taken his car from the parking lot without telling him and had clipped a parked car. Someone got the license number; this was traced to Dr. Dreiserward — the police came to the hospital with a hit-and-run charge. Tommy could establish an alibi, having been in surgery, and he could only "surmise" to the police that someone had taken the car. By then, one headlight broken, it was back in the hospital lot. Later, of course, he had had a scene with Carol.

"I hope he broke *her* headlight!" said Laurie fiercely.

Aaron laughed. "Is that what I should do to you?" he asked.

"*If,*" she said firmly, "if I ever would treat you so! Remember that!"

"I'll remember."

"And you might tell Tommy."

Laurie asked him about Linda Marshall and Dr. Miller. One evening Sam had come into the cafeteria and Aaron had introduced him to Laurie. He had been charming, and she was greatly impressed. "Two such nice

123

people," she said to Aaron as he walked her to the outer door. "What are they going to do?"

"I don't know," he said. "Maybe they don't know either."

"They are very much in love."

He turned to look at her. "How do you know that?" he asked.

She smiled. "I can tell."

At these dinner meetings Laurie told Aaron about her new job. Not every phase of it. For the time she had decided that Aaron was much too busy doing important work to be bothered with her own small affairs. Things like the way she had trembled when she called the office of Mark Hulsey to ask for an appointment about the position. She managed to control her voice and to speak with brief efficiency. She mentioned her father-in-law's suggestion that a secretarial position was open; she told of her previous employment, her reason for leaving it — and she got a fixed date when "Mr. Hulsey will see you." She put the phone down and sighed.

"That's one step taken," was what she told Aaron.

"You're climbing ladders too?"

Laurie laughed. "Mine is more a step stool."

"It looks big and important to me," he said soberly. "Laurie — do you mind, terribly, going back to work?"

She had anticipated this question. "Oh no," she said readily, "not if you're to be too busy to spend much time with me. I really like working in an office."

"You look like a doll . . . "

"But I type like a demon," she assured him.

In the three days she must wait for the interview Laurie considered the matter of clothes. During the spring she had let her "office dresses and suits" wear themselves threadbare. Her trousseau had been made up of "pretty" things. The silk suit in which she was married, ginghams, a skirt and blouse, all chosen for the things she expected to do as a bride. Housekeeping, supermarket shopping, a weekend picnic with Aaron. She had very little that would be right for her as secretary to a successful lawyer.

She spread out the meager display of things that might do. Her gray linen, for a hot day. The office would be air-conditioned. There was one of her old suits that could be furbished — but it was too heavy for now. And that was all.

She would need at least two suits and a minimum of three plain, smart dresses. Good heavens! How could she buy even the first of these things?

She then went into a flurry of budget-making. She expected to get a good salary, and she could charge things against it — but she still must be very careful. From the first she must build up a little reserve.

As carefully as she budgeted her money, she must plan a wise and full use of her time. On Aaron's free days and evenings she must be able to set everything aside. So she must plan — so much time at work, when she would get up, her daily dinner date with Aaron, the duties she would allocate to each evening when she would be alone — laundry, shopping, hair and other beauty rituals . . .

If only she knew what salary she would get . . .

If only she knew what Aaron's schedule would be . . .

Well, she could call him and find *that* out!

He had left her a number to call in any emergency. So she curled up in the corner of the couch, a barefooted girl in blue denim shorts, white blouse, and a bandana tied around her hair, and she dialed the Center number. Aaron had told her that the Center had the largest private switchboard in the city — it served all the various hospital units, the medical school, the university.

In a voice as clear as water she gave the extension number. And then, still limpid, she asked to speak to Dr. Battle, please?

She could hear him being paged, and she smiled. "I can fairly smell the hospital," she told herself. From the noises — the voices, the sound of another phone ringing —

"Battle here!" Aaron's voice came gruffly, a little breathlessly. He'd been at the far end of Emergency — he had an injured woman in hysterics. What in thunder could require him to come to the desk telephone?

The place was jumping that morning, and they were short two nurses. He —

"Oh, Laurie," he cried in despair. Then his attention tightened. "Is anything wrong?" he asked sharply.

"Oh, no, dear. I'm fine. Don't worry — "

Aaron rubbed his forearm up and across his face. "Laurie . . ." he said. "What did you want?"

An old man had fainted and fallen from the bench not ten feet away from Aaron. He — someone — should go to him.

She put her question, explaining that she wanted to budget her time. She could have talked to him this evening — at dinner. He swallowed his exasperation. It seemed quicker to explain to her that he never could leave the hospital on Monday, Wednesday, or Thursday nights. The third weekend of each month he would be free from Saturday noon until Monday morning early. He gave her the date of this first break.

He reminded her that this schedule could always be interrupted or changed.

"But just now," she said brightly, "I can count on the times you *won't* be home?"

He should joke with her about making other dates. But there was too damn much to do.

"Look, Laurie," he said, as patiently as he could. "I can't talk now. I'll see you at dinner, won't I? And, honey, *please* don't call me while I am at work, except when there is a crisis of some sort?"

She was rebuffed. "I thought this was a crisis," she said in a small voice.

He knew she was hurt. But, "It was no crisis," he said shortly, and hung up.

"The little wife burn her biscuits?" asked the intern when Aaron came back to the cubicle.

"Let's stick to the job, shall we?" suggested Dr. Battle coldly.

"Oh yes, sir!" said the intern. "By all means, sir!"

Aaron was ashamed of himself. He should have been more patient with Laurie, and he should *never* chew out an intern who was as willing and hard-working as this chap.

The next day Laurie went downtown to be interviewed for the position in Mark Hulsey's office. She had decided to wear her gray linen. The collar, her gloves, her small shell hat, were snowy white. Her pale hair was burnished, close to her head; her cheeks were pink and her blue eyes darkly shining. She knew that she was too excited and counted on the bus trip to calm her down.

Of course, then the only seat empty was beside a loquacious woman who was free with questions and even more generous with volunteered information about herself.

Laurie handled this graciously and calmly — and when she got off at her stop, she felt that she was back in stride as a businesswoman, able to handle the people whom she would encounter.

The office building was a fine one, not brand-new, but well maintained. Laurie consulted the Directory in the brown marble lobby. There it was. Mark Hulsey and Associates. Attorney-at-law. Twelfth floor.

Well . . .

The elevator was attended, which Laurie liked. The man running it gave her the eye, but that was routine. He was entirely courteous and indicated the Hulsey offices at the end of the corridor.

"You the new secretary?" he asked then.

Laurie smiled a little. "Perhaps," she said, walking away.

The offices were plush and in good taste. The receptionist also looked Laurie over in a thorough manner. She was a young woman with long brown hair, cut into bangs. There was no PBX. The girl behind the desk lifted the phone, pressed a button.

"Mrs. Battle to see Mr. Hulsey," she said softly.

Laurie watched her.

The girl nodded, said, "Thank you," and hung up. She glanced at Laurie. "You may go in."

Laurie hesitated, and the girl pointed her pencil at a door near the corner of the reception room. A waiting man, seated against the wall, looked at Laurie as she crossed the carpet.

There was a short hall, there was a small office with a desk and a low bowl of pink roses, and there was an open door into a much larger office. Laurie hesitated at the threshold. Behind the big desk was a bank of windows which stretched from floor to ceiling. This gave a magnificent view of the city and the river. And the light from those windows was like a spotlight upon the slender blond girl in gray linen.

The man behind the desk smiled and rose. "Mrs. Battle?" he asked.

His voice was deep, and it vibrated. He was

130

a tall man, with broad shoulders.

Laurie moved toward him, across the thick carpet, acutely aware of the rich, dark furnishings, the leather chairs, the painting on one paneled wall.

The man's handclasp was warm, and he smiled down at Laurie. His smile lifted one corner of his mouth higher than the other. He was well-scrubbed, well-groomed — and kind.

Laurie found herself sitting in a leather chair, not too big, and talking to him. His gray eyes watched her intently as he asked his questions. He had checked her references — he mentioned her father-in-law. Did she think she would like legal work?

"If I can spell the words," she told him.

"You've had enough experience . . . "

She had. She also had training in being discreet. The salary was what she had expected, the hours —

"Sometimes I run over," Mr. Hulsey warned her. How old a man would he be? He seemed youthful, but to have reached his place in the profession . . . Anyway, he was entirely charming, and Laurie hoped —

"I need a secretary very badly," he confessed. "A couple of the office girls can type, but my work — Would you consider the place?"

Laurie smiled at him. "I'd love to work

131

here," she told him.

"Good! You can settle some dreary details with Mr. Fehlig; he's one of the law clerks and somewhat manages this office. Where do you live, Mrs. Battle?"

Laurie told him and about Aaron's being a resident at the medical center.

"Oh, you're one of those wives!" said Mark Hulsey admiringly.

"I'm glad to help," Laurie said demurely.

The interview was over, and Laurie should have left. To speak to Mr. Fehlig, to —

She took a step toward the wide desk. "If you need a secretary so badly," she said in a rush of words, "perhaps I could start right now."

He gasped. He rubbed his finger tips across his brow. "Would you?" he asked, leaning toward her.

"Of course." She pushed the white hat from her head and took off her gloves. "Where do I begin?"

Mark Hulsey gazed at her. "Laurie Battle," he said solemnly, "I love you."

The day had gone well, she told Aaron that evening. She was going to like working in that office.

She did like it. Mark Hulsey was a successful lawyer, and Laurie thought she knew why.

His quick mind, his deep attention to detail, his willingness to work, his thoughtfulness of other people . . .

As for his opinion of Laurie . . .

"I hardly know just how it came about," said Mark to a friend, "but I find that, somehow, I am becoming actually infatuated with my new secretary."

"At your age, too," drawled the friend.

"Never you mind about my age. It's exhilarating to know that I can still stir up a pulse over a lovely young girl. And she is lovely. Pretty as a picture, most attractive in every way. Of course, there is one fault — she is married to a doctor."

"Then I need not mention Mildred?"

Mark laughed and drained his glass. "No need. I mention her to myself each time I buzz for Laurie."

His friend's eyebrows went up.

Laurie did not mention the matter to anyone, but she could have said somewhat the same things about Mark. She was, within herself, a little startled by the impact made upon her by this older man. She knew at once that she liked him, that she wanted to do a good job for him. To that purpose she studied his likes and dislikes.

He wanted anyone's full name written out,

rather than initials used, in any letter. He had a graded scale of letter endings — "Cordially," "Very truly yours," "Sincerely yours," "Sincerely."

She quickly learned to understand why and when he would use these terms. And he was always right in his estimation.

Oh, he was right in everything he did or said. In the way he wore his clothes, in the jokes which he enjoyed, his quick appreciation of an extra favor. Almost at once Laurie decided that he was handsome, his face brown with swift trips in the winter — he mentioned them casually. "We spent three days in Acapulco . . ." "I must keep room for some skiing this winter. I didn't get any last year."

Now, in the summer, Laurie reminded him of golf dates. She knew that he tried to swim or play handball every day.

He was older, of course. Forty, she decided. A slim-waisted, erect forty. His slanted smile was attractive, his dark hair expertly trimmed close to his head. His alert eyes . . .

She tried very hard to please him and succeeded, she thought. Within the first week he was calling her Laurie, which she liked. The other girls in the office — Marie, who filed and did the bookkeeping, Sandra, the legal stenographer, and Sally, at the reception desk — were gratefully glad, they told her, that

Mr. Hulsey did like her. It seemed that the previous secretary had often made him bristle. "So, as a favor to us, Laurie," they urged, "keep the boss in good humor."

"I can't imagine him cross."

"That's what we mean," said Sandra. "Keep him that way."

It wouldn't be hard to try. Each day Laurie went eagerly to the office. After she was through in the evening she thought about Mark Hulsey. At that stage she readily would have admitted that she had a crush on him.

Everyone who saw her congratulated Mark on his new secretary. His friends, his wife — a busy, brisk woman as old as he was, with tinted red hair and tired eyes.

"Take good care of him," she told Laurie. "He works too hard."

"I'm afraid so," Laurie agreed.

The clients who came to the office all admired Hulsey's secretary.

"And she can type, too!" was Mark's way of answering their words of praise for the pretty blond girl.

"She'd better!" said Mildred firmly.

Dewey Langston, Mark's closest friend, and the man to whom Mark had first confessed his infatuation with Laurie, kept a close check on things. "Better watch your step," he told his friend. "Mildred would raise hell . . . "

"Yes," Mark agreed. "She would, wouldn't she?"

Laurie was shocked — startled — when Nancy Parks, with whom she sometimes ate lunch, pointed out that she was, perhaps — well — too crazy about her boss. Wasn't she?

"What are you saying?" Laurie demanded, her cheeks quickly crimson.

"That you flush up as easy as not," teased Nancy.

"Oh, I do not!"

"Well, yes, you do," Nancy told her. "But he must be quite a boy."

"He is a prominent lawyer," said Laurie with dignity. "And he is kind to me. He gave me a job when I needed it."

"And you're just crazy about him," completed Nancy.

Laurie sat thoughtful. "Yes," she agreed, "I am. I do think he is perfectly wonderful. But, Nancy, there isn't anything else to it. Besides, there can't be. I'm still a bride. I've been married only two months."

"I remember," said Nancy.

"And you think I don't?"

"I'd hope you would."

Laurie finished her sandwich. Nancy meant to be kind.

"Aaron's gone a lot, isn't he?" her former

roommate asked.

Laurie nodded. "But that's no excuse — I knew he would be gone. I eat dinner with him each evening — at least I try to. He gets his meals free, and while the meals at the cafeteria aren't very exciting, dinner for me there is cheap."

"Is money a worry?"

Laurie leaned toward her. "Of course it's a worry, Nancy. Aaron works so hard and gets so little! His check pays the rent, that's all. Mine — I've had clothes to buy. This suit and a couple of dark dresses. I can't wear pink gingham to Mark Hulsey's office."

"Maybe he'd like it."

"Oh, Nancy! Don't tease! But I have had to charge a lot of things against my pay checks; then there's bus fare, and Aaron's haircuts, and shoes — the money just doesn't go anywhere!"

"How do the other wives manage?"

"I don't know — "

"Maybe you could ask them."

Laurie did not think that she would do this, but three evenings later, when she was waiting for Aaron — they had an agreement that, if either was delayed beyond six-thirty, the other would not wait — Laurie found herself talking to Carol Dreiserward.

She didn't like Carol; the young woman

137

was supposed to be very sexy and attractive to men. Laurie could never see why. She was a tall girl. Her hair had been stripped and tinted a neutral gray-blond color; it fell across her face and hung lankly to her shoulders. Her manner was vivacious and enthusiastic about everything.

Oh, she cried, Laurie's job downtown must be marvelous! Did she wear things like the cute little seersucker job she had on now?

Laurie smoothed her seersucker shirt. "No, I change when I get home," she said quietly.

"You have that much energy?" asked Carol, wide-eyed.

"I don't have that much money!" said Laurie, laughing. "Office clothes cost so much — "

"You wear basics, don't you? Yes, they would cost. Of course, there are millions of ways to pep them up — scarfs and jewelry — so you don't need many. Or do you? I wouldn't know. I've never worked in an office."

"Haven't you?" asked Laurie. "How do you manage?" She did not like Carol! And she was provoked at herself for letting that sort of girl needle her into feeling like a day laborer.

"Manage?" Carol repeated, lighting a fresh cigarette. Her red-monogrammed, white linen shift had cost a lot too. "If you mean money," she said airily, "I don't even try to manage."

"But — " Laurie shook her head. "I don't

understand what you mean," she admitted.

Carol smiled. She did this brilliantly, her eyes darting about the room. People came and went — mainly doctors. "You can't be so innocent that you don't know about charge accounts?" she asked. "And loan services? Of course I get my clothes at a discount — I work in a specialty shop, you know? But even then — " She shrugged.

Bills! Bills piling up and piling up — with no prospect of paying them. "Going into debt would kill Aaron!" Laurie blurted.

Carol smiled at her and shrugged again.

Aaron came then, and Laurie said good-by to Carol and went toward the cafeteria with the tired-looking man in white. He had taken off his jacket, and he looked hot, even in rolled-up shirt sleeves. She decided that she would not mention bills or money to him.

He asked what Carol had had to say, and Laurie in turn asked where Carol worked.

"Oh, in one of those glitter shops on Maryland. I think she doesn't get much more than her clothes out of that job. What are you going to eat?"

At the end of the week Aaron got his first forty-eight hours free, and his mother invited him and Laurie to eat Saturday-night dinner with the Battles.

Laurie didn't want to go; she wanted and she needed to be alone with Aaron. She felt that it would take his whole time at home to get back into her serenity as a wife, a feeling that had been drifting away from her during the past month. There were things to talk about and to do. She wanted just to be *with* him. But — still — there was the budget. A good dinner at her mother-in-law's would save several dollars. With that under their belts, she and Aaron could have a good brunch on Sunday and make a couple of chops do for Sunday evening. She told Mrs. Battle that they would be there.

"Aaron is eating like a horse these days," she warned.

"I know," said his mother. "I've planned a standing rib."

The dollars saved mattered tremendously. It was because of them that, on Friday of the next week when Laurie rode down in the same elevator with Mr. Hulsey — both of them on the way to lunch — and he asked her to eat with him, she agreed. Why not?

There was no reason half as important as the dollar she usually spent for a sandwich and a glass of milk. She was ashamed that such an item should loom so immensely big for her, but it did.

Mark took her to the Tenderloin Room at a nearby hotel. This was a pleasant place of wood-paneled walls, red-checked tablecloths, and generous helpings of steak sandwiches which they ordered, salad in a wooden bowl, cheese and crisp crackers. Mark smiled when she shook her head at his suggestion of beer.

"I'll stick to milk," she said.

"How old are you, Laurie?" he asked, nodding to the waiter.

"It's on the office record. I'm twenty-four."

"You look eighteen."

She shook her head and smiled.

He made the hour interesting, talking about a variety of subjects. Where she had grown up — and his boyhood. The difference in the way boys were and did things now. He had two sons, and they lived in a city apartment.

Twice men came up to the table, and Mark introduced them to Laurie. No one seemed to think much of anything about his having lunch with his secretary. So Laurie should put no significance to it. Just the same, she meant the first time to be the last time she did it. Though she was enjoying herself, and it was pleasant, all afternoon, to think about the break in her routine.

Friday should be Aaron's night off, and he had said he would come home if he could, so

Laurie didn't go to the cafeteria for dinner that evening. He would eat there.

He came in about eight, and dead-tired. He was working without an intern, and he talked a little about the Admissions staff who was, he said, such a perfectionist that a man had to run his tail off to meet even grudging approval.

It was a hot and humid night, and Aaron took a long shower, coming out in his pajamas to suggest that they turn out the lights, open the blinds, and go to bed early.

Laurie made cold lemonade, and he drank it thirstily. There, in the dark, she told him about having lunch with Mr. Hulsey that day, about the Tenderloin Room, and the steak sandwich — she had a feeling that he was not listening to her. He sat with his head back, his legs stretched out. Before she was really finished, he yawned mightily. Laurie took his glass to the kitchen. "All right," she said, "we'll go to bed." It was only ten o'clock. He fell into bed and was asleep at once, lying there like one dead. Laurie tiptoed about, took her bath, and lay down beside him. He might as well have stayed at the Center. She felt tears sting her eyes. She knew that he was tired, because he had said that he was tired, but she could neither understand nor comprehend the extent of his fatigue. He hadn't cared if she went to lunch with an attractive man — well, of course, there was nothing to "care" about. But he could at least have been interested. Couldn't he?

CHAPTER 5

Not slowly, but so routinely, so firmly fixed in a pattern that one stopped noticing the days and counted only the weeks and the months after they had gone, suddenly it was January. Aaron Battle had been a resident in surgery for six months. He had worked in Emergency, then he had spent three months in Urology, which he did not like, though he had learned quite a bit about surgical techniques there. Now he was assigned to Thoracic Surgery which was where, he decided, he wanted to be. He liked it very much.

There he felt he actually was a member of the house staff of University Hospital, as his name was listed in the directory. The clinical department where he now served was headed by Dr. Daniel Barr, with other specialists also on the staff. These skilled men were regular members of the faculty of the University School of Medicine, and Dr. Battle — like the other residents, including Dr. Dreiserward — helped in the instruction of the students in the medical school, both in classroom and bedside. Doing this Aaron was able to *feel* his own knowledge and experience forming into a solid core within himself. Which was good.

He would be on Thoracic Surgery for three months, which from the beginning seemed too short a time. When it would be over — in April — he was scheduled to go to one of the state mental hospitals where he and a chief resident would handle the surgery for the five thousand inmates. This would mean living away from the city, and Laurie would really squeal when she found out about it. Which need not be now.

Meanwhile he worked and enjoyed every minute of it. He talked to patients, he talked to his colleagues, with nurses; he read and observed, and made reports at conferences with other surgeons and specialists. He learned to evaluate what he already knew and how to add to that knowledge. He seldom rested and was seldom alone. Yet when he was alone — as, a resident on call, he found himself alone on the ninth floor, late at night, the shadows furry black, the lights blooming eerily, his lonely responsibility heavy, the first responsibility for forty patients — he confessed that it "kind of shook him." Yet he liked even these solitary moments of duty, when he sat alone in the pool of light at the chart desk. It was a welcome pause amid sustained activity. If that night should remain quiet, he might get as much as a five hours' sleep. A resident seldom asked for a bigger gift.

At work he was responsible for a share of the post-operative patients. He attended conferences every day, usually at noon, where Dr. Barr or Dr. Gage, or both, was present, and the work done, the surgery in prospect, was discussed. Aaron scrubbed for surgery, sometime serving only as second assistant, but as his experience increased, he could be first-assistant, and at times he would operate, with his superior — Dr. Miller, or even Dr. Barr — assisting *him*. Gage, he understood, never accorded this privilege to a first-year man. Which was all right. Heart surgery was for the experts.

One day Aaron would be such an expert, though he still thought he would follow Daniel Barr rather than Ivan Gage. The latter was a whizz-bang doctor, and as such Aaron admired him. But he did not inspire Dr. Battle as Dr. Barr did.

Barr could be rough to work with, but — well, Aaron had never seen him rap an assistant's knuckles as he was told Gage had done to Tommy. Aaron wondered what he would do under such circumstances. Take it, as Tommy did, quietly, saying nothing — his

146

eyes getting darker and a bead of perspiration popping out on his forehead? Or . . .

Aaron talked about this a little to Sam Miller. Sam was prime; he was all Aaron had expected him to be as a superior on the floor. Busy, able, fair — with time always to straighten out a kink for a young doctor. In return a resident would expand his last ounce of effort for Sam.

Even Tommy, who affected a pose of doing the minimum in the way of work and the maximum in the way of relaxation. Assigned to Thoracic Surgery, Aaron had become Tommy's roommate, which pleased him.

"I hope you like having me in here," he said to Tommy a week after he had moved his things up to the ninth floor.

"Why should I like it?" asked Tommy. "I'd got used to having a room to myself."

"Where did you park the guy before me?" Aaron had learned not to believe all that Tommy said.

"The guy before you was a girl," said Tommy.

Aaron looked around. "And you objected?"

Tommy smiled sweetly. "Sam Miller's a prude."

"How'd she get along?" asked Aaron.

"Gage is convinced that no woman is capable of doing surgery."

"Was he right?"

"About this girl? Yes. Her back ached."

"Doesn't everyone's?"

"In heart surgery it does," said Tommy feelingly.

Aaron laughed. "Is Miller easier to work with than Gage?"

"I've never stuck my big fat fist in his way," said Tommy.

"Is that what you did?"

"Must have. The great Gage makes no mistakes."

"I've heard that Miller is as good."

"And one day will be better. But Sam didn't tell you that."

Aaron sat down and put his feet up. "No," he agreed, "he didn't."

"Like everybody else," said Tommy musingly, his eyes on the ceiling, "Miller has his faults."

"But you like him."

"I like him fine. I'd hope I could ever be the doctor he is. And the man, too, if you back me up against the wall."

"So — "

"I still think he has his blind spot. I still think he is crazy to risk his career for a woman."

"But — "

"Any woman," said Tommy firmly.

Aaron reached for a book. "I take it you wouldn't do such a thing."

"Not me," said Tommy. "Would you?"

"Oh — I don't know. Of course I could point out that Laurie is not Carol."

Tommy said nothing.

Aaron glanced at him. "Nor is Linda Marshall," he persisted.

Tommy swung his feet to the floor and sat up. "You're right," he agreed. "And do you know, I'm pretty sure I hate somebody for *that!*"

He walked out of the room, as if he was in no hurry at all to do the things he had to do on the floor, check the patients, look at the chart boards, receive any problems and handle them. But Tommy was a good doctor.

They needed good doctors on Thoracic Surgery. It was one of the "big" departments of the immense hospital complex. Their burn unit was another. But lung surgery and open-heart surgery were very, very big. From the first surgeon at the Center who had dared to remove a man's lung, with the man living for a score of useful years afterward — the Center had given this department the money and the personnel it wanted. As the technique of such surgery, as the refinements of heart and lung surgery developed, the work done had increased in amount and in success. In fame.

149

Humbly Aaron knew this, humbly he was grateful that he had been judged worthy of working and learning here on this floor. He was keenly and exactly aware of how and why he had been coaxed, and coerced, into doing his first residency. Miller — Dreiserward — he knew that all personnel was so carefully chosen. And being grateful for the chance given him, he worked as hard as was necessary. Which was hard.

The work could be exciting, or it could be a grinding series of routine scrubs. He could be kept up all night supervising the giving of blood to a hemorrhaging patient, checking on pressure, watching for the many signs of failure — or success — or he could nearly fall asleep over the chart books which he must read every day and sometimes several times a day. And be shocked at himself for getting drowsy. It was his place to note every detail, to think about those details — while he worked, while he rested, while he walked across one of the driveways that separated the various buildings of the complex, a small figure in white as seen from the penthouse of the intensive-care unit. But without him, he came to realize, some vital bit of work would not be done, some warning change would go unnoticed.

The complex was "enormous." The ninth floor was "big." The flashy work, the great work, was done by Gage and Barr and Miller. But Aaron Battle was there, too, and needed. Some day, his luck holding, he would do the big work.

He called it luck, though knowing where his gratitude belonged and where he placed it. He never scrubbed and faced the mirrored gaze of his eyes above the tautly stretched mask but what he acknowledged his gratitude to Dr. Barr and the hospital, and to Laurie. Here his eyes would smile tenderly. That game little girl, going downtown every day, spending her lonely evenings furbishing her clothes, keeping her collars and gloves snowy white, her hair in shape, just to earn her living — and Aaron's — so that he could stand here this morning and scrub his hands, his knuckles, his wrists.

There were others who had a claim on his gratitude. His father — for his help while Aaron did his pre-med, his med school, and his internship. So a father did owe things to his children! But not the long years and the thousands of dollars which Philip Battle had devoted to his older son. Not the warm coat which he had bought for Laurie. Last night she had shown the coat to Aaron when she came to eat dinner with him. It was a big coat, of red-plaid wool, warm, and thick. There was a bushy fur collar that would surely keep her ears and throat warm.

"Did you pick it out, Laurie?" he asked her. It was — different — from her usual simple, unadorned things.

"No," she said. "Your dad brought it to me in the box. I think your mother may have helped select it."

"Does it fit?"

"Oh yes. These coats are supposed to look big."

"Is it warm?"

"Very."

She would not, he decided, have bought this particular coat. She would not have spent the money in this particular way either. But going downtown every day, waiting for buses and things, she needed a warm coat. He must find a free minute after they got out of surgery to call his father and thank him.

That evening as they ate dinner, he told Laurie that he had done this.

"I'm glad," she said. "Your dad is really sweet."

"They keep in touch with you, do they?"

"Oh yes. If they don't call me, I call them. They know they can't call you — "

"Well, they could . . . " He shrugged.

"You are working hard, aren't you, Aaron?"

She had on the slim green wool dress which she wore to work. There was a narrow scalloped collar of white linen and bands of the same white at the wrists. She had also bought a knit suit — Laurie always looked bandbox clean, even at the end of the day. Aaron was acutely aware of his crushed shirt collar. "I'd worry if I didn't work hard," he said.

"Why?"

"Well, that the hospital was going broke. Or that I wasn't being called on — for reasons."

She smiled. "Jokes."

"Mmmmn. Not entirely. But don't worry. I am working hard." His eyes brightened. "Hey!" he cried. "There's Sam!"

It was Sam, and he came over to their table for a minute to speak to Laurie. Didn't she have a cold? he asked.

She smiled at him. "Just a little sniffle. It's nothing."

"I hope not. Aaron, did you compare those x-rays?"

"I did."

Laurie sat back while the two men talked technically for three minutes. Then Sam went away, greeting others in the room as he passed between the tables.

"We should have asked him to eat with us," suggested Laurie.

"He'd know he was welcome. Do you have a cold, Laurie?"

"Just as I told Dr. Miller. Only the sniffles. I'll be all right. My throat isn't sore."

Aaron's hand reached for her wrist; there seemed to be no fever. He smiled at her. "Go to bed early —"

Laurie nodded. "Is Dr. Miller still interested in Linda Marshall?" she asked.

"I'm afraid so."

"Why should you be *afraid?*"

Aaron put butter on his rye bread. "I've told you. She's Dr. Gage's girl."

"Not if she likes Sam better."

Aaron smiled patiently. "I don't know about that. But I do know, for the past couple of years, she has been as good as married to Gage."

"As good as being married isn't *being* married."

"No, it isn't, but —"

"Why doesn't he marry her? Why hasn't he?"

"I don't know. But they have been — close. She's gone places with him, he has given her things — and he isn't apt to like it if another man should step in and take up her time and attention."

"If he has no claim upon her —"

"Maybe you could argue that if the second man were someone other than the chief resident under this same Gage, a man who has

154

been privileged to be hand-trained by Gage to carry on the great man's work. Oh, Laurie — "

"I can see it wouldn't be the tactful thing or the diplomatic thing," she said. "But once Sam's fallen in love with her, and she with him — "

"That only adds to the risk," said Aaron.

He sighed. "A risk that could include Sam's staff appointment for next year," he said flatly.

She stared at him. "But, Aaron!" she cried. "That's awful. Dirty politics and personal grudges, in a *hospital!*"

"Why not in a hospital? We're human beings, working hard, and working very closely, very dependently, upon one another."

"It still doesn't seem right . . ."

"It still doesn't seem smart for Sam to stick his head in the bear trap." He stood up. "I'm getting some ice cream. Want some for your gingerbread?"

She shook her head. "I can't afford to get fat. My clothes wouldn't fit."

He laughed and went off for his ice cream.

When he returned, he talked about Tommy. "He's an odd one," he told Laurie.

"I like him."

"Yeah, sure. But he's strange too. The way he seems to mope around; he walks slowly and talks little — "

"But he *looks*."

"Oh yes, he does that!"

"Those eyes of his. And his *hair* . . . "

"Someday I'm going to cut that hair while he's asleep. Imagine a dutch bob on a grown man."

Laurie laughed. "It isn't down over his face. And a beard would be worse."

"You're right, since there is a word being passed around here that beards are not to be encouraged among the students, interns, or resident personnel. Which means no beards!"

"Because they aren't sanitary?"

"For one reason. But — that's a funny thing. Years ago the symbol doctor always wore a beard. Remember the old paintings and lithographs?"

"Yes. You wouldn't look good in one."

"Oh, I don't know . . . " He pretended affront.

She laughed, glad that his spirits were restored. "But, Tommy — "

"He'd better lay off. That guy is in trouble enough."

Laurie looked concerned. "I thought you considered him a good doctor."

"He is good. And his work is not involved. I was thinking of that wife of his."

"What's Carol done now?"

"Nothing new, I think. The same old matter of money — and she dates men, I believe."

"She does," said Laurie. "Or at least I've seen her with men — perhaps not real dates." Though Carol had been date-dressed, and date-mannered, going into the big hotel which Laurie passed as she walked from the apartment to the hospital. "One can meet up with a man, you know — and nothing wrong . . ."

Aaron was not listening. The enunciator had begun calling a series of names. "I'll be on that," he told Laurie. "That's my o.r. team."

"Oh, Aaron . . ."

"There!" he said, his eyes beginning to shine. And there it was indeed. "Dr. Aaron Battle. Dr. Battle. Dr. Aaron Battle."

He pressed Laurie's hand. "Take care of that cold," he said. And he was across the room to the telephone. Hanging up, he waved to her and disappeared.

Laurie shrugged and pushed her gingerbread, half eaten, away from her. There went her evening — or at least the hour she had counted on having with Aaron.

She was disappointed and let down. She was tired too. And her cold was a nuisance.

When she went out of the building, there was a taxicab at the door. On impulse she hailed it. These dark winter nights she was sometimes a little afraid of the walk home. There had been incidents of women's purses being snatched right in front of the hotel —

and young women pulled into driveways for assault. She could not afford taxi fare. Sixty-five cents was sixty-five cents. But — well . . . She leaned forward and gave the address of her father-in-law's home. She would go visit with them for an hour. She could tell from the lights if they were at home or not.

They were at home. Laurie paid the driver and hurried up the steps. Now she knew that she would not have another long and lonely evening.

The Battles were surprised to see her. And glad. Mrs. Battle asked if she'd had dinner; Philip said something about not liking her on the streets at night.

"I took a cab."

Edward was at home — his parents called him Eddie, which he disliked. He was an overly tall youth who just missed being hand-some. The light-gray eyes which were inter-esting in Aaron's tanned face, and behind his heavy dark lashes, in Edward were just pale. His features were all a little blurred; his skin had been bad and even at twenty-two was still blotchy. He was thin, and he had not learned to coordinate. Aaron told Laurie that he would soon learn to handle his height. Tonight he wore light corduroy slacks, a yellow shirt open at the throat, and a fuzzy green sweater. He was beginning to study law and seemed very well pleased with himself.

So why should Laurie worry about him?

There were reasons. Eddie always acted as if she were some country girl who needed to be taught the facts of life. He said things of *double-entendre* and then would explain them to her. Under other circumstances Laurie would not bother with Eddie Battle.

Tonight, when there was mention of coffee, she followed Mrs. Battle into the kitchen. She had already told how Aaron was and what they had eaten for supper.

Spanish rice — gingerbread. She shrugged. It hadn't been especially good, but it wasn't bad either. "Aaron gets his meals free, you know, and my eating there gives us a little chance to talk. But tonight he was called to surgery."

Mrs. Battle poured the coffee. "At night?"

"Well, I suppose it was an emergency."

Mr. Battle came out and sat down at the table. "Aaron's working, I suppose," he said.

Laurie nodded, sniffled, and hunted for a tissue. "You've got a cold," said her mother-in-law pityingly.

Laurie smiled. "Just a little one."

"I should put you to bed."

"Yes!" cried Philip. "That's a good idea, Mother."

"Oh no," said Laurie. "I have to go home. I

159

must get my clothes ready to go to work to-morrow."

"But with a cold you should stay in."

"It's not bad."

"If Aaron knew . . . "

"He does know. And he isn't worried. I wouldn't want him to be either. He works much too hard."

"So do you," said Mrs. Battle, "if you can't take care of a cold."

Laurie smiled wryly. "You may be right," she agreed. "You know? Sometimes I wonder if medicine is as important as Aaron seems to think it is." The overhead light shone upon her pale hair and threw deep shadows about her eyes and in the hollows of her cheeks.

"Have you asked Aaron about that?" suggested Philip.

Laurie smiled at him. "I know what he'd say, and so do you. But my question is: Is Aaron right? He seems glad — happy — to work like a ditchdigger for it. And the other doctors do too. The young ones, I mean. And I wonder if they really think . . . ? For instance, does Sam Miller think it is worth giving up the woman he loves and wants to marry?"

"Is he the one . . . ?"

"Yes, and then there's Tommy Dreiser-

160

ward, Aaron's roommate. His wife is turning into a tramp, and Tommy must know it. Does *he* think his profession is worth all that?"

"I don't see how he could think so," said Mrs. Battle.

"The girls have to think it is worth while, to do their part," Philip pointed out. "The way you're doing, Laurie. You're a brave little soldier."

Laurie stood up. "With a runny nose. I have to go back. Thanks for the coffee — and the chance to blow off steam."

"You come any time, dear," said Margaret.

"I'll drive you home," said Philip.

Margaret put cookies into a little box; Laurie got her coat and talked to Eddie while Philip brought the car out of the garage.

In twenty minutes he was home again. "The poor kid gets lonely," he said, hanging his coat away.

"I think she wants to quit her job," said Margaret sagely. She had brought her knitting to the living-room couch. Eddie was sprawled in a deep chair, watching TV.

"Oh no, she doesn't," he said softly.

"Doesn't what, dear?" asked Margaret vaguely. Philip found the newspaper and sat down at the other end of the couch.

"Laurie doesn't want to quit her job," the young man repeated.

"She seems tired . . . " said Margaret.

"Here she does. But you should see her downtown, little mother."

Margaret looked up, frowning.

"When do *you* see her downtown?" asked his father, annoyed, and apprehensive because of Eddie's tone. Aaron had never given his parents any trouble, but this boy — What kind of lawyer would he ever make?

"I go downtown often enough," said Eddie, "to keep a check on my pretty little sister-in-law."

"Have you gone to the office where she works?" asked his father.

"Oh, no need," said Eddie. "But I see her around. And I definitely would *not* say that she wants to give up her job. Not since she's working for Mark Hulsey. If you can call that work — "

"Eddie . . . " said his father.

"I won't say a word," said Eddie, "but — who-whooo!"

Philip rattled his newspaper. Margaret looked distressed.

"Where did you see her, dear?" she asked in a conciliatory tone.

"Not her," said Eddie, leering broadly. "*Them.* And — if you'll pardon the expression, Mom — it was in a bar on Twelfth Street."

"Eddie!"

162

"I'm old enough to go into a bar, Mom." His pale eyes were wide.

"I mean —"

"Oh, Laurie and Mark Hulsey. Well, they were sure there. Having a drink after a hard day in the salt mines, I presume. But then, Mom, she's old enough too."

Margaret looked at her husband. "Philip . . . ?" she said, wanting reassurance. If Aaron's pretty little wife —

"Eddie's teasing you," said Philip.

"Were you?" Margaret asked him.

Eddie laughed and recrossed his long legs. "I saw 'em," he said. "And frankly I was a little shocked too. Hulsey is old enough to be her father, but then — " He shrugged.

"I'm sure everything was all right," said Philip emphatically.

"If we'd ask Laurie . . . " suggested Margaret.

"No, dear," said her husband. "That would indicate we didn't think everything was all right. Eddie's correct. They just were having a drink after a long day's work. They probably had been at the courthouse and were on their way back to the office — "

"I didn't know Laurie drank . . . " said Margaret sadly.

"Now, dear — one drink. And it could have been gingerale."

163

"In a stinger glass?" drawled Eddie. "Oh, come off it, you two. What did you expect when she started to work in that sort of office?"

"Mark Hulsey," said Philip, with angered — and frightened — dignity, "is one of the city's most eminent attorneys."

"Sure he is," said Eddie. "And he's considered a fascinating person, for all his fifty years. As for our little Laurie — I know she looks like the top angel on a Christmas tree, but those girls can be *cool. Real* cool. You know?"

"We'll not talk about it!" said his father. "And I *mean* that!"

He did mean it, but all that night Philip Battle worried and did not sleep. Margaret knew that he did not, but then she couldn't sleep either. Her worry was more about Eddie than was Eddie's father's. She wished her younger son didn't like to tease and make trouble. Laurie was a sweet girl, ready to work hard for Aaron, and Eddie could at least leave her alone.

While Philip . . .

The next day he went to see his older son.

Sometimes Philip Battle could just about understand his son's excitement over medicine. Going into the big hospital, he could be caught up into the bustle, into the sense of urgency — men moving busily through the wide lobby, two white-clothed men talking earnestly in the elevator, the long expanse of shining floor up on Nine, the nurses station, the people . . . Always the people. White-shoed nurses, the spinning wheels of a chair, a patient moving cautiously along on slippered feet, a bell ringing, a cart coming toward him.

"Could I help you, sir?" a nurse asked him.

"Yes — I am looking for Dr. Battle."

"Dr. Battle? Well, just a minute sir. I think, he may be busy. I'll go see. Your name?"

Philip smiled. "It's Battle too. I'm his father."

"Oh! Well, how do you do, Mr. Battle. I'll go see if *Dr.* Battle can get away — "

Smiling, she went swiftly down the hall, across all the shining pools of light. Somewhere a woman talked in a high, shrill voice. Philip shivered and went to stand against the wall, wanting to be as much out of the way as he could. These busy people . . .

Aaron came very soon, surprised to see his father. Was anything wrong? he asked.

"Not that kind of wrong," said Philip hastily. "I just hoped I could talk to you a little."

"All right," said Aaron. He did look so — so grown up here. None of the little boy left in him. "Look," he said, "can you wait awhile? Ten minutes or so? Is this important?"

"It's important," said Philip. "And I can wait."

"Fine." Aaron pointed to a bench against another wall. "You sit over there, and I'll be back." He smiled a professional smile and hurried away, stopped to sign a clip board, saying something to another white-clad doctor he passed, disappearing around a bend in the hall.

Philip waited. There was plenty to look at. Why, one could figure out the life story of a dozen people just sitting there. He took off his overcoat and waited. Hospitals had used to smell — this one didn't. But it was noisy — in a way. Muted-noisy would be the term, he guessed.

And people. All sorts of people. Down at the far end of the hall a gray-uniformed man used a waxing machine . . . doctors, and more doctors . . . always nurses. In white. In striped dresses with white aprons. Some caps were plain, some had a black stripe or two stripes. Some young women wore no caps. There were men in white who probably were not doctors — Philip wouldn't want to be the one to tell.

Patients — the one in the room directly across the hall from where he sat. That patient lay flat, and a doctor in a white shirt stood gazing down at him, talking to him. There was some sort of framework over the bed. Philip could not tell if the man were very sick or not. But Aaron would know. Even now Aaron knew so much more than his father would ever learn. Book knowledge, that was.

But common sense — and the experience acquired by living — perhaps Philip could still give his son advice. He hoped so.

Aaron had said ten minutes. It was closer to twenty when he again came briskly down the hall. "Let's go in here," he said, opening a door. "We can have a cup of coffee and talk." He waited to catch the nurse's eye, pointed his finger to the door, and went in behind his father.

It was a small room and strange. There were two armchairs, a narrow table on which was a microscope and an opened book, a carafe of coffee and paper cups. Along the wall were bookshelves and a rack which held x-ray film. There was a bulletin board on which were chalked schedules. Philip supposed this was where the doctors could relax or study if they had a minute or two free.

"Laurie came to see us last night," he told Aaron, taking his cup of black coffee.

"Oh? I ate supper with her, and she didn't mention it."

"She had a little cold. Mother called her early this morning, and she said it was better."

"Good." Aaron sat at the table and sloshed his coffee around and around in his cup.

"You're tired," said his father.

Aaron nodded. "I didn't get much sleep last night. We had a police case — a man shot through the lung."

Philip shuddered.

"He'll be all right, and it was an interesting case."

"According to your taste."

"Yes. Dad — "

"That's what I wanted to talk about, son. I wanted to find out from you if anyone has ever bothered to ask Laurie if she wants you to be a big-shot specialist."

Aaron was so startled that his hand jerked and coffee slopped out of the cup. He reached for some tissues and wiped up the mess which he had made.

"No," he said slowly, "I think she probably was not asked. I think I probably never considered asking her. And — I can't recall her saying that was what she wanted. She was, however, the one who decided I should take this residency."

"I know she was, Aaron. Because she realized that you'd have to do it to become such a doctor."

"And that was what *I* wanted," mused Aaron. "Dad, don't think I fail to appreciate Laurie. I know the whole thing means a hard pull for the girl. She's alone a lot; she goes downtown to work every day — she doesn't have much of anything she thought she would have when she married me. However, she hasn't complained to me."

"I don't think she would complain. To anyone. But I just wondered if you knew she was working about as hard at your career as you are." He spoke sternly.

"I know — or try to guess."

"I think Laurie enjoys her work," said Philip.

"I hope she does." Aaron was troubled.

"But — perhaps you haven't thought about this," said Mr. Battle hesitantly. "There are temptations to any young woman working in the sort of position which Laurie has. I suppose there are possible temptations in any job."

Aaron frowned. Was his father attempting to tell him something? "I suppose you could be right," he agreed.

"The girl is alone too much," said Philip.

He *was* telling Aaron something! Though, six months ago, Laurie and Aaron had rejected Margaret's suggestion that Laurie live with Aaron's parents. Aaron was sorry this discussion had been started. The things his father brought to his imagination were things he should talk about only to Laurie.

So he sat silent. Thinking, against his will, of the word which Tommy had passed to him that morning. Tommy had had a free night, and he had returned to the hospital to tell Aaron, as the two walked down to a surgical conference at seven-thirty, that Carol had left him. He'd found her moved out of the apartment, lock, stock, and hair curlers, to quote Tommy's wry phrase. Carol Dreiserward had not been able to take what Aaron was asking Laurie to take.

"How long will this situation go on?" Philip Battle was asking.

Later on this day, at noon — more precisely two o'clock than noon — Sam Miller, in the midst of planning seminars with Aaron, had told the younger doctor that he could have the first-assistant spot in Thoracic Surgery the next year. Dreiserward, he had said, would move up to first-year resident.

Aaron had managed a calm, "Thanks. I'll think about it." And then he had gone on to talk some more about the seminars. In them he would undertake to lead, teach, supervise, the three senior medical students who were doing their twelve weeks on surgical. In groups of three he would so supervise all such students as they were assigned to Thoracic Surgery.

This was an important part of his residency. To teach . . . Appearing and sounding calm, actually he had been swept with wave after wave of emotional reactions. Relief, first. The offer of another year's residency meant that he was doing all right. His work had pleased the staff men — especially Dr. Barr and Dr. Miller.

Then, swiftly, had come excitement. He was started! To be offered that residency was what he wanted! The place he wanted!

And finally had come the sad-sweet thought of Laurie — the things *she* wanted were different. Laurie wanted a home — an attractive house, with a decent kitchen. She wanted a baby, and a coat which she could pick out for herself. She would get none of those things very soon. And Aaron perhaps had not the right . . .

Miller had sat watching him closely. He knew about the relief and the excitement — he had recognized Aaron's conscientious remembrance of Laurie.

"This will mean hard work," he said quietly. "Thoracic is not considered an easy course. So what I am offering you *is* hard work and a chance to sacrifice just about everything you wish you had right now. But if

171

you do take this course, Battle, the results of your hard work and sacrifice will make it all worth while."

Aaron had looked curiously at the man who had picked up the second half of his corned-beef sandwich and was eating it. "Tell me, Sam," he said, "*is* it worth while? Has it been worth while for you? Will it be?"

Sam did not bat an eyelash. "I've made it worth while, Aaron," he answered firmly. "And I mean to continue along that course. I mean to consider first, last, always, the heart patients I've been trained to help and will help."

"You could help heart patients somewhere other than on the ninth floor of University Hospital."

"Yes," said Sam, tight-lipped, "I could." Then he smiled slightly, his face folding into lines that curved deeply about his wide mouth. "I know," he admitted, "that the hospital is gossiping about me and my affairs. I can assume that you know this too?"

Aaron had felt itchy-uncomfortable. Except with patients, he was always unhappy when people revealed the intimate corners of their lives to him. "Yes," he said quietly, "I know what you mean."

"Then I can go on to tell you that Gage is watching us more closely than anyone else in the hospital."

He would be. Aaron leaned his forearm on the table.

"I've seen him work, but — what kind of *man* is Gage, Sam?"

Now Dr. Miller's face was somber, even sad. "The only thing," he said slowly, "that should matter to me is the kind of doctor he is."

"But that isn't all that matters, is it?"

Sam shook his head. "It isn't the whole of it. No." For a second there was naked agony in the man's face. Aaron could not bear to look at it. Instead, he pretended to be concerned with the lettuce in his sandwich.

"I want to marry Linda!" Sam cried harshly. "I want to!"

Aaron glanced at him.

Sam shook his head. "*She* says we should not even see one another. She means off the surgery floor, of course."

"Do you go along with that?"

Sam shrugged. "I just about have to."

"The woman calls the turn, doesn't she?"

"It would seem so. And I guess a man would do well to remember that."

At the time Aaron had thought about the situation in relationship to himself and Laurie. Yes, she had been the one to say that they must wait until he finished interning before they married; she had been the one to decide

173

that their relationship must not take any too intimate turn until that marriage; she had been the one to say that Aaron should continue his medical training.

Now he quickly thought again about all these things. And he quietly answered his father's question. "My being selfish," he said, "Laurie's carrying the heavy load, will go on, I suppose, as long as can be managed."

"I'm not calling you selfish, son," Philip Battle said quickly. "Nor do I think Laurie has minded doing what she is doing. But — well, at my age one stops occasionally to take inventory. I am almost sixty, Aaron. And your mother is getting there faster than she cares to admit." He smiled gently at his son. "Also — we have to consider Eddie. He hasn't done too well in law, I'm afraid. Now he thinks he wants to do some graduate work in business administration. Your mother and I feel we should do for Eddie what we did for you. You boys are different, but we don't want to be the ones to point out those differences."

Aaron nodded. "I guess you're right," he said. He looked at his watch. "If," he added, "there is any right in your helping us at all."

"Oh, now, look!" cried Philip Battle. "We want to help our sons!"

"I know it," said Aaron, standing up. "But

Laurie and I will try not to ask you for any more help. We should be able to manage, even though things may stretch a little thin at times."

"All right, son. Only — remember — we do want to help."

Why had he come? Surely not to worry Aaron. Was he hoping to get Aaron's help in persuading Laurie to live at the Battle home? Aaron wouldn't do that. He agreed entirely with Laurie's wish to remain independent.

He thanked his father, said a couple of times that he "understood" — even though he didn't.

And he walked with Philip to the elevator, promising to see the "folks" on his next weekend. Though even that promise could not be kept if Laurie had made other, and more important, plans. Aaron walked back to the station, frowning his concern for Laurie. Everything his father had brought up had previously occured to *him!* He knew that things were rough on the girl; he knew that she must get lonely and bored — and even tempted to seek diversions such as Philip Battle had, fearfully, suggested.

But what his father did not understand, or take into consideration, was Laurie as a person. He probably did not know what sort of girl she was. Honest, straight thinking, and in love with the man whom she had married six months ago.

Aaron sat down at the chart desk and tried to keep his mind on what he was doing. But if he paused at all in his concentration, it was to frown again and ask more questions. Why *had* his father come to the hospital? It was an unprecedented thing for him to do.

Was he warning Aaron about something? Had he cause to feel a warning was necessary?

Or was he — and Aaron's mother — worried about their son and his wife to the point that Philip had come seeking reassurance? In that case, had Aaron given him what he sought?

Did they really feel that Aaron was unaware of Laurie's situation and that a word must be said in her behalf? Yes, that probably was bothering the older Battles, and Aaron should give some thought to the matter, though he felt it already was pretty well in hand.

CHAPTER 6

With the questions which Philip Battle had aroused still in his mind, on his next free evening — free in the sense that he could go home, yet must keep in touch with the hospital and hold himself subject to possible emergency call — Aaron decided that he would tell Laurie about his father's visit.

He came in later than he had hoped, but Laurie was not visibly upset. Had he eaten?

"Yes. You?"

"Oh yes. Would you like something now? Coffee . . ."

"*Your* coffee?" he teased gently, brushing the fine, golden hair back from her forehead.

She gave him a little push. "Oh, you! It can't be that bad."

"If it's worse than we get in the doctors' lounge, it's bad, honey."

"Is it worse?"

"Mhmmmn." He kissed her shoulder.

But when, finally, they were settled down to her coffee and a plate of crackers and

177

cheese, he did tell her about his father's trip to the hospital.

"I concluded that he felt I was not appreciating you, honey," he told Laurie.

"That night when I went over there I had a little cold and was down — though not much. Maybe he felt I was about to demand something from him and your mother, and since they already had bought me a coat — maybe he even had some second thoughts about that coat. I mean, maybe they didn't want me to get an idea that a lot of such things would be forthcoming."

Aaron considered this. "Maybe — " he said doubtfully. Then he looked up, his gray eyes shining like silver through his lashes. "They like you, Laurie."

She nodded. "I know they do. They are really very nice to me. I'm lucky in my in-laws."

"Just that same day," said Aaron hesitantly, "Sam Miller had told me that I could have a first-assistant residency in Thoracic Surgery next year. It's the place Tommy has now."

"Oh, how is Tommy?"

"Low. I told you Carol had walked out on him."

"I wish he had married a nicer girl."

"I think she married him."

Laurie nodded. "Yes, that could be."

"One day he talked to me about Carol. I am sure he hopes I have forgotten what he said. But I didn't or couldn't." He glanced at Laurie. "He said that she was the sort of girl who was outwardly feminine, without being womanly — and that could mean total disaster to the man in her life. Husband, son . . . He said that she — such a girl, was his term — was, under the surface softness, pure flint. Girls like Carol lack generosity and tenderness. They know how to wheedle and coax and flatter, but they know nothing of comfort."

Laurie put her face against his arm. Her cheeks were wet. Aaron cleared his throat. "The thing is," he said gruffly, "being saddled with such a wife, maybe Tommy shouldn't plan anything like the medical career he is planning."

Laurie looked up into his face. "Do you think Sam Miller's way is better?" she asked.

Aaron shook his head. "Not better. Both men would benefit from a good wife."

Laurie's face was pink. "Like me?" she said softly.

Aaron grinned. "You said it — I didn't."

"Aw, Aaron — spoil me a little."

He reached for her hand. "I guess I should," he admitted. "But I do think Tommy is under a tremendous pressure. Trying to do heart surgery in spite of all the things Carol throws at him."

"He doesn't show any pressure."

"Oh yes, he does! The reason Tommy so often stands in a corner, not saying much, is that he doesn't trust opening the flood gates."

"*Aaron!* Does he often talk to you?"

"Not often. Sometimes, a little. Generally in a sardonic way, saying one thing, meaning another. But that can tear a guy to bits too."

"Yes, it could. Maybe we should hope Carol really has left him."

"If he has any plan to make good in heart surgery, he should hope that too."

"It's hard, Aaron?"

He could not, he thought, go into the intricacies of heart surgery — or any chest surgery — with Laurie. She simply would not comprehend the dedication required of a man doing it, the long hours he must work in o.r., with his entire attention focused on what he was daring to do. She would not appreciate the need for meticulous diagnosis, the close and personal relationship such a doctor must have with his patient . . .

"It's a long, hard course," Aaron answered her. "Tommy happens to be good at it, but he would have an impossible handicap if he tried to do it in spite of his wife."

"Did he know this when he began his residency?"

"I'm not sure he knows it now. But *I* know

it — and that's why I think I should tell Barr that I won't take a second year."

"But — " Laurie stared at him. "Do you think *I'm* a handicap?"

Aaron leaned forward to put his half-eaten cracker back on the plate, then he put his arm about Laurie and pressed his cheek against hers. "You are not!" he cried. "I just think I shouldn't take any more training at this time!"

Which was not making any effort to explain to her how he felt about thoracic surgery, his excitement, and the need to learn that difficult specialty over a slow, long time. But Laurie didn't understand — she wouldn't understand. He recalled the time she had chanced to open one of his books. It was made up almost entirely of comparative chest plates. She had looked through it, and she had glanced up at Aaron. "Is that all it is?" she asked. "Just ribs?"

Well, yes, it had been just ribs. So now he kissed her and leaned back against the couch cushion.

"Don't tell Dr. Barr a thing," Laurie told him. "I know that you want this . . ."

"Yes, but — "

"Then we'll manage," she said definitely.

"It's too hard on you."

"You work very hard, don't you, Aaron?

181

As tired as you are sometimes when you come home — "

"I work hard," he agreed. "And I get tired. But I am keeping busy — and I am doing the thing *I* want to do."

"It's the thing *I* want too. Or don't I feature?"

"Of course you feature," he cried. "Too much, maybe. Because you have the hardest part. I know you must get bored and lonely — "

"So I'm old enough not to mind," she said staunchly.

But Aaron looked dubious. She was wearing one of her summer cotton dresses, with a sweater around her shoulders. She had known that they would not be going anywhere on his free night. And they were not.

"Look," said Laurie. "Suppose we had not been married last summer."

"Why should I suppose such a ridiculous thing?"

She smiled at him. "Thank you, darling. But listen to me. I'm serious. Suppose you were alone now — not married to me, or to anybody — just you, by yourself. Understand?"

"I still don't like it."

"Maybe not, but suppose it. If that were the case, you would be getting along on your seventy-five a month, wouldn't you?"

182

Aaron grinned and lifted his shoulders. "I guess I'd have to."

"And you would. You would live in your room at the hospital, and the seventy-five would buy your clothes and haircuts and things. Then take me . . . "

"Any time!" he said, clowning.

Laurie tried to look stern. "Listen to me. If I were not married to you — if I were not married at all — I would have to support myself on my salary. Wouldn't I?"

"Yes. And you would be doing all right too. You'd have more fun — dates and things. Free meals. Hey! Now *I'm* a handicap!"

Laurie's cheeks were bright pink. "Quit that!" she cried.

His smile was gentle. "I was only teasing, honey."

"I know, but I'm trying to be serious. What I mean is, if you could get along, alone, on seventy-five dollars, and I could get along on my salary — being married, and together, shouldn't make any difference."

But both of them knew that it did make a difference. There were such small things as the cheese bought for Aaron, and which Aaron had just devoured. Their apartment — as unattractive as it was — cost more than would Laurie's room shared with some other girl in the hotel for women. Because gifts must be

183

made to Laurie as well as to him, Aaron's Christmas presents from his parents had been smaller this year.

Laurie would not let Aaron go about in bad shoes or a too thin overcoat. Things like that.

On his part, he wanted to give his girl small presents — a handful of yellow jonquils from the corner flower stand, a cute little pin which he'd seen in the lobby gift shop. He couldn't spend her money on such things, though on his own he would have squeezed it out of the seventy-five.

Later in the evening Laurie asked him again about Tommy. Were things really — well, finished for him, so far as Carol was concerned?

"I don't know how to guess about a rat like Carol, Laurie. She can come back — she can make things rough for him in many ways."

Yes, she could. "Well, then, what about Sam? Isn't he going to *do* something?"

Aaron laughed shortly. "You know?" he said. "I don't seem to know very much about decent people either. Just now I'd say Sam is trying to be wise."

"Oh dear. I know what you mean by that," said Laurie. "And that can't be easy either."

"Of course it isn't easy."

Laurie rubbed her finger along his arm.

"You know what I think?" she asked. "I think you and I have all sorts of company."

Aaron glanced at her. "Does that make you feel better?"

"I understand there's strength in union."

"But — is there?"

"Oh, Aaron! You're too serious. Can't you hope there's strength in the fact that other people have troubles and manage?"

He pursed his lips. "I can hope that," he conceded. "But what I'd rather do is see that you have a little fun."

She tossed her head, her fine golden hair spraying. "Oh, pooh!" she declared. "I'm a big girl. Do you have fun?"

"Oh, there are moments. Just now we have a fat old girl in for a mammectomy. She's taken a shine to Tommy, and his efforts to escape — as well as ours not to let him — are a pure riot!"

"I can imagine," said Laurie. "So let's us both have some fun. Let's go down to the corner and eat pizza."

"I can't go down to the corner and eat anything. I'm on call."

"Well, then, I'm going to pop some corn! And don't you dare ask me if we can afford it!"

He reached for her and kissed her. "You're wonderful, Laurie," he told his girl.

Around ten o'clock Aaron was called back to the hospital. He did not want to go, but Laurie was sure he didn't feel the same way as she did about his having to leave. For one thing, he would be busy at the hospital, while she had only the apartment to look at, the loneliness to see and to listen to. She could put up her hair; she need not bother with any kind of robe — there was nothing to do but lie in the middle of the lumpy bed and think.

To have Aaron come home and then leave again after an hour or two — well, the letdown was terrific. And the loneliness, instead of being a gray shadow to which a girl became accustomed, turned into a mist about her, swirling with all sorts of frightening ideas and longings.

Last year, when she had loved Aaron and had agreed to marry him, she had had moments of being lonely for him. But that was different. Things would be different now if Laurie were not married. She would be sharing a room or an apartment with some other girl. She would have company; she could, on her own, go places — to a movie, or she could skate on the rink two blocks away — there were various things which she could do.

But now, unless she could do those things with Aaron . . .

Of course, she was still more or less a bride.

Six months was not long enough — not the six months which she had had — to make her ready to fill her time with other interests. If she had been married longer, things might have been easier — they might have been. She thought. But as a bride she did not want to settle down to doing crewel work or taking night courses at the university, or —

No! She wanted to be with Aaron! To see him, touch him, love him — and have him love her. Had Aaron been disappointed at all that he was called this evening? He had sworn a little and said something about his not being *that* vital, but he had moved swiftly to get into his coat, to kiss her, and when she watched from the window, he had been running down the street.

To what? If she only knew more about his work! If she only knew anything about what he did! There were words — chest surgery, heart surgery. One evening he and one of the other doctors had talked for an hour about "mesh." Listen as intelligently as she had tried to do, Laurie could only gather that it was something of use in healing a large incision.

What ailments led to the need for heart and chest surgery? Children with malformed hearts — men with lung cancer . . . Tonight, in mentioning his chance to do a second-year residency, Aaron could have, but had not, told her about his work. It was a chance for him to say specifically why he wanted that second year, and a third, and a fourth. She would have listened to him and perhaps understood. But as things were now, she had many questions to ask and few answers.

Was there so much to learn about chest surgery that it took as much as five years of a man's life? Five years after he was accredited as a graduate doctor? Five years, each made up of 365 days, each made up of many hours in the operating room? Were there that many different cases? Or did a man need to practice the same thing over and over? For five years? Or six? Or seven?

That was a question which Aaron could answer for her, and specifically. She would not even suggest the question which Eddie had once planted in her mind. Wasn't the hospital, he said, just hanging on to cheap labor which it secured through its intern-residency system?

Laurie had immediately discarded the idea as unworthy, but she remembered his saying it. Other than that, there were dozens of things about Aaron's life and his work which she did not comprehend. Thinking about those things, she always came to the basic question: Why did Aaron want to work like a slave for medicine? Why should any virile young man be willing — no, glad — to immolate himself, to work long, long hours, to go without sleep, and often food, for his profession?

What spark was there? What lure?

Was it because of the patients? Were they people so interesting, so intriguing — Did they make their individual claims upon the kind man she knew Aaron to be? But there were other doctors in training whom she knew and who did not seem to be especially compassionate. Yet they too endured the training which Aaron seemed to think was so desirable. Why?

Aaron's face lit up whenever he spoke of Dr. Barr and Dr. Gage — and Sam Miller. Were these older doctors the reason for his dedication? They did great work, he said, and performed tremendous feats of surgery. He appeared to be like a stage-struck youngster, happy to bask in their presence. . . . But Laurie knew the glamour of those great doctors was only a part of Aaron's interest. He primarily wanted to learn from them so that one day he, too, could do tremendous things and teach other generations of young doctors.

Dramatic things happened in a hospital. Laurie knew that. The drama itself could be the lure for men like Aaron, and Tommy, and Sam Miller, and even that footsy-playing Dr.

Boccardi. If there was drama and good work, too . . .

Tonight Aaron had said something wryly about not being needed that much! But he had been sent for, so he must be a necessary component of the work being done. Being needed would be spur enough for Aaron, she thought.

Of course the hospital was probably being conscientious about its obligation to teach the young resident. Laurie must remember to ask if this was a significant case which had called him back.

All these things — glamour and drama and a feeling of being needed, a wish to be a part of the *big picture* — all of them together — were they enough?

They must be. Aaron was entirely happy to be a slave, and he would be unhappy if next year he could not continue to be one.

Sighing, Laurie got up and drank a half glass of milk. Perhaps that would make her sleep. She came back to the bed, smoothed the sheets, straightened the blankets, and lay down again. She took the second pillow and hugged it in her arms, trying to feel that it was Aaron. . . .

She had often tried to talk to Aaron about his work. She asked interested questions and would have listened with interest — and growing intelligence — if he had answered her. He seldom did. Not in any detail.

It was somewhat the same when she tried to talk to him about her work. He was polite but not really intrigued when she told him of some notorious client who had been in the office, or tried to tell him something funny about Marie, the file girl. When she told him that she had had that first lunch date with Mark, he hadn't seemed to care or to listen.

Now Mark — Mark was a good listener. She meant Mr. Hulsey, of course. Though she called him Mark now in her thoughts. If the name ever slipped out, he would like it. But she must not let it slip out, though everyone called him that. His friends. The clients which came to him. His associate lawyers.

In the six months and more she had served him as secretary Laurie had come to know the man very well. There had been other lunches eaten together — one could not call them dates. They were too casually suggested, too natural a development.

"I have to go out to Clayton, Laurie, and I'll need you. If you don't make a fuss, I'll buy you lunch."

She couldn't refuse. She didn't want to refuse.

One night when she had waited late at the office — as late as eight o'clock — for him to return from a court session which had dragged out interminably, he had bought her dinner. He had, he argued, asked her to stay until his return; he couldn't do less than feed her.

The dinner had been a good one, in a famous Italian restaurant where tables were at a premium. He had pointed out various celebrities to her and had talked in a most interesting fashion about those people. The meal over, he had taken her home, going with her into the building and up to her door — he thought she should live in an apartment house where there was a doorman. For her safety, he said.

Mark Hulsey was a criminal lawyer, but there were borderline cases where he did divorce work. Laurie had typed various statements and depositions in such cases. Some of them ran:

"I took her out to lunch and enjoyed her company very much. We hardly realized at first that we were growing so attracted to each other, for the feeling was quite mutual."

Could that testimony . . . ? It might apply to Mark and Laurie. Because she and her boss were growing to like these excursions they made. He became interested in showing his secretary different restaurants and watching her while she tasted new foods. Vichyssoise. Steamed mussels. Guacamole. One day — a

192

suddenly springlike day in mid-February —
he drove her clear out to the other river, to the
Three Flags Restaurant, which was built like
a boat on the edge of the bluff above the slow-
moving, ice-flecked brown water, and where,
indeed, flags of three nations whipped in the
breeze. They ate crisp-fried catfish that day
and corn bread that was more like cus-
tard. . . .

It was fun to go, to spend an hour in the
restaurant, to drive back to the city, talking
about "native" foods and customs. It was
pleasant that night to think again about the
adventure. Things like that, as they happened,
gave excitement to her days and her lonely
evenings.

Laurie scarcely noticed what was happening
and would have said that Mark put no weight
to their little expeditions. He was just being
kind. She could not be prim or unresponsive
when her boss meant only to be kind. . . .
Certainly she enjoyed the good lunches, but
she enjoyed working in the comfortable offices too. She enjoyed the other girls who
worked there and had fun when a couple of
them would go with her to the nearby, and
very good, cafeteria for lunch.

Then, one late afternoon, when she had
been with Mark in court, walking back to the

office, he had asked her if she would mind going into the Jefferson Bar while he had a cocktail.

"I need it the worst way!"

Of course she had gone with him, and of course she, too, had had a cocktail. Only one.

But the glass sat, half empty, before her, and she was laughing at something absurd which Mark had told her about their client, when Tommy Dreiserward came over to their little table. He had been at the bar; he had seen them come in, he said. "I kept waiting for Aaron," he said. "Though he'd better not show up, as I know the floor schedule . . ."

Laurie introduced him to Mark. She thought it was the first time she had ever called Tommy Dr. Dreiserward. And she stumbled over the name, which made her provoked and turned her cheeks bright pink. Tommy saw her confusion. His finger touched her cheek; his very blue eyes were intent. "You girls are all alike, aren't you, sweetheart?" he asked, and then he went away.

Leaving Laurie distressed.

Mark had not seemed to notice, though of course he did. But Mark would not embarrass her further by speaking of it. In ten minutes they went on to the office, and within the hour Laurie went home, where she changed and hurried to meet Aaron for supper.

She was almost breathless in her urgency to tell him what had happened. He was quite calm.

"Don't mind anything Tommy may have said," he told her. "He's having a rough time these days. Carol is suing for a divorce and has claimed his car."

"Oh no!" cried Laurie.

Aaron shrugged. "She would put a lien on his salary, too," he said, "if he got one big enough to be so dignified."

"Is this his day off?" Laurie asked.

"Carol made him fighting mad when she tied up his precious T-bird, so he got a few hours — to go to see a lawyer."

"Well, he saw one," said Laurie wryly.

Aaron laughed. "He wasn't looking for a criminal lawyer. Not yet, anyway."

He didn't seem to think it at all significant that Tommy had encountered Laurie and Mark in that bar. As perhaps it was not. Aaron would know more about such things than she did. She guessed she could surprise him having coffee with one of the nurses here in the cafeteria and think nothing of it. So . . .

The next week, when she got her pay check, Laurie bought a new suit. She didn't really need it — the three office outfits which she already had were sufficient. She could not afford an eighty-dollar suit just now, and she

195

should not even consider buying one, but she bought it anyway.

Because she wanted to look nice if she went to any more restaurants with Mark. She wanted to look as well as did the other women in the places where he took her. She soothed her twinges of guilt over such reasoning by telling herself that she stood ready to explain this to Aaron if he ever noticed the new suit. She almost always told him when she had a drink or lunch with Mark.

Sometimes she wondered if Mark told his wife about such things? Well, of course he didn't! There was no need. No reason for him to mention the matter at all. Nor for her to say anything especially about them to Aaron. It only put significance to what was without significance.

However, the meetings were becoming more frequent, and a feeling of warm interest was building between them. After seven months Laurie could communicate with Mark Hulsey with a smile and no words required. He could say many words to her with a glance. They had accumulated a great store of knowledge about each other. Laurie knew what colors he admired; she knew that he disliked horse-radish and coffee-flavored ice cream. . . .

They shared certain likes — a folk singer who had a clear, good voice and sang her songs clearly, a Steuben owl in the jeweler's window, the way a rainstorm advanced along the river toward the office windows.

All these little things made for an intimacy that was entirely different from her intimate knowledge of Aaron. She was with Mark Hulsey more than she was with Aaron, and some sort of intimacy was inevitable.

Laurie knew exactly how Mark looked, the pulsing vein in his forehead, the tiny scar in front of his left ear; she knew the way his voice would rise and seem to vibrate when he was angry about something. She supposed he knew equally unimportant things about her.

One day she forgot her gloves. A minute late, she ran out of the apartment in a panic to catch her bus. Her fingers were cold, and when he buzzed for her the minute she came into the office, she had to rub her hands together before she could take notes on the things he wanted her to do "right away, Laurie. I've a plane to catch at noon — you know about that! And we must get eight hours' work into this morning."

She was sorry about her cold hands and murmured an apology.

When he returned from his quick trip to Chicago, he brought her a pair of gloves. Not horribly expensive gloves. They were leather palmed, with cotton-string knit backs — they were made in Italy.

She looked at them and up at Mr. Hulsey and shook her head. "I can't accept them," she said softly.

"For heaven's sake, why not? Monday your hands were freezing."

"Only because I had forgotten my gloves. But I have gloves." She closed the box and handed it to him.

He shrugged and went on into his office. Later she saw the box in his wastebasket.

And she knew that she had made a fool of herself. Her refusal had made the gift much more important that if she had accepted it in the spirit in which it was offered. Mark was being only kind and thoughtful.

Though that was not exactly true . . .

He was a man — an older and exceptionally attractive man — and with him she was well aware of herself as a young and pretty woman. She felt feminine and thrilled by the fact that she was a woman. She brushed her silver-gilt hair, she put on lipstick and fragrant hand cream, she chose her clothes — with Mark's approval in mind.

It was exciting each morning to go to the office, to arrange his desk, to tear off the calendar sheet, set out his appointment pad and three pens, to check on the bowl of fresh flowers on the table against the wall; she carefully adjusted the blinds at the great window. This all done to his exact taste, she sat at her own desk, the typewriter keys rattling, alertly ready to answer the phone and to smile, rise at his coming, immediately available to take dictation or to talk to Mr. Hulsey.

It was exciting to see him in the courtroom, handsome, clever, quick-thinking. She admired his maturity, his sureness of his own abilities. During a trial he was capable both of great courtesy and slashing, even vicious, attack. He could, before and after a court session, be friendly with the opposing attorney — genuinely friendly — and yet be deadly serious when attempting, during the trial hours, to circumvent and defeat this same man.

Mark Hulsey's was a complex character. That he had time to show kindness and interest to Laurie aroused within her a feeling akin to worship. That he should ever say to her:

"I like you, Laurie. I like you very much."

She could only look up at him, worship dark in her violet-blue eyes, her lips parted . . .

"Do you like me, too?" he persisted. "A little?"

Her cheeks flamed. "But, of course . . . " she gasped.

He shook his head and smiled. "Not as your boss," he specified.

"I've never known anyone like you — "

He chuckled then, bent over, and kissed her cheek. Lightly. But —

It was as much as two weeks later when the subject was mentioned again. They left the office together; they went down in the elevator and around to the lot where he kept his car. They must go out to the county courthouse for a hearing. He had decided that Laurie could be most useful at such times, to make notes, to take down a bit of evidence, to find things among his papers . . .

He put Laurie into the car, handed her his brief case, smiled his crooked smile at her, and went around to his own seat. "When I get a lift from a girl at nine-thirty in the morning," he announced, turning the key in the ignition, his eyes turned to look at Laurie, "I'd say there was quite a bit of attraction present. In fact, I do say it!"

But Laurie said nothing. Mark backed the car, turned it expertly into the street. It was a fine car, and he drove it in a masterly fashion.

"Laurie," he asked, "could I hope that the feeling is mutual?"

She took a deep breath. "I . . . " she said softly.

He nodded. "What are we going to do about it?"

She turned her head. His scarf was puffed

up a little under his right ear. She longed to smooth it back into place. "We're not going to do anything," she said firmly.

He nodded. In the mirror she could see that his lips were tightly set. He was accepting her decision.

And she felt let down that he should — so quickly — accept it.

But, of course, that was the way things should be and would be. Laurie was not Tommy Dreiserward's wife! If only Aaron knew what temptation had come her way and could appreciate her behavior . . .

She did not mean to tell him, but that evening she did wish he could be at home. As he could not. He was on duty, and he didn't even get down to the cafeteria for dinner. Laurie waited, then dawdled over her bowl of thick soup, hoping he would come in late. He did not.

Aaron had been held late in surgery — too late to try to send Laurie word. He called her when he came out, but a phone call was not like seeing her and being able to touch her, however briefly. He explained his defection to her. Yes, he was tired. Yes, he would remember to eat some dinner. Yes, he was on duty.

He still wore his surgical gown and cap; at the desk Dr. Barr talked to him for ten minutes about the surgery just done and the prognosis for recovery.

"You could keep a check on that boy, Battle," he said. "Mark the chart —"

This would mean regular, frequent trips to the recovery area. Around nine o'clock Aaron managed a sandwich, and at eleven he came into the residents' lounge, looking bushed, and still wearing his scrub suit.

The other men rallied him about this. He tried to explain the assignment made him — that, and the floor, and —

"I hope your record tallies with that of the man on duty in Recovery," drawled Tommy.

"I'd copy his when he wasn't looking," said Leon Boccardi.

Aaron filled his coffee mug and smiled wanly. "If I knew what Barr's idea was . . ."

"You'll probably be assigned to Recovery any day now," Tommy assured him.

"Night, not day," amended Boccardi.

Aaron nodded and sat down. The chairs in here were all well broken in, the springs sagging from many weary bodies. He drank thirstily of his coffee and laid his head back.

Tommy sat in the corner of the couch, erect, his face impassive. It was hard to get Tommy to show any of the things he had to be feeling. Boccardi should have been in bed — he was on emergency call. But evidently he felt in the mood for a bull session. Evidently, too, the residents had been briefing the new intern on what to expect from his just-begun duty on chest surgery. By the time Aaron came in, they had the lad pretty well scared. Dr. Battle was in no mood for an involved project, but he listened to the things which Boccardi and Tommy thought up to say. Tommy's air and appearance of earnest intent could persuade a timid intern into almost any belief.

"Those two," Aaron finally said to the lad, "are residents only through a court sentence and leg irons hidden under their neat white ducks."

"Can you find some good things to say about the system?" drawled Tommy in a reasonable tone.

"I'm surviving. And so are you."

"But how man *how?*" demanded Boccardi.

Aaron shrugged. "It's turned out some pretty good doctors."

Tommy's eyes flashed. Now he was getting interested. "Have you ever considered," he asked, in his close-clipped manner of speech, "what kind of doctor a non-academic system would produce?"

"Mhmmmn," said Aaron. "The old diploma-mill type."

"Agggh!"

"There must be some reason why all medical students — repeat, *all* — do their damnedest to get appointments to university hospitals."

"I thought research was the reason," ventured the intern.

"You bet it is, from the intern's position," agreed Boccardi. "But maybe you should ask Dreiserward, and Battle — maybe even *me* — how much research we are doing."

"It's being done," said Aaron mildly. "And we are in it with each case of inter-thoracic birth defect that comes to our floor."

"All this means money to the layman," said Boccardi.

Aaron grinned. "But not to us," he agreed.

He got up and went back to the recovery room.

While he was gone a myocardial infarction came in. Tommy took the intern with him on the case and, an hour later, the young doctor was ready, wide-eyed, to tell Dr. Battle about it.

"I had no idea of the strength with which one must pound the chest," he said. "Dreiserward just doubled up his fist and let fly."

Aaron glanced at Tommy.

"Man's all right. He lost heartbeat and there was no blip for a few seconds. But we got it started."

"Brain damage?"

Tommy shrugged. "How's *your* boy doing?"

Aaron poured coffee, adding a fourth cup when Boccardi came in again. "One of your congenital chest defects," he said, "is crying for his mother."

Aaron looked sorry. "We hope we can do a lot for him."

"Look who's saying 'we,' " drawled Tommy. "Does that mean you're taking on next year, Aaron?"

Aaron drew a deep breath. "Laurie thinks I have to."

"Laurie's dead right."

"What sort of thing do you get," asked the intern, "from the birth-defect research program?"

Tommy was allowed to answer him. "Anatomical defects," he said. "Any number of congenital heart deviations — *patent ductus*, the whole thing — valve misplacements, things like that. T.B. comes in on this, because of environmental predisposition — and of course there are some physical characteristics passed on. Boccardi's pigeon breast in nine-twenty — "

"Don't call him that!" cried Aaron sharply.

Tommy lifted his long, thick eyelashes. "What's eating you?" he asked mildly.

Aaron shifted in his chair. "I just don't like

205

patients listed as 'Ward Three's' or 'skulls,' or 'carcinomas' — or 'pigeon breasts.' Excuse me, but I don't."

Tommy made no comment.

"I'll bet I've taken long case histories on a dozen of that boy's relatives," mused Boccardi, as if the little interchange had not taken place.

"Were any of them . . . ?" asked Aaron with interest.

Boccardi nodded. "In fact, there wasn't a good profile showed up in the dozen."

"That's helpful," said Aaron with satisfaction.

The intern looked at him in protest, then colored. "I see what you mean about research," he said in apology.

"But no money rubs off," Tommy assured him.

"No — but then, we know when we elect medicine that we won't earn anything for a dozen years."

"Residents are paid better in some hospitals," said Boccardi.

"You thinking of changing?"

"No. Because I want to stay with University Hospital."

"So do we all," agreed Aaron. "And that's what's so hard on our families. The *system* takes them very little into account."

206

"I guess a man really should not get married before he's through his training," said the intern. He was an exceptionally boyish-looking one, short, stocky, pink cheeks, and curly blond hair.

"Well, that settles a lot of questions," said Boccardi. "And after it I hate to bring up the fact that our being residents is just about as hard on our *girls* as it is on our wives."

"How's that?" asked the intern.

"You haven't had any trouble with the girls you tie up with a date and leave waiting for you to show up?"

The intern smiled widely. "I've been married since I was a senior in pre-med," he said blandly.

The other men chuckled. Even Tommy laughed. "Do you have problems?"

"Not too many. My wife's a nurse."

"Well, you must have it made, boy."

"Not really. My wife wants six kids, and we're beginning to count on our fingers."

"Benjamin Franklin was born when his mother was fifty-six," Tommy said.

The intern eyed him skeptically. "Really?"

Tommy shrugged. "I've not counter-checked the information," he admitted.

"My wife was telling me — she's down in Orthopedics — that there was a thing of some sort between the surgical supervisor and our chief resident up here on Thoracic. She heard that they were going to be married and then that they weren't . . . "

"Which states the whole thing about as succinctly as could be done," said Boccardi.

"Speaking of residencies being rough on families," agreed Aaron.

The intern frowned. "Shouldn't I know what goes on?" he asked. He was going to make a good doctor, even if he did stay looking twenty.

"I think you should," said Aaron. "We get enough boo-boos up here on Nine without your adding any to the heap." He looked at his watch, then swiftly outlined the situation between Dr. Miller and Miss Marshall.

Young Dr. Wall pursed his lips into a soundless whistle. "What are they going to do?" he asked.

"About the only certain thing," said Aaron, "is what they are not going to do. He can't marry her . . . "

"But why not?" asked the young man. Boccardi made sounds of applauding his stand.

"You don't think his career is important?" asked Aaron.

"Because this nurse has been Dr. Gage's girl? But wouldn't you say that Gage is entirely too big a shot to persecute a man — "

"Maybe he wouldn't persecute," Aaron

conceded. "But think of what the hospital would say, his friends — and Miller's friends — even the city, for all I know."

"What would they say?" asked Dr. Wall.

"Why, that both Sam and Linda owe something better to Gage. He's brought Miller up by hand, you know."

"As a heart surgeon, you mean?"

"As a Gage-trained heart surgeon. I couldn't mean anything bigger."

"He seems awfully nice."

"Miller is an exceedingly nice guy, Wall. Grand. And he is just about the perfect doctor."

"I've heard that. It's too bad, isn't it, that he — well, picked the wrong girl?"

"At least too bad. For him, and for Linda too. Because she also is a grand guy."

"Aw, she's too much woman to be called that," demurred Tommy.

"If she's young," said Bob Wall thoughtfully, "and I suppose she is?"

"Thirty-five, maybe. Smashing good looks."

"Then, if she is Gage's girl, why doesn't *he* marry her?"

"You know," said Dr. Boccardi, "I think someone should ask him that. Maybe you could do it, Wall."

The other men laughed.

"I'll ask some damn fool questions up

here," said the intern. "But maybe I'd better lay off that one. I've had one interview with Dr. Gage, and somehow I got the idea . . ."

Aaron stood up. "You keep that idea firmly in your mind, son," he advised.

"Yes, sir. I gather that Dr. Miller will specialize in heart surgery."

"Yes, that will be his place on the team. And he should have a fixed place as clinical professor of cardiac surgery."

"He could, I suppose, go into private practice."

But Tommy was shaking his head.

"No?" asked Dr. Wall.

"You'll learn," said Tommy. He was a most capable doctor, and his instruction of young medics always impressed Aaron. "Patients these days want team medicine. They flock to the hospital clinics and emergency rooms to get it, where, as little as twenty years ago, they used to see a doctor in his own office. It is said that people like the impression of confident skill which the team conveys."

"A surgeon has to have hospital affiliation, anyway," Dr. Wall pointed out.

"Yes, he does, and there the private-practice man isn't hurt by the competition from the university hospital."

"Which isn't as good as it sounds," said Aaron, who was working on his chart board, getting his records in order.

But Wall wanted answers. "Why not?" he insisted.

"Well, hospital affiliation used to be a part-time responsibility. Office hours were easily managed. Today — and yesterday, too — there is increasing pressure toward full-time staffing of all hospitals."

Wall thought that over. "Then how . . . ?" he asked alertly.

"How can a private practitioner keep himself medically alert?" Tommy voiced the question.

"Yes! How can he?"

"I'll answer that when you tell me the answer to how a full-time medical-school faculty member can retain his clinical skill without patients of his own."

Dr. Wall shook his head and got up to answer the buzzing wall phone. "We need a pronounce," he told the group. "Who . . . ? He nodded. "I'm on my way," he agreed.

The men left behind smiled wearily. Boccardi decided that he would go to bed. Aaron went back to Recovery. Tommy went to look at his infarction. Wall's education had advanced a distance this night.

CHAPTER 7

By the end of that week Bob Wall was able to say that he felt he had always been on Thoracic Surgery and had things well in hand. Aaron suggested that he not invite fate by making any such declarations. "Your *things* can go boom without warning."

"Yes, I guess they can."

"Better snatch some sleep," Aaron told him, smiling.

"Yes, sir."

"And don't call me sir!" said Aaron automatically. There was no more than a year's difference in age — and knowledge — between him and this likable boy.

Dr. Wall disappeared into the shadows of the darkened corridor, and Dr. Battle sat on in the pool of light at the chart desk. He was the resident on call; this was only a pause amid sustained activity. Responsibility for all chest-surgery patients now rested on him. On a quiet night he could hope for a little sleep — sometimes he even got several hours of sleep. Tonight was not dramatically busy, but there were things that kept constantly happening — a death, an emergency admission — a heart patient threatening to fibrillate, who must be watched. One of the nurses cut her hand . . .

It was five in the morning before the resident could seriously think of his room and bed. He walked down the hall, his eyes already half shut, welcoming the sleep to come. He was due in surgery at seven-thirty. Breakfast could be skipped. He yawned.

The lamp was on in the room which he shared with Tommy. Aaron either did not notice or gave it no thought. A tired resident could sleep under floodlights.

Aaron pulled off his tie, shed his jacket, lifted his arms and shoulders to flex them, to relax — then he leaned forward sharply.

Tommy . . .

The man lay on his side, his long, fair hair across his forehead. One hand dangled from the mattress edge. There was a dark spot — a stain — a dark and viscid stain — across the pillow and the sheet. Below his hand, something on the floor caught the light —

Aaron, feeling that he could scarcely move at all, took a step — another — not to touch his friend, but to reach — and pick up — that little knife.

He held it in his rigid hand. It was a very little knife. Really, just a bright edge of steel, fastened into a handle. A scalpel. Aaron probably had one just like it in his jacket pocket. Along with scissors, a thermometer, and —

He drew in his breath with a sharp hiss and cast the knife away from him. It clattered on the tile floor.

At the sound Aaron shuddered, glanced over his shoulder at the door — yes, he had closed it. Then he moved slowly, with chilling dread, closer to Tommy's bed. He could not touch him — yet he must touch him. Though he knew before his fingers ever reached the wrist —

Still, he did lift it, and then he held it, looking down at Tommy's face where it lay in that pool of life's blood. The thick, dark lashes made a crescent upon the man's cheek — the lips were parted just a little . . .

Aaron put his finger tips to his own lips. What . . . ? And why? *Why?*

Later he knew he had been looking for a note. But the only thing on the small desk, under the down-bent lamp, was an issue of JAMA — open at page 1181 — the page of Deaths in the American Medical Association.

Aaron began to read them, because he could not yet do what he knew he must do. The little paragraphs marched down the page in three columns, the names lifted into prominence by darker type:

ARCHER, ROBERT WILLIAM . . . Denver . . . 1932 . . . age 57 . . . pulmonary emphysema.

CARROLL, LEO HENRY (M) . . . Dermatology. . . age 55 . . . Coronary occlusion.

And right here should be, would be, a paragraph that would read:

DREISERWARD, THOMAS (M) — U. of California 1963. . . died February 26 . . . age 28 . . . of hemorrhage due to self-inflicted laceration of common carotid artery.

Aaron drew in his breath, hearing the sob-like sound in the room. So it would read next month, or the next — where it could, fifty years from now, have read so differently.

DREISERWARD, Thomas (M) — U. of California 1963 . . . Certified by the American College of Chest Surgeons . . . affiliated with . . . died, age 76, of heart attack suffered in connection with an automobile accident.

Aaron shut his eyes. His hand reached out to the magazine and gently closed it.

He should not touch a thing — the scalpel, or the magazine. He should not touch Tommy again.

Tommy!

He must tell someone.

But *he* was the resident on duty. Of course there was Sam too. And the floor head . . .

Again he pressed his finger tips to his lips. He picked up his jacket and made a struggle of getting into it. Without looking again at Tommy's bed and what lay upon it, he went out into the hall. The clock said fourteen minutes after five. A nurse was hurrying down the corridor; the night head sat behind the desk. Aaron knocked on the chief resident's door and then opened it. Sam was stirring, sleepily.

"What's up?" he asked, still not really looking at Aaron.

Aaron tried to speak; his voice croaked in his throat, and he coughed to clear it. "Something — awful — has happened . . . " he managed.

Now Sam was looking at him. "What's happened to *you*, Battle?"

"Get your clothes on — something will happen to you too."

As Sam dressed quickly — the way a doctor learned to do almost the minute he acquired his stethoscope and thermometer — he cast concerned glances at Aaron, who leaned, as a man exhausted, against the wall. He guessed his face showed how he felt, though how could it? Because he had *no* feeling! He was in complete shock — and the chief resident knew that probably.

Sam sat down to tie his shoestrings. ". . . can't imagine what could have happened . . . " he muttered. Then his head snapped up, and he got to his feet, his hand seizing Aaron's arm. "Linda?" he cried. "Tell me . . . "

Aaron shook him off. "No!" he shouted. Then he was sorry for the man. Aaron would have felt the same apprehension about Laurie. "It — it's Tommy," he said. "And it's bad . . . "

"All right," said Dr. Miller. "Let's go."

They walked swiftly, automatically conscious that they must not betray, or create, panic. Aaron opened the bedroom door and stepped aside. Dr. Miller went in — and it was bad.

At once a hundred things needed to be done, with no more flurry apparent out in the hall than would be created by any emergency, which that floor was able to handle without any flurry.

Always with the lump of personal grief suffocatingly in his chest, Aaron must quietly tell the floor head what had happened. He phoned to Dr. Barr and to the Administrator and told them.

They would need a stretcher.

No. The police would come first, and they did come. Aaron told them of how he had found Tommy — when —

There was not much to tell, but that little must be said to each one. Yes, he had picked up the knife — and put it back. He had tried to find a pulse — nothing else. He would not, he decided, mention the Journal's being open at the page of Deaths.

He had found no note.

All this was said over and over, his agony and his disbelief multiplied by the people he had to talk to and the things he had to do.

The work of the floor must go on. Already the floor schedule had been altered to eliminate Tommy's name. Aaron stared, gritty-eyed, at the blur made by the eraser and the new name written in. *He* was scheduled for surgery, but Dr. Barr said he should be excused. And always there must be more talk.

"The newspapers . . . ?" suggested someone.

"Not yet!" snapped the Administrator.

Of course the word had swept the floor and was beginning to seep through the entire hospital. Orders went out; until Dr. Dreiserward's family had been contacted no discussion of his unfortunate death was to be permitted.

Tommy's family — a grandmother in California, and Carol. His wife. Though no one could find her. She had moved from the apartment where she had lived; she no longer worked at the specialty shop.

Aaron said he did not know where she might be; she and Tommy had been separated for several months. There was a lawyer whom Tommy had consulted about the car, but Aaron did not know the lawyer's name.

Dr. Barr, looking very sorry, asked him if he would go through Dreiserward's papers — his billfold . . .

This was the practice of medicine. This was the pain of being a man's friend.

Sometime in the gray mist of those first hours a student nurse brought Aaron breakfast on a tray. He drank the coffee and attempted the toast.

He thought of the surgical schedule. No, he was to stay on the floor. The patients of course must not know . . .

Of course.

At ten o'clock, when a spontaneous pneumothorax came up from E. R., Dr. Miller told Aaron to "take care of it." His tone was brisk. His manner said, "Snap out of it, son.

The hospital work must be done."

Aaron was glad enough to go to work. The patient was in pain — and distress. Aaron took him to the floor o.r. and scrubbed. He had never done this particular bit of surgery, but he knew what was needed, what must be done. He studied the x-rays on the scanner and went to work. Relief of course was immediate, and he could tell the man, as he took him back to his bed, that the bleb — the bubble — would not re-form.

"Thank God!" said the patient fervently.

Aaron smiled at him, patted his hand, and went out to chart the small event. Small as this floor went, small when he thought of the open-heart surgery on which he had been scheduled to work that morning. He was glad Sam had made him do the pneumothorax. It had jolted him where he badly needed a jolt.

He could now, more calmly and more assuredly, talk to the new policeman who waited for him at the desk. This was a detective sergeant.

No, Aaron said, he did not know of any real reason for Dr. Dreiserward —

Yes, his wife had left him. But that was months ago.

And claimed his car . . . ?

Yes.

How about any professional difficulties?

Absolutely not! Tommy was an excellent doctor, by record. The hospital would confirm that.

Yes, they were friends. Dr. Dreiserward had many friends. He was Dr. Battle's roommate, but the hospital had arranged that. Yes, Dr. Dreiserward had been best man at his wedding.

Last June. . . .

Yes, again, they were friends.

On the basis of that friendship Aaron was summoned to the Administrator's office. And questioned. About the possible places where Carol could be found, without a police alert. Aaron thought of asking Laurie and discarded the idea. She probably would not know, and she had better be kept out of the whole mess.

This was turning into a long day.

Dr. Barr asked him if he thought he could carry on for Dreiserward.

"I'll try, sir."

"We'll get another resident in — I understand you are not opting for heart surgery."

"That's right, sir."

"Would you pack up Dr. Dreiserward's clothing and personal effects, Battle? I don't like to ask this of you, but you might rather do it than have a stranger — "

Aaron would rather, but the task was a dif-

221

ficult one. So to invade a man's privacy, so intimately to handle his personal belongings — Aaron was tempted just to tumble the drawer contents into a box and sweep his clothes — Tommy's navy worsted suit, his tweed sport jacket — everything! — over his arm and carry them downstairs. He made himself carefully pack the bags, put the books into a box. The microscope, the two stethoscopes . . .

He would never need to go to Tommy's funeral. He had buried his friend this day.

After he was finished, and sometime after two had eaten a sandwich, he made rounds, wrote orders, attended a floor-staff meeting, and wondered how he would get through his second night on call. Sam stopped him as he went toward his room, thinking that he had better shave and put on some fresh clothes.

"Have you looked at the board, Aaron?" the chief resident asked.

"No — "

"You've been relieved of tonight's duty. You look bushed. So go home and get some rest."

Aaron nodded. "Thanks a lot, Sam. The thing shook me, I'll admit."

"It shook us all."

"Can you manage?"

"We'll manage. That new intern is pretty good."

"Wall is very good. He — All right, I'll take off."

"Right away."

Aaron looked at the clock. It was not quite five. Just twelve hours since — "Thanks," he said quickly. "Thanks a lot. I'll see you in the morning."

"You'd better. Barr has an exploratory. And you're scheduled."

"I'll be there."

He was glad to be given these free hours. If he hurried, he would catch Laurie before she would start toward the cafeteria. They'd manage something to eat at home. He was so considerably "shook" that he did not believe he could tolerate one more nurse coming up to him and saying she was so sorry about Dr. Dreiserward. "He was such a darling . . . "

As Aaron went past the elevator, his numbed mind read the sign, "Department of Thoracic Surgery." And he thought about the game which he had used to play — with Eddie and his parents, and his friends — of transplanting the letters of one word to make another.

Thorax, he thought. T-h-o-r-a-x. Well, let's see. There was ox . . . yes! And hart. Ox hart.

Now there was a useful bit of information.

Did it make any sense?

Absolutely none.

223

Nothing made any sense.

Meanwhile little Laurie, too, was hurrying home, sitting on the edge of the bus seat to get there more quickly, her piquant face concerned with her plans, to get home quickly, to change her clothes . . . She would wear her new suit, the pretty light-blue one with its cocoa blouse. That was why she had told Mark she must go home first; she could not go on her first real date with him wearing her green wool, the cuffs not entirely fresh after a day's work.

Well, really, it was not a *date,* though it would look like one, and he would make it seem like one too.

Two weeks ago he had had her get him a couple of seats for the Royal Scots Tatoo, which was going to show at the Auditorium tonight. He'd talked enthusiastically about the prospect. He did love drums, he said, and marching men . . .

"So do I," agreed Laurie. "And trumpets!"

"You should go."

"Oh, I can't count on Aaron's being free."

"Too bad."

But this noon, just as she returned from lunch, Mrs. Hulsey had phoned. Would Mrs. Battle please tell "that husband of mine that I have a lousy cold? He'd better not count on

224

my going to his Tatoo thing."

The cold was genuine. Laurie could tell from Mrs. Hulsey's voice. She said this to Mark when she delivered the message. "It's too bad. I don't see how she could bear to miss the performance! All those kilts . . . "

Mark had nodded and shrugged. Then his attention had quickened. "Look!" he said. "If you're free — I mean, if the doctor is going to be busy at the hospital, and you'd spend the evening alone — why don't you go with me?"

It sounded reasonable, but Laurie shook her head. "Oh, I couldn't," she said firmly.

"But of course you could."

"I don't think so." She turned to go back to her desk.

"Wait a minute," he said. "If — well, if you're having qualms, I'll have Mildred phone you."

Laurie felt the blush rise hot upon her cheeks. "Oh no!" she said. She would not show herself to be that young and prudish.

"All right, then. We'll have dinner — "

But she was firm about dinner. She must go home first, change . . .

He gave in and said he would pick her up at seven-thirty.

It was Laurie's plan to eat quickly with Aaron and get back to the apartment in time to slip into the pale-blue suit.

She certainly had not expected to find Aaron in the apartment waiting for her; something must have happened. He never got home this early on even his free nights. He —

Her confusion made her unable really to comprehend the story he was telling her.

What was she going to do? How could she reach Mark and tell him . . . ?

She listened to Aaron, she said she was so sorry — and she thought about her need to break the date. She would just have to phone him at home — there wasn't anything else to do!

She didn't actually say that she had planned on seeing Nancy Parks, but she was guiltily aware that Aaron thought she was breaking such a date.

Fortunately for her, Mark answered the telephone when she dialed his home number. If she had had to ask to speak to him — But he did answer. "There's been a death — of a close friend," said Laurie. "I'm sorry."

Mark was sweet; he said that he understood. Laurie hung up. *Now* she could give her full attention to Aaron. "Tell it to me again," she urged. "I just can't believe — This is an awful thing, Aaron. I'd never have expected it of Tommy. Would you? He was such a dear person!"

Aaron nodded. "And now he's dead," he said wearily.

"But what happened? Oh, I know about Carol and the way she's done — but she's been that way all along. Something special must have happened last night, don't you think? To trigger this?"

Aaron took a deep breath. Laurie now was sitting beside him, her pretty face deeply troubled. "Almost anything could have triggered it," he said. "I don't know of anything. But it could have been — maybe some medical incident, or just the accumulation of the over-all situation suddenly got too heavy for him. He did it in a quiet, professional manner —"

Laurie clapped her hands to her cheeks. "Don't tell me!" she cried. Then she saw the look in Aaron's eyes. "Oh, Aaron," she sobbed. "It's been terrible for you, hasn't it?"

He bit his lip, got up and walked out into the kitchen, came back with three crackers. "I don't think I've eaten much today . . ." he said uncertainly.

"I'll fix something. I have soup — bread — eggs . . ."

"Later." He sat down again beside her. He took her hand in his. "It's been rough," he said, his tone dull.

"The thing that is frightening me," said Laurie, "is — could this happen to *you?*"

Aaron glanced at her.

227

"I mean — you — when you're overworked, and tired ... Sometimes you do seem so tired, Aaron!"

"I know. But you should remember one thing, Laurie. I am not the man Tommy was. And you are not his wife."

"Why not?" she asked blankly.

He smiled a little. "In both instances?"

"Yes, I think so."

For a moment he sat thinking of his friend, the languid grace of the tall, and seemingly indolent, man as he went about his duties in the hospital, his white clothes crisp, the ceiling lights shimmering upon the helmet of his too long golden hair. Aaron thought of Tommy's vulnerable mouth, and the way his thick, dark lashes veiled his always watchful eyes. . . .

"He was an exceptionally able doctor," he told Laurie. "He was quick to observe, to act. I know he tried to seem lazy. But in the operating room Tommy's hand and instrument were always where they were supposed to be; in any conference Tommy wasted few words but could always come up with the right conclusion, usually before the other men were ready to do more than look at the symptoms or lengthily consider the situation in hand. He was doing very well in his profession; the staff men liked his work, and the patients fairly worshiped him. His co-workers — you, tonight, called him a 'dear man.' People felt that way about him; he was sensitive and overly emotional. He knew that himself and tried to disguise it by an air of lazy indifference. Today I have had a dozen people speak of him as 'darling.' "

"Well, he was," said Laurie, her voice trembling.

"I suppose he was. Which was what made him so vulnerable to the hurts he would not let show. He always seemed more interested in the hurts and the pleasures of others than interested in his own affairs."

"I did like him."

"Everyone liked him, honey. And made tremendous demands upon him. I've known patients to ask him to stay with them during the night before surgery — and he's done it. Coming into the room a dozen times during the night, holding a woman's hand, quietly reading to a man — he did that way. Losing his sleep, and his own feelings torn."

"I think it was wonderful," said Laurie.

"Maybe. But it was not especially realistic medicine, my dear. And now he is just a name on the Deaths page in the Journal — when he could have contributed a great deal to medicine." Aaron got up, found his own copy of the magazine, and told Laurie how he had found it open on Tommy's desk. "Under the lamp — he had been reading about the deaths of all these doctors. Men like himself, men he did not know."

Laurie pushed the thick magazine away. "So that's the doctor Tommy was. Now, what about you?"

"I am a good doctor, too, Laurie," Aaron said gravely. "But I am the kind to do my job first, last, and in between."

Laurie nodded. Yes, that would be Aaron.

"I have friends," he told her. "I think people like me — but no one has ever called me a 'darling.' "

"You're different, Aaron."

"Yes, I know I am different. Now Tommy — he had another weakness, Laurie. He couldn't wait for things to come to him. Not the way I can be patient. He knew he was doing all right, and that things would come, but — well, in his work, once he had learned a technique, it bothered him — bugged him, was his word — to have to do the same thing over and over. He wanted to go on to other tasks.

"I don't know that this is true, but it seems possible that Tommy was impatient — last night — about the time it was taking for him to learn to be his own man, to do things on his own, rather than patiently take orders from other doctors.

"Of course his troubles with Carol must have been a part of this. She was making trouble, and in the spot he was in Tommy couldn't go out and handle that trouble. He had to continue to live in the hospital, his hours long, his pay small — his hands tied."

"Carol . . ."

"We couldn't find her today. At least, she had not been found at the time I left the hospital."

"She's a terrible person."

Aaron laughed shortly. "We didn't like her, because of what she did to Tommy. She should never have been his wife. She hated all aspects of medicine — the smell of his clothes, the battery of pens and thermometers and stuff a doctor carries in his breast pocket, the talk his friends engage in. She was completely without understanding of the demands made upon him. I understand she could throw a screaming, dish-breaking tantrum when he would be called away from some small party.

"She constantly did things to make him jealous with men she cared nothing about. She ran up tremendous debts against him, and she finally walked out on him and took his car. She — well, as I said, she was not the wife you are, Laurie.

"You're having a rough time too. Just as rough as Carol ever had. And I know it. As

Tommy knew it. He would have been grateful — *I'm* grateful for your putting up with all you must endure."

Laurie took his hand, turned and put her face against his shoulder. She was weeping, and he held her tenderly. She clung to him almost desperately.

Laurie was desperate. And in almost complete panic. Should she tell Aaron, here and now, about Mark? About her near-date with him tonight? Tell him how she had come to feel about her boss — excited, and eager . . . ?

Another time she might tell him, and he would be patient and understanding of her "crush" on the older, successful man. Tonight, though he was not ordinarily an "emotional" man — tonight Aaron was one.

What should she do? She was so painfully aware that she was not being, and might not turn out to be, the girl he thought she was.

CHAPTER 8

The next morning Aaron left for the hospital as early as six o'clock, not letting Laurie get up to fix him any breakfast. He seemed his usual self; his face was still grave — but he had slept and would probably be all right.

Very soon Laurie did get up, ate some breakfast, straightened the apartment, dressed, and went to work. She felt tired — as if she had worked too hard the night before. Though she was determined not to think of the night before. She would subdue it in her mind. If she possibly could . . .

At exactly ten o'clock Mark Hulsey buzzed for her. With a determined show of efficiency, which did not to any extent cover her dread, she went into his office and closed the door behind her. Mark sat at his big desk, his chair turned so that he could look out at the sun-tinted mists that swirled above the river, the chimneys and tall buildings, the great bridge, probing blackly upward through the glow.

Laurie stood in front of his desk, her heart

racing, her face held firmly into lines of calm waiting. As always, her plaid suit was trim, well-pressed, and attractive. Her pale hair was brushed into a smooth twist at the back of her head.

Mark only glanced at her. "What happened last night?" he asked. The pulse in his forehead was prominent; his hand seemed tight upon the chair arm.

Quietly Laurie told him what had happened. "When I got home I found Aaron there. His friend — his roommate — had committed suicide yesterday morning. There's a story about it in the paper today. I could not leave Aaron — "

Mark nodded and swung around to face her. Now his face was in shadow. "Of course you couldn't," he said warmly. "What a terrible thing it must have been."

He went on to say all the properly sympathetic words. Though, Laurie knew, he could not have any real understanding of the event, its impact upon Aaron and upon her.

Laurie sat down in the chair, listened, and answered as was needed. Once her finger ran around the collar of the knitted shell which she wore as a blouse. The neck was not tight . . .

That day Mr. Hulsey was wearing a dark-blue jacket with gray trousers. The collar of his white shirt was soft-looking — he was not due to appear in court. Laurie opened her notebook; he would soon get down to the day's business.

But — he did not.

After he concluded his really kind words of sympathy, he sat for a long minute, tapping his fingers on the chair arm, and looking at Laurie.

"I felt sorry about last night" he said then. "I missed having you go with me so much that I realized how greatly I enjoy the times you *are* with me. Your youth — your prettiness — your enthusiasm. You make me feel young and enthusiastic again. I thought about this a great deal last night. So I have a suggestion to make — see how it strikes you. And that is, that we each — the two of us, Laurie — might conceivably love each other and might eventually marry each other, Laurie. We — "

The notebook slipped from Laurie's grasp and fell to the floor. Automatically she bent to retrieve it; she was a little dizzy when she straightened. "You're joking!" she gasped.

He shook his head, one corner of his mouth drawn in. "Oh no, I'm not. I think it presents a wonderful prospect."

Again she shook her head, the golden hair rippling. "How could we ever . . . ?" she gasped.

He nodded. "This is a law office, my dear. Divorce is a word we know quite well."

She opened her soft lips to speak and had to make a second effort. "It — it's a shocking idea!" she cried. Swiftly she wondered what Aaron was doing at this minute. In green, in the operating room? In white, at a patient's bedside?

She could not find any reality in her own presence in this quiet, paneled office, the carpet soft underfoot, the winter sunlight like gold dust filtered through the blinds.

"You'll adjust," said Mark softly, at his most charming. "I was shocked, too, when the idea first came to me. I have a truly wonderful wife and two fine children. College for them is just around the corner. This means, of course, that I am older than you, Laurie —

"I know all those things." He got up and walked the length of the big room and came back. Laurie sat with her head down, her thoughts whirling.

"I considered them," said Mark, close beside her. "But in spite of that I succumbed to the idea of you and me — acceptance of the idea has grown very rapidly, Laurie."

Now she was shaking her head again. "You know that it is a crazy idea!" she cried. "You know that we should not give *any* thought to it."

"Ah, yes," he said again. "Conscience. You have one, I know. And, believe it or not, I do too. That problem is all that has held me back from speaking of this before. But last night I was so disappointed that you were not going to spend an innocent evening with me — so frustrated — that I knew I must speak, that I must determine what lies ahead for us, Laurie. There could be no need for me to 'court' you. We already know each other, we like to be together — we know what we could make of this."

Laurie stood up. And she faced him, though even then she looked only at his mouth, not into his eyes. She took a backward step, away from his outstretched hand. "You are mistaken, Mr. Hulsey," she said briskly. "Nothing lies ahead. And I won't listen to anything more on the subject." She turned on her heel and went back to her desk.

Where she sat in a complete vacuum, her hand holding a pencil, her eyes down toward the papers she should be checking. She could not even think. . . .

Within a half hour she knew that Mark left the office; she heard him speaking to Sally, the receptionist. Laurie sighed with relief. She could not, she would not, have talked with him again. That morning.

She made a genuine effort to work, but she

still pushed any thinking to the back of her mind. Thinking about herself, that was. When the exact time came, she went to the washroom, then put on her little hat, her coat; she found her gloves and purse and went out of the office, to lunch.

But she did not go into any of the places where she usually ate her sandwich or her bowl of soup. Instead, she walked along the city streets, not seeing the people who jostled past her, who waited at the corners for the WALK signs, who streamed out and carried her with them on the tide of humanity, all hurrying somewhere. She hurried, too, though she was going nowhere.

She passed the windows of the big department stores. She looked, unseeing, at cruise wear, at golf clothes for men, at a superb fur coat thrown across a white love seat, gloves and a diamond bracelet, a purse, laid casually upon a low table.

And against her will, thoughts seeped into her mind. She heard the voices of these thoughts and could not shut them away. It was as if some close friend were whispering to her.

"If you married Mark," the voice said, "you would have a fur coat. Mrs. Hulsey has furs. She comes into the office — superb suit, shoes, a coat like that one on the brocade

238

loveseat, or the short white beaver you saw last week and drooled over . . .

"There's Mark's big car. You'd have one of your own. Any kind you wanted. No more running for the bus and shivering in its drafts as you're bumped and shaken on the trip downtown.

"You wouldn't have to wear this horrid coat which Mr. Battle bought for you — the huge fur collar. You could pick and choose your own clothes.

"You could have children. A baby. And you can't have that — yet — with Aaron. Though you do want children. . . .

"You'd live — not in a city apartment as he lives now. Or —" Here there was a really nasty laugh. "Or in the apartment where you live now. You could have a house with a big bowed window, hung in pinkish thin stuff, that would draw into close, pleated folds. A bedroom with white furniture, painted with flowers — a thick blue carpet and a deep, green velvet armchair.

"You would not have to work — or worry about a budget —

"You —" She had gone down along one street for several blocks and now was coming back; if she crossed this intersecting street, she would be at the door of her own office building. She —

She was swept hotly with shame for herself! To let thoughts of cars and fur coats — and babies! — come into her mind! To let herself even consider temptation.

She was already married! She was Aaron's wife, and she loved Aaron! She did! There, on the windy, gritty street corner, she thought of intimacies which were pure wonder with Aaron but which would not be —

The light changed, and she started across, feeling tears, hot and burning, behind her eyelids. Aaron trusted her. He appreciated what she was doing, the way she rode downtown in the bumpy old bus every morning and wore the coat which her father-in-law had selected for her — the way she faced the temptations of men like Mark Hulsey. He knew all these things were hard for Laurie, and he loved her for enduring them. He had said last night that he appreciated her.

So why should she feel sorry for herself and even *look* at a darned old coat thrown seductively across a white brocade love seat? She was the one who had decided that Aaron should do the residency. He was working very hard at it — could she do less? Could she cheat on him? And turn him into a Tommy Dreiserward, a name in JAMA? Or, since he said he was a different man, make him into a doctor like Sam Miller, all for his work, with nothing else given him?

Of course Laurie didn't want that!

So —

She need not ask anyone else, either, what she should do about Mark. She *knew* what she must do!

She went into the drugstore on the ground floor of her office building and was lucky enough to find a stool empty. She perched upon it and ordered a "quick" malt. She even found jokes to make with the counter boy, who knew her from various coffee breaks.

She drank her malt and went upstairs, where she managed to get some work done, though now her mood was one of letdown. She was definitely in the doldrums.

It was all very well to determine to be a "good girl," but where was the rewarding feeling of lofty virtue?

Mark did not return to the office all the rest of the day, and Laurie was glad. Though of course tomorrow he would be there, and on the days after that. There would be the occasions when they might, reasonably, lunch together during a court recess, or share cocktails while waiting on a jury. Now Laurie would not enjoy these things. She would be most uncomfortable, trying to seem friendly, but impersonal — and probably appearing only prim and young.

But she must steel herself to endure such a time; she could not afford to leave her good job — the figures of her budget danced crazily between her and the paper in her typewriter.

Cleaning, $50

Food, $720 . . .

No, she could not afford to leave. And certainly she could manage the situation. It would be, she supposed, a continuing conflict between intelligence and emotion.

Perhaps she could persuade Mark as to the true nature of the contest for them both. He had mentioned his family. There were other reasons why he should not throw his cap over the windmill. If he would consider them — the opinion of his friends, his position in the legal community . . .

This morning he had been considering only how he felt and how Laurie might feel. But the logical conclusion of such consideration must be based on something deeper than excited emotion. She would tell that to Mark, if the subject should ever come up again. She hoped it would not.

On her part, suspecting that she possibly would get no help from this man, she must keep it firmly in her mind that there could be no chance, no thought, of her ever marrying Mark Hulsey. And having a pale golden mink coat.

242

Of course, temptation would arise; down on Olive Street this noontime it had swept over her. And confusion would engulf her; she knew that a sense of her youth and — well, innocence would bring on its familiar confusion. She hated to feel young and unsophisticated, so she had better set out a firm anchor against being swept off her feet by such embarrassment.

Besides, Mark was a most attractive person; she would be less than honest not to recognize his impact as a man upon her as a woman. She had "loved" working in this man's office; she had "adored" going with him into smart restaurants and bars.

She had been having what, before this morning, she would have acknowledged to be a "crush" on her boss. He had known those things and acted upon them.

The emotional draw of his attractiveness would continue and perhaps grow. It might even become stronger and exert a force which could overcome all her intellectual reasoning. If she would let herself think about Mark's charm, his kind thoughtfulness, his ability to talk in a flattering way to her —

She must find a weapon against this. Or use the one she already had. Mark had mentioned her conscience. Well, laugh at it or not, she did have one. She knew what was the right thing for a wife to do. She must be loyal to her husband, whom she loved.

Whom she loved.

Again words were echoing in Laurie's mind. She closed her desk, went in and tidied Mr. Hulsey's desk — from now on he would firmly be Mr. Hulsey — and she prepared to leave for the day. She did love Aaron. She had married him because she loved him, and she still did. So there was her weapon. Her feeling for Aaron was stronger and could be made — could be kept — stronger than any feeling she might have for Mark.

So, other things being equal, there would be no contest. Of course things were not precisely equal. For instance, things could be easier for her if she were with Aaron as much as she was with Mark. There lay a very big trouble. She knew that things would be easier if she were with Aaron more.

Tonight she would eat dinner with him. He would be tired. He had entirely too much work to do at the hospital. His hours were too long; he must read and study . . . He didn't eat properly, even when she was with him for dinner and tried to persuade him to order the food he needed. Meat, and salads — desserts high in sugar and milk —

She ate dinner with him often, trying always for five nights a week. And he had come to expect her to tell him what to put on his tray. But halfway through the meal he could be called away, the food uneaten, and there were some evenings when he did not show up at all. Those evenings she suspected that he ate no dinner. Those evenings she *knew* she went home and felt sorry for herself.

This evening she tied a plastic hood over her hat and hair — it was raining — and hurried out to the elevator, out of the building, to the bus stop.

The weather was really getting foul. Any other night she would not have much trouble persuading herself to stay in, but tonight —

She thrust her feet into red boots, wrapped a thick wool scarf around her head and throat, and ran all the way to the hospital. She hoped that Aaron would not be late; she hoped that he would not be too tired to talk to her, or too cross —

Aaron was waiting for her. He scolded her mildly for coming out on such a night and hung her wraps on a coat rack, then followed her to the food line. Before they reached the counter, he predicted what nourishing food she would pick out for him.

She glanced around at him, unbelieving. He seemed to be in high good humor — though there were shadows about his eyes and lines about his mouth. He was making all this effort for *her*. She reached back for his hand and squeezed it. He nodded.

"You choose," she said.

"I'll take chili . . . "

"Oh, not chili, Aaron!" she said quickly, then laughed a little in acknowledgment of the trap he had set for her.

"O.K.," he agreed. "Pot roast, huh?"

"I think so — and ask for extra gravy."

They could not find a small table, so they must sit at a large one already occupied by two doctors, a medical student, and two nurses. Aaron named these people to Laurie, who nodded and smiled.

She was sorry that she would not be able to talk to Aaron, though maybe this was better. She really didn't have much of anything she could say to him. The other young people talked about the lousy weather and how busy Emergency would be. The med student said the trick was to imagine you lived in Sweden, or Russia, then this rain would seem amazingly springlike.

The older of the two nurses said she really did not think they needed a Pollyanna in the hospital.

"But *you* like me, don't you?" the student appealed to Laurie.

"You bet," said Laurie, accepting one of Aaron's rolls.

Carefully — very carefully — there was no mention of Tommy Dreiserward. Laurie was both shocked and relieved to realize this. Aaron busily cleaned his plate and took his part in the talk going around the table. Laurie didn't quite comprehend it; she touched his arm, and he nodded.

"They're talking about Linda Marshall," he explained. "She asked for a change of duty."

"Nobody can imagine Surgical without Marshall," said the eyeglassed doctor. Laurie had immediately lost the names of these people.

"There must be other nurses capable of holding down her job," said the student, with an eye on the nurses now present.

"Tell that to Dr. Gage," one of them suggested.

The student shook his head.

"Why did she ask to change?" Laurie asked Aaron.

"I'll explain later," he murmured. But the others at the table would have none of this. They, in detail, told Laurie why the surgery head thought it expedient that she see less of the chief resident in Cardiac Surgery, so —

"Where did she ask to work?"

"P.N."

"Psychoneurosis," Aaron interpreted.

"Which even I can see is the waste of a good surgical nurse," said the student.

"*That's* what Gage thought," agreed the handsome doctor.

"Did he ever make a row!" marveled the younger nurse.

"I don't believe I ever heard the grapevine so busy either." The second one laughed. "I understand there were meetings at all levels. Was it stormy up on Nine, Battle?"

Aaron nodded. "When Dr. Gage is upset — " He shrugged.

"Well, I guess he plenty was," said the older doctor, "because Marshall's name has gone back on the Surgical duty roster."

Laurie looked up at Aaron. "Couldn't she change her work if she really wanted to?" she asked.

Aaron tried to explain. The hospital was a machine, he said, with each component part finely geared and meshed. Time was lost, even lives endangered, if one of those parts was lifted out of its place and an attempt made to fit it into —

Laurie waved her hand. "Doesn't the fact that your old cogs and gears are human beings make any difference?" she demanded.

Aaron again tried to explain to her. She listened, but she really was more interested in looking at him, at his gray eyes behind his dark, stubby lashes, at his mouth when he talked. And, looking at him, she thought about how much she loved Aaron; she remembered the way she first fell in love with him. Because of his smile, she thought — a flashing white smile in his dark face. And the gentle, delicate way he used his hands. He was a strong man, and pretty big, but his body was slender, his limbs taut with muscle. His voice — she coughed a little and ate the peaches she had selected for her dessert. This was not the time or place to get physical.

The other doctors, the eyeglassed one called Bunk, and the handsome one — he really could offer competition to Ben Casey *and* Dr. Kildare! — were talking to Aaron and the nice young student about some sort of meeting — a session, they called it, where Aaron had "taken the podium."

Laurie looked up at him.

"It was a staff-resident conference," he explained. "I just found myself talking."

"Compulsion," said the handsome doctor dryly. He glanced at the enunciator box, then tipped back in his chair and lit a cigarette.

Aaron smiled. "It was something like compulsion," he agreed cheerfully. "I had those things to say — and I said them."

Laurie touched his sleeve. "You had to say *what*, Aaron?" she urged. "And *where* was it?"

Everyone answered her at once. The med student mentioned a man named Flexner.

"He put medical training in charge of the universities, all right," agreed Aaron, "but who has been responsible for isolating the medical schools *from* the university?"

"You tell 'em, Doc," said the handsome doctor.

"I did tell them," Aaron admitted ruefully. "There I sat with the dean of our own medical school, and he's an officer of some sort in the Association of Medical Colleges as well, and I told him how to raise the level of medical practice in this country, how to get, and produce, more doctors and better men as doctors."

"You were among friends," the eyeglassed doctor comforted him.

"Yes, I was," Aaron agreed. "Maybe even our dean knows that something must be done to erase the present stodgy concept of medics."

"It takes a man to fight AMA," said the doctor called Bunk.

"I wasn't taking on any such a fight alone," Aaron hurried to retort. "A lot of doctors — and non-doctors — think that the Deans' Club is a bad thing. But, because of its exclusive nature, there is our best chance for change."

"Radical change."

"I did not mention the word radical."

"No," said his challenger, who sat smiling receptively. Laurie, puzzled, looked from one man to the other. The nurses had departed. "You just told one of the deans how his club could break the chain of circumstances that has left the American people short of doctors."

"I said the level of medical competence could be raised if the university medical schools would assume the responsibility for training hospital interns and residents. I said they should also assume the responsibility of keeping doctors up to date after they enter private practice.

"I said, too, of course, that they should give some power in the American Association of Medical Colleges to presidents and faculty of the universities, that this would result in more scientific and some humanities-discipline of thought in the study of medicine, and would add social perspective to the old concept of treatment and prevention of disease."

Bunk shook his head. "I thought I heard you say all those things," he marveled.

"And you thought I was making trouble for myself," countered Aaron. "But don't you chaps think the deans of the medical colleges know they'll have to make some changes in the system? For all you know, I was only saying things that have already been discussed thoroughly in their meetings. We have to have more doctors — our doctors are going to have to be better — in all ways."

Laurie sat appalled at what she was getting out of the interchange. And when she and Aaron left the table and went out to the hall, she tried to talk to Aaron about it. "You shouldn't make the big shots mad, Aaron," she told him. "Should you?"

"Oh, now, look, Laurie — "

"You keep telling me that Sam Miller can't be in love with Linda because it will make his boss mad. All right. Then why should you criticize the doctors, or deans, or whoever they are who are your superiors?"

He smiled at her and took her coat from the rack. "Stealing a man's girl is one thing," he said. "Criticizing the system under which he works is another. Anyway, don't worry, honey." He patted her cheek with his finger.

"Why not?" She let him button her coat under her chin.

"Because, first," he said, "you wouldn't know what you were worrying about."

She didn't want to be talked down to, she — It had been a long day! So she flared out at him in a manner that was not like Laurie. "I *know* I don't know what any of this is about!" she cried, snatching the scarf from him and wrapping it about her head. "But why don't I?"

Aaron sighed and shook his head at her. "I don't have time right now," he told her, "to put you through a medical course."

She dropped a glove and stooped before he could to pick it up. "Sometimes I wonder if you have time for me at all," she gasped.

"We had a nice, leisurely dinner together this evening," he pointed out. "That is, it was nice until you got cross."

She whirled to glare at him. "I am not cross!" she cried.

He shrugged. "It comes out cross."

"And you don't like it."

Now his eyes were gray steel. Aaron had a temper too. "No, I don't like it when you are cross over nothing. The little we are together — "

"That's it," said Laurie, going to the big door and tugging at the handle. "We are together very little!"

"Which you didn't know about last July?"

"There were a lot of things I didn't know about last July!" she cried.

"I'm sorry." He opened the door for her, and that, too, infuriated her. That he should be strong . . .

She went outside without kissing him or even looking back at him. Aaron stood at the door until her wind-blown figure disappeared into the blackness. Then he rubbed his hand back over his hair and he walked, fast, toward the tunnel. He'd straighten things out tomorrow. Though he wasn't entirely sure just why they had quarreled *this* evening.

Laurie hurried home, glad when she reached the lobby of the apartment house, more glad when she could unlock her door and go into her own home. Suddenly she was tired, and she felt like weeping. So many things had happened this day. To end it by quarreling with Aaron — and over nothing. As she remembered them, the words she had said sounded very silly — and she had not been given any time to apologize, to make up or discuss what had made them quarrel.

The next day — Mark was out of the office again; he had a cold — she called her mother-in-law midafternoon and invited herself for dinner. This suggestion was always cordially received.

"Why, of course, Laurie. We're having hash, but I'll make a pie. What kind would you like?"

Laurie told her, knowing that this would please Margaret Battle. Then she called the hospital — as always thinking of the complicated switchboard — and left a message for Dr. Battle with the nurse, or whoever, up on Thoracic Surgery. "Please tell Dr. Battle that his wife is going to eat dinner with his mother this evening."

"Oh, that's nice," said the woman's voice. "I'll sure tell him. How are you, Mrs. Battle?"

Laurie said she was fine and hung up. She hoped Aaron would not think she was still peeved at him. She wasn't. Just tired — and she occasionally did eat with her in-laws. About twice a month.

Tonight she went straight out there from the office, having stopped in the corner candy store to buy Mr. Battle a half pound of the glazed nuts which he liked. It was a bargain at the price; she would not need to spend anything for dinner.

The evening went pleasantly. The dinner, of course, was delicious; she said she wished Aaron could have shared it.

"How is Aaron?"

She told them about Tommy — yes, Aaron had taken that hard. He had got an extra night off because of it. But she had eaten dinner with him last night, and he seemed to be enough over the shock to appear normal.

"Of course I don't really know. That's the trouble for us. We don't see enough of each other to know even how we *feel*. It's almost like strangers meeting — he tries not to worry me and I try to be pleasant with him." She laughed. "We don't even have time to quarrel and make up."

"Then you'd better not quarrel," said Philip Battle.

"Oh, we don't. Not big quarrels. Mainly over my coffee." Laurie smiled. "But I do wish I could see more of him. I know his work doesn't allow this. That is, I'm told that it doesn't. Aaron doesn't talk to me much about his work. I really don't know anything about it."

"Is this weekend his free one?" asked Aaron's mother.

"Yes . . . It should be."

"Well, you two kids had better come here for Sunday dinner."

Laurie thought she saw an escape. "Oh, we couldn't," she said quickly. "There's to be a memorial service that afternoon for Tommy — in the chapel. Aaron and I would have to go. Of course we *want* to go!"

Saturday morning Mrs. Battle called Laurie and said firmly that she was expecting her and Aaron for dinner that night. Laurie decided to let Aaron manage to refuse if he were so inclined.

But when he came in at one-thirty he groaned, then said he guessed they'd better go. "We'll go late and come home early," he promised.

Laurie had decided that their little spat had not been important enough to bring up. She agreed when he suggested that they go over to the rink and skate. This was fun; it got Aaron some fresh air and exercise. He said he'd suggested it because she looked so cute in a hood.

"And sitting on the ice?" She laughed.

"I'm usually right down there too. I can't tell."

Their cheeks were red and their eyes bright when they burst into the Battle home at five o'clock. Laurie offered to help her mother-in-law. Yes, she could cut up things for salad.

Philip Battle took his older son down to the basement to see his new jig saw. "It's the slickest thing . . ."

Then, under the lights of his workbench, with the smell of sawdust in the air, the new saw having been demonstrated and tested, Philip, in his most well-meaning, and bungling, way, tried to talk to Aaron about how hard things were for Laurie.

"Oh, Dad," Aaron protested, "not again."

"Yes, son. And then again, if I need to."

"What is it you think I can do?"

"Not much, I know. But then, it wouldn't take much for you to talk to her when you are together, to show her that you trust her."

"She knows I trust her. If trust is needed."

"It may or may not be. Then I've been thinking — how much does she know about the work you do?"

Oh-oh! Laurie must have said something.

"How much does Mom know about the textile market?" Aaron asked, keeping his tone cool.

"This is a little different. I'm with your mother twelve or sixteen hours out of each day. We can talk to each other, explain about things whenever we want. But Laurie's alone — she has time to think and maybe to imagine things."

Aaron was exasperated; he was both guilty and innocent. And he could not, possibly, in the short hour before dinner, make his father understand.

"If," he said, in a vain attempt to vindicate himself, "if I had time to talk to anyone, it certainly would be Laurie. I'm not too sure that a doctor's wife needs to know very much about his profession — "

"Just enough to understand why she must be alone so much."

"Yes," Aaron agreed. "There's that. And if she doesn't understand it, I should try to help her understand. She has been very brave about this — she is a brave girl, Dad. An honest girl . . . where some wives are not."

"She told me about your friend. We're sorry."

Aaron nodded. "I give Laurie what free time I have," he told his father. "I know it isn't enough — but that's a little tough on me, too!" His voice rasped.

His father stretched out his hand. "No need to be cross . . ."

"Well, I get cross, just thinking of all the things I should do and never seem to do."

"Perhaps all it takes is a little better management, Aaron. I'm glad you took her skating this afternoon. You two don't have enough fun."

"The whole thing is," said Aaron, still crossly, "the study of medicine isn't funny. Not very often."

"I can understand that, son. And your mother and I would like to be able to help out in this, more than we do. We'd like to take Laurie to the theater, you know — or on a little trip. But Eddie's tuition and his allowance just about use up any cash we have."

"Nobody has asked you to do more for Laurie!" Aaron shouted angrily. "If she and I can't manage this together, well — we'll acknowledge that we can't. It's not your problem!"

On Sunday, having slept late and eaten a big breakfast, Aaron and Laurie dressed in their best clothes and prepared to go to the memorial service in the hospital chapel. Tommy's body had already been sent across the country to his grandmother for burial.

The small chapel was filled. There were white flowers on the altar, and the nurses' choir sang. Dr. Gage was there, and Dr. Barr. Aaron pointed them out to Laurie. She looked critically at Dr. Gage and was in a position to acknowledge the appeal this older, elegant man would make to Linda Marshall. Sam Miller came in at the last minute, wearing whites. But Linda was not there.

Though Carol, Tommy's widow, was there. A black mantilla on her platinum hair, she wore a black suit and even black stockings. People looked at her curiously. Did she really grieve?

The memorial service used up a lot of Aaron's free time, but this weekend things had not been too bad. Sunday evening he let Laurie talk about everything — Dr. Gage, and Linda Marshall, Carol Dreiserward . . . "If she didn't care enough for Tommy to be good to him in life, I think she should have stayed away entirely."

"Oh, Laurie, things can be very tough for a resident's wife."

"I know," said Laurie cheerfully. He glanced at her. She was curled up in one corner of the couch, doing some kind of sewing. She had spoken in a tone of calm acceptance. For a minute he was inclined to bring up the conversation which he had had with his father . . .

He said nothing.

But something about Laurie troubled him. He sensed that she was being careful of what she said; he suspected that her calm, pleasant manner was one which she had determined to use so as not to spoil this weekend. He would have rather —

No. He did not want them to quarrel. He did ask her how her work was going. She said fine and added that Mr. Hulsey had a cold, he had not been in the office for a couple of days.

So — why did he worry? Why was he still worried when, in the chill of early Monday morning, he must hurry through the dark city streets to the hospital? There was an unsavory-looking man at the corner bus stop. He spoke to Aaron, who passed him quickly, returning the greeting as he passed.

The incident reminded him of a cartoon which someone had clipped from a medical magazine and had pinned to the bulletin board. It showed one man being held up by another, masked, young man. The caption read: "I'm only doing this until I finish my internship."

It was a funny cartoon, though not really.

Aaron came into the lighted, steam-warm hospital, already bustling with Monday's busyness. He spoke to the people he passed; he jiggled with impatience as he waited for the elevator. . . .

Money was the biggest part of any troubles he and Laurie had. It was as simple as that. He should, on his weekends, be able to give the girl a whirl. Take her down to the lake, perhaps, or to the theater. All Aaron had managed this past weekend was an hour at the free skating rink in the park. And she had had to produce her own quarter to check her long coat. She didn't mind — but Aaron minded. It put him in the wrong family position. If he could think of any possible way to earn a little money himself on the side! There were, regularly, cases where an intern or resident was accused of taking narcotics — either just plain stealing them from the medicine shelves, or overprescribing them, then retrieving them, and selling them — this was not a difficult thing to do, and it would bring in some money, but Aaron could never do it.

He checked in, consulted the schedule, and went to work.

He worked all day — rounds, three hours in surgery, a conference — a half hour midafternoon to sit in his room and read up on a problem they were later to handle in surgery. Already he wore the baggy scrub suit, a mask dangled below his chin. He rubbed his eyes to keep awake . . .

And he thought about Laurie and himself. In the interns' dormitory, in the residents' lounge, during coffee breaks, or around the table down in the cafeteria, there was much talk of moonlighting.

But how, in God's name, did a man manage such a thing? In the hours when Aaron was off duty he was so tired — not as tired as he had been as an intern, thank God. Then he had been little more than a husk of a man. But still he was tired. Right this minute, after a good sleep last night, he could have blissfully dozed off over his heavy book. Of course bronchogenic carcinoma was pretty heavy study . . .

Within the hour he would be part of a team to take out a tumor in a man's chest and half of a lung — they would determine cancer. And then there must be surgery later to care for a brain lesion, this dependent upon their patient's recovery from massive chest surgery. The prospects for this were not rosy — so what did *Aaron* have to worry about?

He thought he did have something. Money — moonlighting — how could any resident doctor consider such a thing? He couldn't count on being free if he took any kind of job! Aaron knew of one chap who had conducted a class in anatomy at some school for embalmers.

Or he could, just possibly, do work in some

commercial laboratory. Or a technologist's school — instructing, perhaps.

How much money would he earn from such a job? Five dollars? Even ten extra a week?

That sounded good as extra cash in his pocket. But it would mean giving up the free time he now spent with Laurie. So would it be worth what it cost?

No. Their troubles, if any, lay in something bigger than the money problem itself.

They . . .

He glanced around at the knock on his half-open door. "O.K.," he said briskly. "I'll be right with you."

He put his mask up over his mouth and started down the hall. He would take their patient up to surgery; he would spend three hours, at least, as one of a team of doctors around the operating table. Barr would be doing the surgery, and that was all it took to excite Aaron. He didn't think any more about moonlighting; he already was busy doing the job he liked to do!

CHAPTER 9

Because of Tommy's death, and the decision not to get a replacement for him this late in the hospital year, Aaron was working harder than ever in chest surgery. He didn't really mind. He liked the work, even when he was assigned to assist Gage in the operating room, and on the wards. Gage was a brilliant doctor, and working with him was an inspiration. Though Aaron had never wavered from his first determination to make thoracic surgery his specialty, with particular attention to the lungs and bronchi. There was work enough for anyone! He wanted, he hoped, to train under Dr. Barr, to become one of his "bright young men." And there was dream enough for any doctor!

When the March assignments were coming up, and Aaron was asked again if he would do his second-year residency as surgical assistant in Thoracic Surgery, he said yes, almost without stopping to think. He wanted to do it; he must do it.

265

But ten minutes later in his room again, and sorting out his laundry — of all things! — he was appalled to realize what he had done. How could he take on another year?

Yes, they had talked about it briefly, he and Laurie. She had said he could do it.

But her consent was not the whole of it, as they had learned — or should have learned — during this first year. Things had been fine for Aaron! But for Laurie — and he must consider Laurie. He loved the girl, and he had married her to take care of her, not to let her take care of herself. And of him.

She had not been happy this past year — certainly not lately. Though she valiantly tried to conceal this from him, he had guessed. She was lonely, she was frustrated. Lately he had thought, a time or two, that she was unhappy in her job, and he had wondered if it was not proving too hard for her. But any job — Laurie didn't want to work; she wanted her own home to keep and a child. He should be able to give those things to her.

It wasn't that he had any feeling of his marriage's being endangered. His situation was nothing at all like Tommy's. Laurie did not complain; she did not two-time him. She was loving to him and patient with him when he came home too tired to offer her much of anything in the way of husbandly care and affection. They had some good times together. His just past free time — he had exchanged weekends with Boccardi because of a wedding or something in the other resident's family — Laurie had been happy to have Aaron free so soon again; she arranged for him to use his father's car and for the two of them to stay overnight in a cabin at one of the lake resorts. It was still too cold to fish and certainly to swim or rent a boat. But they had had a roaring fire in the cabin; they had taken a long walk. And they had talked.

It had been a good break; both enjoyed it. Laurie had stifled his one question about whether they could afford such luxury, and he had gone along with her.

Now of course they must face six weeks before his next big break. And that would be hard for the girl. He knew that she got bored; so many lonely evenings must mean boredom. A stack of library books could not possibly substitute for companionship and fun.

Though companionship, he thought wryly, did not mean entirely clear sailing. He had managed on their weekend to tease Laurie one time too many about the coffee she made, and when she had accepted his apology, and his embrace, he had almost ruined the whole project by slapping her hip affectionately and saying that her slacks did seem pretty tight, was she putting on weight?

He'd meant only to tease her, but she had been really hurt.

It had taken some doing to get himself out of that spot. Laurie tearfully admitted that she had put on five pounds — and they could not afford it! Not if such a thing meant new clothes. But what was a girl to do? She spent her evenings with a book, or the radio, and of course she nibbled. Potato chips — crackers and cheese. Her mother-in-law kept giving her candy or cookies. "And of course I eat them!" she said defensively.

He tried to comfort her. She wept for a little, then was angry "about the whole mess!" He guessed they made up, but . . .

Laurie guessed they had made up too. She had really wanted that weekend to work out well. For her own sake, as well as Aaron's. Laurie was still being very tense and wary about her job. Mr. Hulsey's cold had given her respite; it had been a heavy one, and the week before he had said, "Maybe what I need to get rid of this cough is ten days in the sun. Of course I'd have to take my secretary along . . . " He had looked inquiringly at that secretary.

But she had managed to remain cool, and she shook her head.

"No?" he had persisted.

"No. You can always get a Manpower girl. I couldn't leave."

He gazed at her for a long minute. "Oh, Laurie," he had said sadly.

Laurie wished he would go away for a couple of weeks. He'd get rid of his cough, and she —

But on Monday he was in the office, and at noon he came out to say briskly, "Come along, Laurie. We'll eat lunch and then go courting."

"Thank you," she said brightly. "I'm not eating lunch these days."

"Oh, now, look, girl — "

"I drink a can of Metrecal," she explained. "To keep my weight under control."

"Would you say you were fat?" he asked, comically concerned.

Laurie laughed. "Oh no. But others might say it."

"If you're bothered about your weight — Is that really why you won't let me buy your lunch?"

Cool as cool, she took the letter out of her typewriter and ran in another set of papers. "Maybe not," she agreed. "But it's a big reason. If you like puns . . ."

"I don't." He came and sat on the corner of her desk, which was not so large that it did not put him uncomfortably close to her.

Laurie bit her underlip and hoped she could handle this — this —

"Look, Laurie," Mark was saying. "Having lunch with me isn't any big deal."

She said nothing.

"I thought you liked doing things of the sort — "

"I did."

"But now?"

"No, Mr. Hulsey. Now I'll stick to my Metrecal and meet you at the courthouse." She let herself glance up at him and found that he was looking at her very intently.

"You know," he said, taking one of her pencils and balancing it across the fingers of his left hand, "there are all sorts of reasons why you should let yourself be attractive to, and attracted by, men. Other men. That's a very natural process, my dear, since neither men nor women are born with blinders."

Laurie listened. She had heard some of the arguments before.

When he paused, she again glanced up at him. "The thing is, Mr. Hulsey," she said firmly, "I happen to love Aaron."

He dropped the pencil and got off the desk corner to retrieve it. "All right," he agreed. "I 'love' my wife too. But I still like to take you to lunch and to talk to you."

"A week or so ago you said something about divorce."

He nodded. "I did. And you were shocked."

"Certainly I was shocked." She typed in the address and salutation of her letter.

He put his hand on her wrist. "Don't you like me, Laurie?" he asked. His tone was only reasonable.

"You know that I do like you."

"But my mention of divorce, and possible marriage, shocked you."

"Of course it did."

"All right, then, we'll be friends. As a friend, can't we have lunch together?"

She said nothing.

"As a friend," he persisted, "can't I kiss you occasionally? Buy you some pretty thing? Enjoy being with you?"

She sighed. "Things don't stop there," she pointed out. "They wouldn't."

"No," he agreed, "they wouldn't. But is that bad? Would it be?"

"You know it is bad." She would not look at him, but she knew he was shaking his finger at her.

"*You* know that," he said. "You — what you're trying to do, Laurie, is to make your mind rule you, set the pattern of your life, and not your feelings. But that doesn't promise very much fun, does it? So why not relax? You're a young and beautiful girl-type creature — "

Her chin lifted. "And I suppose that is an

argument for me to act like an animal?" she demanded. "Forgetting that I have a human's intelligence?"

He shrugged. "It would be fun," he insisted.

"To feel, instead of reason?" Now her blue eyes looked directly into his face. And indeed, she was a young and beautiful creature. She felt that way.

"Yes," he said consideringly, "it would be a lot of fun."

Laurie shook her head. "I think," she said, knowing that she sounded sententious, and unattractive, "I am sure" — she firmed her voice — "that we were made human, with a reasoning brain, to know some moral laws and standards."

"I expect you're right," Mark agreed. "But we still feel too."

"Yes, we do!" cried Laurie. "But there are circumstances under which we should *make* the brain function for feeling."

He stood looking down at her. He held out the pencil to her and she took it. "Don't get smart on me, Laurie," he said sadly. "You're too cute a girl."

Laurie made a wry face. "I doubt if I'm cute," she said, "and I know I am not smart. Not smart at all. Not in comparison to you, Mr. Hulsey, ever! But it does seem clear to me that I have to choose between emotion and reason. I am afraid, for me, just now, I cannot possibly live under the influence of both." She spoke almost pleadingly.

Mark nodded and took a few steps away from her, then came back. "I say again that emotion surrendering to logic does not offer much to a girl like you."

"Well, neither does logic lost to emotion!" she cried spunkily. So spunkily that he laughed.

"We could make a lawyer out of you, Laurie!" he told her.

Then she laughed, too, though somewhat uncertainly. "Oh, Mark," she begged him, "won't you let me alone? I shouldn't have to give one thought as to whether I'll be loyal to Aaron . . . ."

He pursed his lips. "I've never met — or seen — your Aaron, Laurie. Do you think he's worth all you're giving him?"

Her eyes were wide and dark. "Well, of course he is worth it!" she said. "He's a really wonderful man, kind and serious-minded. And he is going to be a really wonderful doctor. Everyone says he will be."

"What kind of doctor, dear?"

"A surgeon. Of course I don't know very much about his profession, but he is planning to specialize in something called thoracic surgery. That's the heart and the lungs and stuff.

I really don't know too much about it — or anything at all, really. But Aaron says it is very worth while, and since I trust him in other things, I guess I had just better believe that it *is* worth while!"

She spoke earnestly; she looked sincere.

Mark Hulsey nodded. "I don't know the man," he said again, "but I can tell from here that he's a lucky guy. All right, then. Enjoy your canned lunch, and I'll see you in court at two. O.K.?"

"Yes, sir," said Laurie, her fingers flying over the keys.

It was a day for self-arguments. Aaron had one with himself almost at the same time that Laurie was going over again the things she had said to Mark. She was right — she knew that she was right.

But Aaron was not nearly so sure of himself. That morning, about eleven, Dr. Barr had summoned him to his office. This was a fairly routine thing and Aaron had gone there without any anticipation of what might be discussed. They had that exploratory surgery scheduled for three. Their patient was a world-famous psychiatrist — Dr. Barr would want his operating team well briefed on procedures.

Now Dr. Barr offered Aaron his choice of the fresh fruit which heaped a wooden bowl on his desk. Aaron took a pear and sat down. Dr. Barr handed him some tissues, saying that the fruit would be juicy, then he mentioned the fact that Battle was about through his allotted time on chest surgery. "Aren't you?"

"I have to the end of the month," Aaron agreed.

"I understand that you plan to continue with us next year."

"Yes, sir." Of course Barr "understood" this.

"We talked a little about you in staff conference this morning," his chief told him. "Dr. Gage suggested that you might as well start in right now as our first assistant. We've never filled in for Dreiserward, you know."

"Yes, sir, I know."

"Gage seems to like your work."

"Well, I'm glad of that, sir."

Dr. Barr laughed dryly. "It's a help," he agreed.

"But I'm opting for lung rather than heart, sir."

"I know you are, but you'll still work some with Gage. We chest men have to know the whole field."

We chest men . . .

Aaron's pulse skipped.

"I think," said Dr. Barr, "that you would

lose some valuable experience if you didn't go on and do your three months at the state hospital, as originally scheduled."

Aaron wrapped the pear core in what was left of the tissues. "Yes, sir," he said quietly.

"There was enough discussion on the subject that we decided to let you make the decision, Battle."

Now here was a switch! If only Tommy were alive, so that Aaron could tell him about this!

Aaron considered what his answer would be. He could sincerely say that any work done with Dr. Barr would be of prime interest to him. And he would sound like a veteran apple polisher! He could say —

"You'd know better than I," he did say slowly, "how much value there is in the three months' work at the state hospital."

"It's valuable," Dr. Barr told him. "You'll be down there — you and a chief resident — and you'll have the surgical care of several thousand inmates and personnel. You'll be on your own. It's valuable experience, Battle."

"Then I think I'd like to have it, sir."

Dr. Barr sat back in his chair, regarding him, level-eyed. "The men's wives don't usually like this term of duty, Aaron."

"Well — our residencies are tough on them in a lot of ways."

"Yes, they are. I wasn't married when I did mine. We medics didn't marry very young then. I suppose there is something to be said on both sides."

Aaron waited. There was much to be said. Miller had waited. Aaron — and Tommy — had not.

"You've a very pretty wife, Battle," said Dr. Barr. "I saw her in the chapel a week or so ago. She's young."

"Yes, sir, she is."

"How old . . . ?"

"Laurie is twenty-four, almost twenty-five."

"Oh? She looks younger."

"No, sir. And she *is* twenty-four. I mean, she's mature about the things that take such judgment."

"That's good for you. How does she feel about your leaving town for three months?"

"I am sure I have mentioned the schedule to her — but I don't believe she has thought too particularly about it. She doesn't know very much, really, about any of my work."

"Maybe you had better talk to her about it, eh?"

"Yes, sir. I've thought I should."

They did their surgery; a mass was found in the chest of the famous psychiatrist. This was probably a lymphoma, and after their patient had gone to Recovery, Dr. Barr instructed his residents and interns on the difference between lymphoma and malignant cancer, on the treatment with x-rays and chemotherapy. . . .

Aaron was assigned to stay close to their patient, and this gave him some chance to think about what he would say to Laurie to bring her into some greater understanding of the demands his profession made upon him and would make. Personally he felt what he should do was to put more weight to the fact that he loved Laurie and owed much to her.

If he could manage to tell the girl that in a way to make it stick, everything else would fall into place.

He knew, and perhaps he could make Laurie know — more particularly than she knew now — that, in the long run, what he was now doing — the long hours, the loneliness each of them knew, the financial straits — all this would eventually work out best for Laurie as well as for Aaron. A well-trained doctor, a busy doctor, a successful doctor, could afford to give his family everything they might want.

He did his thinking even as he made regular checks on his psychiatrist. He had long been the great man's admirer, and he hoped that things could go well for him. In o.r. a child was undergoing open-heart surgery, with the full panoply of machines and teams. This was a second session for the little girl. The men in the hall — intern, orderly, Aaron, and a nurse or two, the one at the scheduling desk — all talked about the pro's and con's of a second operation.

"I was pretty well sold on the notion that a child could have only one open-heart," said young Dr. Wall.

"Do you suppose Gage has been told about that?" asked the recovery-room resident drolly.

"Of course they can have second surgery," said Linda Marshall briskly. "They often do, and the trouble corrects."

Aaron wondered if many women would look as handsome as Linda did in a baggy gray-green gown, tight-fitting cap, and shapeless canvas shoes. She too was keeping an eye on Aaron's psychiatrist.

Together they went into Recovery and came out again. "How about some quick coffee?" Linda suggested.

The Recovery resident had passed them going into the room.

Aaron nodded, and they went into the head nurse's glass-enclosed office where Linda produced bright green mugs. "How are things with you, Aaron?" she asked cordially.

He shrugged. "Pretty good," he said. "Barr's put a choice up to me that will need some explaining, maybe, to Laurie. Whether I'll go to Eads the end of this month or start right now on a fifteen-month tour as first-assistant resident in Thoracic."

"To fill Tommy's place," said Linda.

"Well— "

"That was a very rough thing," she agreed. "Were you able to explain it to Laurie?"

"I don't know," said Aaron. "She was upset and grieved, of course. And she asked if it could happen to me."

"What did you tell her?"

"Oh, I pointed out the differences between Tommy and me as men . . . "

As he talked, Aaron was thinking that he liked the sympathetic listening woman. He liked her a lot! And in just about the same way as he liked Sam Miller. Both were hard workers and understanding of all the aspects and contacts of their profession.

Those two were in love with each other, and the consummation of such a love would seem to be the only conclusion possible. Yet those same two were considering the logic of their position over and above their feeling toward each other. Perhaps Linda could show Aaron where it was right so to apply logic.

He mentioned the fact that he knew that he and Laurie must undergo difficulties now in order for him to achieve complete control of his chosen line of work.

"And don't forget what you are doing, even now, for your future patients," said Linda.

Aaron nodded. "It often seems to me," he said solemnly, "that too much of the idealism of medicine is lost in the need to consider finances."

"Oh yes!" she said quickly. "Yes, indeed. Your pay, for instance, is *nothing* — and that is not right, Aaron. Though I suppose I should mention the argument that the cost of all you are learning these days, and years, should be considered as pay."

Aaron's cheeks creased into a grin. "Tell that to the barber the next time I need a haircut."

Linda leaned back to study him. "You could use one now, Doctor," she decided. "It's sprouting out all around your cap."

"That's no way to judge, just on length. I wait until I am told to cut it off!"

They both laughed, and Aaron looked at his watch. "I've been thinking," he said. "Medicare is going to mean a much bigger load, isn't it?"

"Oh, heavens, yes! It surely will."

"I'd love to think," said Aaron, "that the pay for interns and residents would be increased. Since, from what I've read, they are the ones to be paid by Medicare."

"I guess you may have a point, Aaron."

"Should I mention it?"

"I don't think you mean to me . . ."

"No."

"Well, then, I'd say to move cautiously. You must remember that all our staff members have gone through the same mill where you're being polished and honed."

Aaron got up to refill his mug. "I know it," he agreed. "I know, too, how any staff doctor will answer my question."

Linda watched him. She thought Sam was right about this young doctor; he was definitely a comer. For one thing, he could think!

Aaron was standing facing her, his green coffee mug in one hand. "We are, gentlemen," he said, in the tone, exaggerated, of the lecture platform, "here at the university, a hospital of one thousand and fifteen beds, one third of which are occupied by patients who pay little or nothing of their hospital costs. Those are the teaching beds served by the hospital staff, including physicians in training."

Linda smiled at him.

"The costs of caring for those patients," Aaron continued, "are paid from the charges we collect from the full-pay patients in the other two-thirds of our beds. We do have some endowment and charitable funds to pay part of the costs of indigent patients.

"Along with paying the costs of caring for our teaching or ward, patients, we pay the — excuse me — salaries of the interns and residents on those wards. We estimate that the loss to the hospital from our teaching program each year is a million and a half dollars.

"Now when the law goes into effect, gentlemen, our indigent patients over sixty-five will be largely paid for under the new health-insurance program. If there is any great increase in such patients, and the government pays us on a cost formula based on hospitals which do not have a teaching program, we are going to be in trouble.

"We have only a certain amount of money with which to operate the hospital. If the government doesn't take into consideration the cost of our teaching program, we'll have two choices. We can pass the increased cost on to our paying patients under sixty-five. Or we can cut our teaching program."

Linda watched him and listened, fascinated. "I don't see much chance of a pay raise in that, Doctor," she told him. "You must already have talked to staff men about this?"

Aaron drained his mug. "They've talked to us."

"Are you really worried, Aaron?" she asked.

"Sure. Why not?"

She laughed and stood up. "I guess there's no reason. Do you have time to worry?"

Aaron rinsed both mugs at the small sink. "I don't have time to do anything about it."

She came to him, put her hand on his arm, and looked intently into his face. "Learning to be a surgeon," she said wisely, "presents a rough go. But remember all this, Battle, so when you are a big-shot specialist, you can tell your patients why your fees are so big."

Had she and Sam worked this out with each other?

"It seems pretty rough," said Aaron, "to take it out on my future patients."

She walked to the door. "Oh no, it isn't," she said. "Not really. Consideration of them, the thought of what you will be able to do for them, is why you stick with the thing. And then, too, when a patient comes to you — to any specialist — this is what he wants from you. These years of experience."

Aaron looked at her, then put his hand on her shoulder. "You're a wise girl, Linda," he said warmly.

She nodded. Suddenly there were tears in her eyes. "I'm getting that way," she said. "I hope."

CHAPTER 10

The first of March blew in like a rather coy lion, breezy, but warm. The city perked up, deciding that spring had arrived. At the hospital there were changes in intern and resident duties, but Aaron Battle stayed on Thoracic Surgery, assigned to the children's ward this particular week. He told Laurie that he found care of the children especially rewarding. "We get some stinkers, but not nearly so many or as bad as we do with the grownups."

"Do children get things wrong with their chests?" she asked. "That need surgery?"

"Oh, sure they do. Heart defects, birth defects —"

She put her hands over her ears. "I guess I don't want you to tell me," she said.

Which was just about as far as Aaron ever got in talking to Laurie about his work. "Have you heard from the folks this week?" he asked.

"Yes. I'm going over there tomorrow — it's Saturday. I'm going to do a washing."

He laughed. "Does Mother know you're coming?"

"Yes. She suggested it. She thinks the laundromats are possibly not very hygienic."

"Well, maybe they're not. I'll give you a call out there. Maybe I could even wangle an hour or two."

On Saturday? Laurie smiled at him. "I hope so."

She was already planning her busy day at her mother-in-law's. She would do the washing and then iron. She hoped she could take a long tub bath, and use the sewing machine . . .

That evening she stacked the things she would need in a big basket, and when Philip Battle came to fetch her at nine on Saturday they both laughed at its size.

"Are you moving out?" he teased.

"No. But I do have a full day planned."

She wore her gray stretch pants and a loose green shirt. She pulled on the plaid coat. "Though I don't really need this," she said. "It's so warm."

"Better wear it if you're going to stay all day. It may turn cold tonight."

She did the washing — three machines full. Then she washed her hair and put it into small curlers. She would, she planned, iron after lunch.

286

"Don't fix me a big lunch," she told her mother-in-law.

"Aren't you hungry, dear?"

"Yes, but — " Laurie turned away. "Just a sandwich," she said tensely. "Please!"

"I'd think you'd enjoy a good lunch, with time to eat it."

"I would," said Laurie. "But like a lot of things, I can't have what I enjoy!"

Mrs. Battle looked at the girl who stood gazing out of the window. "Aren't you — well, a little nervy these days, Laurie?" she asked gently.

Laurie was. She was trying to lose five pounds; she had her problems with Mark — yes, she was nervy. "I'm sorry," she murmured.

"It isn't that I mind, dear," said her mother-in-law. "But I wonder what causes it."

"Just a mean disposition probably," said Laurie, trying to laugh.

"Oh, now, Laurie, you know it isn't any such thing! But — well, I've noticed that you are some wider through the hips . . ."

Laurie clapped her hand to her thigh. Aaron had said that! But five pounds! It should not be that noticeable!

Mrs. Battle laughed comfortably. "Now, that was a terrible thing to say to a girl, wasn't it?" she asked. "Though not if what I suspect is true."

Laurie turned to look at her, suspiciously inquiring.

"Couldn't you," said Aaron's mother, "be — maybe — pregnant, dear? That's where it first shows, you know. A woman gets a certain look across her seat."

She was being pretty darn cheerful about it too! Laurie stared at her. Stunned. Shocked. "Oh, it couldn't be that!" she said loudly.

"Couldn't it, dear?"

"No! Absolutely not!" But even as she denied the charge, her fingers were counting . . . She went across the kitchen and confronted the calendar which hung upon the wall.

It just couldn't be possible, though — of course — it could be . . .

She stared at the calendar. She put her finger on a date and looked down along the line of numbers. Ye-es, Mrs. Battle could be right. So much had happened lately that Laurie had lost track. There was all the turmoil which Mark had started and kept up — her finger moved — Tommy had died. And — now —

It was five weeks! Almost six!

Oh, it *couldn't* be! But, yes, it could . . . She gasped. A great tear rolled down her cheek, another, and another. And she sobbed.

"Oh, my dear — " Mrs. Battle comforted

her, wiped her face, and hugged her shoulders. She said what she could . . .

But of course Margaret Battle was worried too. She was remembering what Eddie kept saying about Laurie and her boss. As upset as the girl was, could it possibly be that the baby — might not — be Aaron's?

Oh, for heaven's sake! Of course it was Aaron's! Laurie was a sweet, dear girl.

Laurie sniffed and sat down at the kitchen table, shaking her head. "I just can't be pregnant," she said mournfully. "We — we just can't afford it!"

Mrs. Battle tried to laugh. "Well, I don't suppose you can," she agreed. "And right off I don't exactly see how we will manage, but I suppose we will, of course."

She began to prepare lunch, insisting that of course Laurie must eat something. "I'll keep it light," she promised. "An egg-salad sandwich? A bowl of soup? I baked brownies."

Laurie nodded. She would eat the lunch; she would iron . . .

"What about your job, Laurie?" Mrs. Battle asked when Laurie came upstairs with the basket of freshly ironed sheets and pillow cases, Aaron's dress shirt . . .

"What about it?" Laurie asked. She glanced at the clock. It was three o'clock.

"Well, I mean, could you keep on working? Is your boss the sort to let his secretary be pregnant? Do you like him, Laurie?"

Laurie stared at the woman. Somewhere, somehow, had she perhaps heard gossip about her and Mark? Through the men at the Athletic Club probably. Mr. Battle went there often. He had found the job with Mark in the first place. Men chattered about such things more than women, she had decided.

And if he — and Aaron's mother — thought for one minute . . . "I think I'll go home," she said in a small voice.

"Oh, Laurie!"

"Yes, I think I had better." She was really scared. What if his mother ever said any of these "things" to Aaron?

What if any of these "things" were true?

She had to wait, of course, until Philip and the car came back from his golf game. Meanwhile Aaron called and said he wouldn't get any free time that evening. They had an injured child . . .

"He'll sit up with that child all night," Laurie told his mother. "And work over it — things called chemical balance and stuff like that."

"How do you know so much about Aaron's work, Laurie?" asked Mrs. Battle. "As little as he's home — "

"I know Aaron!" said Laurie stubbornly.

When she could leave, she must make an effort to be polite and sound grateful. Mrs. Battle had put a package of food into her basket. Two chops, some fresh strawberries, and the rest of the brownies.

But Laurie was too angry, too upset, to feel grateful. She would never spend a day with her mother-in-law again!

All that evening Laurie kept herself busy, shying away from thoughts about the day's developments. She avoided thinking about Aaron, too, and her eventual need to confront him, to tell him —

She was safe for better than twenty-four hours. He would not expect her for dinner, thinking that she was with his parents. So — well — anyway —

She put the freshly laundered things away. She cleaned the apartment, even to scrubbing the kitchen on her hands and knees. She didn't know how she would ever tell Aaron, but she need not worry about that. Just now.

She scrubbed vigorously and thought about other things. About Mark. Well, it was all right to think about him. He was a tremendous factor in the lives of the Aaron Battles. He was Laurie's boss, and he paid the freight . . .

Laurie straightened, scrub brush in hand;

her face was flushed, with a smudge across one cheek. She had tied a green scarf over her hair curlers.

How was Mark going to react to this — this news? These last days he had been exerting more and more pressure on Laurie. It was, he said, silly for her to go to the courthouse alone — and return to the office alone. Why couldn't she, much more reasonably, ride with him? People would talk, he said.

And they would. The prosecuting attorney came in with his secretary. Laurie was just a part of the court proceedings. Like — like — well, like Mark's brief case. It was her job, as Mark defined it, for her to accompany him to court. Some lawyers did not take their own secretaries, relying on the court record.

But Mark was one for quick thought and quick memos — he wanted Laurie with him. Since none of the other office girls thought it strange that she should go with him, he must have taken his previous secretary.

So Laurie would ride with him; if he needed to stop some place — someone's office, or a bar for a drink, or the department store for some socks — Laurie would wait for him.

This he laughed about and argued about; so far she had not gone again to a restaurant or bar with him, though during a trial's lunch break she reasonably could have eaten with her boss. She kept hiding behind the Metrecal thing or the fact that she had brought a sandwich from home; she would get a coke . . .

He waited. He always told her about his lunch — the really *brown* baked beans, the sticky buns, and a ham sandwich, with the meat cut thick and tasting like home-boiled ham.

He was telling her that she was being foolish. And she was, probably. Laurie had decided that she was more often foolish than not. She had innocently, for six months, eaten lunch and had a cocktail with Mark. He had made a suggestion which she had firmly handled. Now —

Well, of course he was an attractive, strong man. She had never known anyone just like him. She had never known a man who so casually could wear a blue cashmere club coat — the material of it was as soft as a baby's blanket . . .

Laurie gulped and bent again to her scrubbing.

Whether it was his cashmere coat or his crooked smile or his vibrant voice — or his quick interest — Laurie had definitely been attracted to Mark Hulsey from the very first. Whether she called it a crush — or falling in love — the fact of attraction was there.

She should be honest about that if she

hoped to be honest about the sincerity with which she was trying to withdraw from the growing relationship with her boss. Mark called that withdrawal foolish — and perhaps it was. But Laurie was valiantly striving for poise and dignity. Righteous dignity, it might be, but dignity nevertheless.

And now *this* had to happen!

Laurie jumped to her feet and went into the bathroom. She turned sideways to the mirror, pressed her hands to her abdomen. No, of course nothing showed there. Next she fetched her compact from her purse, stood on a low stool, and endeavored to see if she really was wider across her hips. It was hard to tell . . .

In any case, at this early stage the whole thing had to be considered as a suspicion. She need not speak of it to Mark for some time yet. But how, at any time, would he take such news?

One thing she could be glad of: the baby couldn't possibly be his. Well, *of course* it couldn't be! Though if she had listened to his Circe song of Arizona or Florida, others might think it a possibility. Her mother-in-law would suspect such a thing.

This afternoon Laurie had wondered if Mrs. Battle had not . . . she had wondered if the older woman had heard some gossip. But she surely would not suspect Aaron's wife . . .

Laurie went back and finished her kitchen, ashamed of her own thoughts on the subject. She could not be unfaithful to Aaron; she would not let another man —

Though, a matter of weeks ago, such a thing had been a possible danger. If she had gone to the theatre with Mark that night, if she had gone with him to Arizona, if she had let him pursue his talk of divorce —

Tommy's death had saved her from the first misstep, and the shock of that saving — well, up to now Laurie had been a little proud of her withdrawal from temptation.

Because temptation had been there. In the form of golden mink coats, and her own home, and children —

Laurie could blush hotly now to acknowledge that temptation. Which had been real, if brief. However, she had forced her brain, her intelligence, to function instead of — or more strongly than — her instant emotion. She was not a girl to play the game from both sides.

So, foolish or not, she had resisted temptation to the extent of refusing to go on any sort of "date" with Mark. She brought a sandwich from home so she would not eat lunch with him. In the late afternoon she would go back to the office and "clean things up" rather than stop for a cocktail. She "liked to walk" rather than always to accept a lift in his car.

Knowing that he called her foolish, she made a valiant attempt to be nothing but businesslike in the office. At first her hands would be damp with nervousness over these efforts. At night she would go home with a headache and weary beyond reason.

But gradually, as the hours passed, and the days, her firmness had increased. Now she sometimes wondered if she was being foolish, but she still maintained the lines which she had set down for herself. She had, as Mark laughingly pointed out, tried to be a "good girl." Once she had argued with him briefly over whether such an effort was as funny as he seemed to think.

Funny or not, he said, it was a waste — of youth and of beauty. Applied as Laurie applied it, such effort was certainly waste.

But Laurie kept on trying. Once, somewhere, she had read that "if a person acts the way he would like to be, soon he would be the way he acts."

It sounded so reasonable that she had made it a law on which to peg her conduct during a very difficult time. She knew she was young; she knew that men thought she was pretty — her slim body and gold and white coloring attracted men. Many sorts of men. She had married Aaron because she loved him and for his stability which she hoped would protect her. But Aaron was away so much of the time! Because of his work she could not tell him her troubles — why, this whole thing about Mark would have driven him crazy!

So she must find something as a guideline, and that sentence fulfilled her need. "If she would act . . . " If she would be cool and business like with Mark — and she should never have been anything else! — she would, in time, feel that way toward him and then easily *be* that way!

She sincerely hoped that this would happen, for Aaron's sake.

Aaron. She guessed she should think about him now. She let down the bed and made it up with the fresh sheets which she had laundered. She smoothed them and sighed. She took a shower, and under the warm water she wept a little at the way her white body had betrayed her. She had wanted — she had tried — very hard to help Aaron.

All she had really done, of course, was to take a job. Maybe there were other ways she could have helped. She could have found things to do in the hospital, evenings and on weekends. She could ask him, though now that wouldn't be a good idea. Anyway, what could she do?

Except for a few weeks of helping in the well-baby clinic, Laurie had no knowledge of hospital work. In the year she had dated Aaron, in the nine months of marriage to him, she had met various ones of his friends. She had sat beside him in the cafeteria and heard the unintelligible hospital talk. Marfan syndromes. Homocystinuria. She wished she did know more about his work! Although she could remember a time or two when Aaron had started to talk about some case and she had begged him to stop. So, though married to a doctor, she knew almost nothing except that his hours were long and his free-time fatigue great. She saw the hospital personnel in their strange garments — Aaron was one of them. She supposed they did important work, but Aaron didn't talk much about it, and he never had.

He acknowledged her lack of insight; he had mentioned it when he had tried to explain to her the Miller-Marshall-Gage situation.

"You just can't understand all the ramifications, Laurie." And another time he had said, "I can't give you a complete course in medicine."

Did he think she couldn't learn about such things? With time and patience, a word here and an experience there, she felt that she was intelligent enough to grasp almost anything he might want to tell her. And some day she would insist that he tell her.

Had he gone on with their original plan of his entering private practice, she had hoped to be close to him in his work; she would serve as his secretary, she would know about his patients. . . .

Then, having decided on the residency, Laurie had become Mark's secretary, and Aaron had become engulfed in the immense hospital complex. About all that Laurie could do in the way of help was to support herself and give him the blind understanding of his problems which he required.

She had endeavored to do just that and recently had accepted the need to carry on for another year.

But now —

How, how, *how* was she going to tell Aaron . . . ?

She got into bed and buried her face in the pillow, to hide, even in the dark, her shame at the way she had failed him. At the way she was about to add yet another burden to his already unbearable load.

How *would* she tell him?

Well, she wouldn't tell him, she need not tell him, just now. She would not tell him until she was sure. A widening of the hips, and a week or ten days — No! She was *not* sure!

And until she was sure, she would not say a word. This would mean that she would see him at dinner; Tuesday night he might be able to come home for a few hours; the coming weekend he was due for a break.

Laurie would make plans. She would refuse to accept any suggestion that they go to the Battles' for a meal. On Saturday they could work on the refinishing of the old blanket chest and catch a movie that night.

On Sunday she would pack a picnic lunch and they would have a day out of doors, if only in the park. Well, there was the zoo in the park and all sorts of interesting things. Of course the weather would need to co-operate. A picnic in the rain might be a diversion all right. But Aaron would have her in the psychiatric ward before the weekend was over.

But Laurie would think of something to keep him away from his mother. And when she was with Aaron, she would act, the best she possibly could, as if she didn't have a care in the world.

"If you act the way you wish you were, then you will come to be the way you act."

There, alone in the dark, Laurie laughed hysterically at this application of her quote. "If I act unpregnant, I just will be . . . " She gulped and let the tears flow. No one would know if she wept. There was the one small advantage of being alone. She need not pretend.

She managed the week. Aaron was able to join her for dinner on only two nights, and his so-called "free evenings" did not turn up at all. There was a wave of flu among the hospital personnel, he told Laurie. They were short-handed. On the weekend he didn't get home until seven in the evening. But, yes, he would have his Sunday.

Could they, she asked, maybe take some sandwiches, catch the bus, and go down to one of the pretty little towns along the river, eat their lunch, and come back? She had the bus schedules.

The weather was not the best. It was a sunny day, but cold. But all week Aaron had suspected that Laurie was worried. Had she had a quarrel with his mother last week? Or with Eddie perhaps? There was something — and he'd find out during the day.

So they started out, Laurie bundled into a thick sweater, much too big for her.

"But it's warm!" she told Aaron, who looked dubious.

"In that case I'll wear a blanket."

"You could . . ."

But he didn't.

They had selected an old town, fifty miles from the city, and they explored it with genuine interest, coming at last to the small park and a canon that overlooked the river. There was a monument — some "geezer," said Laurie — in blackened bronze. He was posed atop a stone pylon which afforded shelter form the wind. They sat in the sun and ate their sandwiches.

And, to Laurie's surprise, Aaron talked quite a lot about his week's work. He told about the famous psychiatrist, and the child which had been hurt in a car wreck, his ribs crushed, a lung punctured. He told about one of the hospital staff doctors who had developed a ruptured, and heretofore unsuspected, aneurysm.

He even stopped to explain to her and draw pictures to show her what he meant by aneurysm. He told her a little about this doctor and his family. He told her a funny story about Dr. Boccardi, whom she knew, and about his — Aaron's — interview with Dr. Barr when he had definitely committed himself to a second year of residency.

"He's a very swell person, Laurie. He noticed you at Tommy's service."

"Oh?" She looked anxious.

"He said you seemed very young to be supporting a big lug like me."

She smiled. "And what did you tell him?"

"I said I enjoyed it."

"Oh, Aaron!"

He grinned. "No. He did say you looked

young and asked if I had made you fully realize what these extra residencies meant to a surgeon."

"I just take it on faith," said Laurie.

"He didn't seem to think that was good enough."

"Well, it should be!"

Aaron looked down at the dull river that slipped along below them, a tarnished-silver ribbon, rippling with brown shadows. "I still wish I could find the words to tell you why it is important to me to do these residencies."

"I know *you*."

"There's that faith thing again. And I have tried to tell you. Of course, too, you've come to know Sam Miller a little. You know how intricately his personal affairs have been woven into his profession. He's about at the end of the course I'm just starting. He's had his six years of residency."

Six years, thought Laurie, her heart sinking.

"He's doing his fellowship work. And what all that amounts to is that he's filled the rigorous requirements of the American Board of Surgery. Because of that he is set up as a surgeon for the rest of his life."

"He'll still have to work . . ."

"Oh yes. And learn too. Keep abreast of new things. But barring physical or mental

303

breakdown, Sam can expect to do years and years of important surgical work. He will make good money — he'll be respected . . . "

Laurie listened. She was thinking that once she had wanted to help Aaron get the same things, and now she was glad that she had let him begin, but — well — She sighed and laid down her uneaten sandwich.

Aaron had been watching her as he talked. Whatever it was troubling his girl, it was not —

He turned full about to face her. He caught the collar of her big sweater and pulled it up around her ears. "Tell me, Laurie," he said gently, "do you, for instance, think you just possibly might be pregnant?"

She was shocked. After all her efforts! And angry.

"Your mother got hold of you!" she cried. "And told you . . . "

He shook his head. "I haven't talked to Mother for over a week. But this — shouldn't a wife tell these things to her husband?"

Laurie's face crumpled. "How did you know?"

"I only guessed. You've been nervy lately. Last night you didn't want to make love. To-day you aren't eating your lunch. For a month you haven't eaten well — "

That was because —

She spoke aloud. "You said I was getting fat."

He gazed at her. Then his arm drew her close. "Oh — Laurie!" he cried.

She clung to him, too frightened to weep. Clumsy at the task, Aaron tried to comfort her. He didn't accomplish much, for he, too, was frightened. If she *was* pregnant . . . What would they *do?*

Well, of course, there would be no second-year residency. Not just now. He would spend his three months at Eads, then find a situation where he could practice and earn some money, and —

Laurie trembled, and he pressed his cheek to her hair. "This is a terrible thing!" she sobbed.

Aaron stared gravely out across the valley to the trees which lined the eastern shore of the river. His young face was stern. "I'm afraid it seems terrible," he said. The taste of failure was bitter in his mouth. The greatest of all failures, the loss of opportunity.

Though was it failure? Really?

He nodded, his lips tight. He never wanted to be closer to that rim.

He drew himself together. "We'll have to talk about this," he said firmly. "First, of course, you must see a doctor."

She shook her head. "I don't want to."

"Don't like doctors?"

But she would not joke. "I don't want to be sure," she said faintly. "Oh, Aaron, I don't want to be *sure!*"

How could his own pain comfort and soothe hers? He tried, as best he could. "We'll manage," he promised. "We hadn't counted on this, but nature has a way of giving us a shake every now and then. To see how strong we are, I suppose."

"Tell your old nature that I'm not strong at all. And I hate myself!"

Then he decided that there was one means only of reassuring her, to tell her how much he loved her, and show her —

"You're good to me, Aaron," she told him.

"Not very. I got you into this, remember."

She nodded. "And we should be happy. But — well, if ever anyone asks you what your medical training cost, tell them that *this* was the price. That we — just can't be glad — about a little baby."

Aaron said nothing, because he could say nothing. He was remembering where Linda had pegged the cost of his training.

Now they could talk a little and eat their lunch. Then they decided that they would go home. Laurie's schedule showed a bus available at three o'clock.

They went home; Laurie prepared dinner,

and they ate. Then they listened to the radio music concert, sitting side by side on the couch, Aaron's arm about her. They did not talk much. Aaron wanted to speak again about the doctor, but he did not want to upset her further.

At nine Laurie sighed and said she thought she'd shower and get ready for bed. Aaron nodded. He'd let the bed down.

"I should never have accepted the second-year residency," he said, reaching for a magazine.

Laurie whirled on him. "And *I* shouldn't be pregnant!" she cried sharply. "But if I am, Aaron Battle, I won't even consider quitting!"

He stared at her. He had not considered such a thing either.

"So what about you?" Laurie demanded.

"No," he agreed. "I wouldn't quit either. I guess . . ."

Though he did not see . . .

That night they slept close in each other's arms, like frightened, tired-of-weeping children.

CHAPTER 11

Three months' service at Eads lay imminently ahead, and Aaron had found no way to tell Laurie about his going there, his being out of the city.

On Monday morning he went to the hospital, tired before he ever went up to the ninth floor. There work immediately engulfed him. Surgery was scheduled for most of the day, but at seven-thirty a conference was scheduled, and quick rounds to make, charts to be read, new admissions noted. Aaron checked on his own duty in surgery; he managed a session with Bob Wall who was still intern on Thoracic. This instruction had to do with the typed reports which every surgeon must make for the Records Committee. Wall always wanted to know *why*. Which was good if he was to learn, but which took time for the resident to answer and explain. But today Aaron managed to tell this young man why the surgeon's report must be dictated immediately after surgery, signed after typing — yes, by the surgeon, not the resident. This report, in its own column, joined the surgeon's pre-operative report, and later his post-operative diagnosis —

"Is his pre-op always correct?" asked Wall, bright-eyed.

"No, sir, it isn't."

"Then — "

"Others ask questions and analyze why there is a difference. One can make an honest misjudgment, you know. But those three reports, along with the Pathology tissue report and diagnosis, hold a good check on a lot of hasty surgery, Wall. Too many acute appendixes, later shown to be normal, can get a surgeon dropped from the privileged list."

"Uh-huh. I see."

"But," said Aaron, "some of the reports should show normal. Else the higher-up will ask if the surgeon is letting too many belly pains go unoperated through caution."

"Gee whiz!" cried Wall, holding his head. "A man just can't win, can he?"

Aaron laughed. "Sometimes it looks that way," he admitted.

He did the work of his long day, on the ward, in o.r., at the chart desk, and in staff conferences, knowing it to be hard work. Yet this hard work on Thoracic was exactly what he wanted to do. It was work which he liked, and it would be his specialty if — now — he could specialize. Leaving her that morning, he had promised Laurie not to give up his second-year residency yet. Though he could not see —

At various times in his training years Aaron had been subjected to lectures on the desirable character for doctors to have. A doctor should have dedication, it was said, and mercy. A doctor must not lack a sense of social responsibility. Yet that same doctor would be trained to act as an individual in relation to his patient who was sick. He would not be especially trained to work with and fit into a group concerned with many patients, and equipped for preventive effort, even though the work he did was done in such an organization, the hospital. The young doctor was told to dedicate himself to serving society before serving himself. Most doctors, Aaron suspected, would claim that they lived by this code. But did they? Could they?

Take himself for an example. He knew that the hospital was counting on his doing the work of the first-assistant resident in Thoracic Surgery next year. He had said that he would do it. But now, was not his first obligation to himself? He *must* take care of Laurie — and his — his family.

He went up to surgery. He changed to scrub suit and o.r. shoes, cap, and mask. He scrubbed. He was gowned and gloved and then was on his feet for hours at a stretch, placing clamps, holding retractors. His shoulders ached, and his neck muscles screamed. The weight of his limbs pushed up through his pelvic bones, and at the same time the weight of his whole body pressed down heavily upon his heels and his ankles.

But, acknowledging the pain which his body felt, longing for relief, he would have chosen no other place or occupation on that rainy spring day. For Dr. Gage was doing pioneer surgery — experimental surgery — brilliant surgery, and Aaron Battle was one of the team.

The bull session afterward crackled with excitement. The nerve of the man!

"But coronary insufficiency has to be handled!"

"But, gee whiz! To build — right there before us — to take a hunk of mammary muscle — "

"Not just *any* old hunk!"

"I know, I know! But it was breast muscle, wasn't it? O.K. So this genius — or idiot — takes the stuff and — "

"It was vessels and adjacent muscles, which would logically be used to serve as a source of collateral vessels in the situation where the coronary blood flow was not sufficient — "

"Yeah! But he built this thing — this — this pedicle, he called it — and planted it into the incision in the myocardial wall — "

"Sam Miller has been doing a lot of work testing arterial pressures to ensure a gradient between donor and recipient arteries . . . "

"I know. Sam's one of the team. He works like an extra pair of hands for Gage."

"You wouldn't think he would, or could . . . "

"I understand they've broken off completely. Him and Marshall, I mean."

"Gage and . . . ?"

"Aggh! *Miller* and Marshall!"

"Oh, that's too bad."

"Yes, it is, but I guess things got rough — "

"If they loved each other, they should have roughed the thing through."

Aaron snorted and went out of the room. If those two had not broken, Miller would have been accused of ingratitude to the surgeon who had trained him so brilliantly. You simply could not win in this rat race. You could not possibly win!

"When anyone asks what your medical training cost, tell him *this* . . . "

Well, Sam Miller, too, now knew exactly what his medical training was costing him. And he was such a nice guy, as well as a splendid doctor. Was the ability to do jobs like the one today going to be worth the cost?

312

Aaron changed his clothes and made rounds. Then he sat down at the desk to write night orders. He was faced with thirty-seven chart books, each of which contained the complete history of a patient in varying degrees of illness. At this minute the rack of them loomed enormous before him.

Aaron wondered if Sam Miller was enjoying his work as much these days as he had before. Aaron was not. Today had been a real drag for him. The worst he had ever known as intern or resident. Too many worries crowded his brain.

He laid down his pencil and rubbed his eyes against the glare of the wall light that shone down on the desk. He had not slept much last night. He picked up the pencil. He had thought he had worries enough before — most of them having to do with money.

But now there was Laurie to worry about, as he had not worried about her before. He could count on Laurie — she was a great girl.

Ah-hum. A great girl. Due to become greater. The stale old joke was metallic in his mouth. Laurie would face motherhood bravely and joyfully — under any other circumstances. But as things were . . . Of course Aaron worried about her.

He made a mistake on a chart and erased what he had written, chiding himself below his breath. A nurse brought him a release to sign, and he did it, managing a smile for the girl. "I'll speak to Mr. Archer before he leaves if you'll warn me, Tina."

"Yes. I'll yoo-hoo."

Aaron chuckled. "You do just that."

Tina was a great girl too.

And now Laurie blamed herself for spoiling things for Aaron. But of course she was *not* to blame! Youth and old Mother Nature were the culprits if any existed.

He could tell himself that he should not have taken on even a first-year residency, and certainly not agreed on a second, but with the opportunities presented to him as possibilities, he would not have been happy with that situation either.

So — let him get through with his charts today. Let him take Mr. Archer down to his car and be as reassuring as he could be to the old gentleman.

"If I thought I could believe you, young man, when you tell me I'll be fine — "

"I'll make a bargain with you, sir. If you'll be fine, I'll be fine too."

"Put it the other way round, Dr. Battle. The odds are better for you youngsters."

"Not these days, sir," said Aaron. "Not always." He shook the man's hand, white and thin from his illness. He smiled, closed the door, and watched the limousine drive away. Mr. Archer was exceedingly rich, but all his money could not give him back the lung which he had lost.

Money could ease a sick man's misery, and it did ease him. He could afford the best of care; he could go to Arizona to recuperate. He need not worry about paying the bills, or —

Money figured in Aaron's present situation too. He stopped at the coke machine and held the cold bottle gratefully to his lips. The money he did not have and the money he would have some day were big items with him. If Aaron continued his training — if he could continue — he might, one day, offer Laurie a notable success as a doctor in place of the failure which her husband now appeared to be. He was not able to pay his family bills; he was not able to be glad about the baby; he was not able even to offer his wife day-to-day companionship.

Aaron went back upstairs and found Dr. Barr on the floor, dressed in a suit of hard gray tweed, with a tie striped in charcoal and pale gold. He was about to depart for a medical convocation in Los Angeles. There he would deliver one of the major addresses, as well as serve on a roundtable seminar of chest surgeons. Mrs. Barr had come for him, and Dr. Barr introduced Aaron to her.

"One of my young doctors, Ethel."

She was charming; she was kind. She was sure they would miss their plane if they stopped one more time! Aaron watched them as they disappeared into the elevator. They were nice people, a successful doctor and his wife.

Aaron could picture Laurie twenty years from now, wearing a smart suit — hers would be blue, or the green which she liked — but the mink jacket would be the same. She would be prettier than Mrs. Barr, but just about as proud and possessive of her important husband.

Aaron drew his lips back against his teeth and spoke to Sam who had just come down from Recovery.

Aaron should tell someone that he could not do his second-year residency, but if he did not do it, all he could give Laurie would be a notable failure.

He went back to his chart desk. He answered the nurse's summons to a patient. He went down to E.R. and brought a patient upstairs. And he thought.

Oh, not a failure actually. He would still have his M.D. He could borrow money enough to get himself established in some sort of practice and, as experience accumulated, he would probably earn enough that he and

Laurie would live rather well. By now he knew that he could be a good doctor. . . .

The thing for him to do would be to talk to Laurie, lay out the whole thing for her, the possibilities, the probabilities. He would discuss with her the possibility of borrowing enough money for him to do further residencies. It need not be too much if she would consent to live with his parents.

He knew she did not want to do that, and he didn't want it either! But it might offer a way . . . The thing was to be sure she saw this matter from all sides. Tonight, when she came to eat dinner with him, he would talk to her. He might even bring her up here on the floor and show her the sort of work they did — that he did and would do . . .

Before this he should have talked to her more particularly about his work and done it more often. He should have kept her knowledgeable about some individual patients, their problems, and their progress.

His work was her work, too, in many ways. For one thing, if she invested her years and her youth in it, as much as he did, she should understand about it.

Tommy's wife had not understood. Aaron could wince now to remember the way Carol had used to nag Tommy, and *nag* him! To take her to some party, to buy her some dress, or a necklace — to go to the Springs for a week. Tommy couldn't do those things, but she was a spoiled and selfish woman, and she had no understanding of his work. So she quit —

Well, of course, Laurie was not spoiled or selfish, but she should understand something of Aaron's work. Then perhaps they could find a way . . .

On that particular Monday Laurie, too, went to work, tired, discouraged, and determined that no one should guess how she felt or the reason behind it. She put on her new knitted suit, the light-blue one with the cocoa blouse; she smiled when the young law clerk whistled at her, and she told Marie, the file clerk, where she had bought it.

"I paid too much — "

She went into Mr. Hulsey's office, made his desk ready for him, adjusted the blinds, fiddled some with the flowers on the side table, and put a single narcissus into a bud vase on his desk.

She took a list of reference books to the library. Mr. Hulsey, she said, had asked to have them on his desk.

"Can't he come back here?"

"He could," said Laurie. "You tell him."

She went out of the library, her heels twinkling, her golden hair bouncing a little. She typed some letters and answered the telephone, her manner brisk, smiling, efficient.

Alone, she looked at her watch and sighed. Mark had several interviews scheduled, beginning at eleven. He would arrive by then. Meanwhile she would catch up on things, forget that she was tired and worried. So worried that it was the only aspect of the baby which she felt. Or which Aaron had felt. Worry about how they would manage.

This should be, she thought resentfully, a lovely time for her. She should be happy, her dreams should be rosy — and, really, she guessed they were. Only —

How *would* they manage? She could not stay in their present apartment. There would be suggestions again of her moving in with the Battles, and now she might have to, but — but —

Mark came in at ten minutes before eleven; he greeted Laurie in much the same tone of cordial friendliness that she had heard him use to Sally out at the reception desk. He looked at Laurie — well, perhaps he had looked at Sally too.

At any rate, he was kind and pleasant. He was "afraid" they would have a long session with his new client. "I'll want you to sit in, Laurie."

"Yes, sir."

His eyebrow went up, and he smiled at her. "You look very pretty today," he said. "A new dress, isn't it?"

"I — yes, it's new."

"Nice. If we run over your lunch hour, I'll make it up to you.

He would try. That, these days, was the trouble with Mark's being nice to her. Underneath there was, too often, the suggestion that he expected her to be "nice" as well.

As she established herself, her book, and her pencil at the side table, as she sat there while Mark did the preliminaries of getting acquainted with his new client — the man seemed to be accused of some very complicated skulduggery in the construction business — Laurie thought, longingly, how good it would be to dump all of her problems on Mark. He was so quick to understand.

This morning he had sensed her mood and, not mentioning it, had offered her kindness. She wished she could lean on him, accept the help he would offer, let him —

She shivered and drew her shoulders together. What was she thinking of? She knew the danger of letting herself be engulfed in Mark's kindness, his — his — well, his interest. It frightened her that she should ever, for one second, consider the pleasantness of surrender to him. Because it would be pleasant, and this was not the first time she had thought longingly of the ease and comfort there would be — in —

She brought her attention back to what was being said there at the big desk. Mark's voice was a fine one; he was careful to speak clearly so that Laurie could set down the important items. He would repeat some answer the client made, mumbling. Mark did not look at Laurie, but he knew she was there. Did he know how aware she was today of this luxurious room, of the view from the wide windows, of the feeling of security in this place?

Oh, it didn't matter what Mark knew! It was her own reaction she must consider and control.

This morning she had come to the office determined to be cool, aloof — and here she was, ready to sway like a grass stem before the first breeze of his charm. Her own wish could *too* easily become his wish. She shifted in her chair and knew that Mark glanced at her.

So she should get away from him, clear away. She must reorient her thinking and analyze her behavior, past, present, and probable. She was making a big mistake to stay around Mark, she knew that she was making a mistake —

She knew what she should do, and, want to or not, she must force herself to act.

Finally the client had told his story. Mark was smiling at him and, walking him to the door, saying something about sending books and records over — he was hearty and reassuring — and he would be back.

Laurie stood up; she gathered her pencils and her notebook.

"Now!" Mark was saying, returning to his desk. "Will those get cold if we grab a steak sandwich before you get to work on them, Laurie?"

"I'll type them this afternoon," said Laurie. "But first, Mr. Hulsey, I must tell you that I have decided to give up my position here, as your secretary."

He turned sharply to look at her. He was surprised and stunned. "You can't do a thing like that!" he cried.

Laurie bit her lip and raised her head high as it would go. "No," she said firmly, "I can't give up a job like this. But — I am doing it."

"Oh, now, Laurie." He came around his desk toward her. "Let's think about this. You need this job, don't you?"

"Yes, sir," she said bravely, "I do."

He stood looking down at her, shaking his head. "Oh, Laurie," he said sadly, "I am sorry."

She nodded and tried to pass him. She was sorry too.

"Wait a minute," he urged. "If I'm to blame — " Charming as always, he sounded as if he were, truly, sorry. "I've never had this sort of thing happen before," he assured her. "You believe that, don't you?"

"Yes, Mr. Hulsey."

"All right, call me *Mr. Hulsey*. But you will stay, won't you? Because I need you, Laurie. I really do!"

She looked down at the book where she had made so many notes. He did need her. But . . . She shook her head. "No," she said again. "I won't stay."

He let her go then. In ten minutes he went out to lunch, saying only when he would be back. While he was gone, she slipped downstairs for a sandwich and a cup of coffee. That afternoon she typed up her notes. Mark returned to the office but was busy in the library. Laurie left without talking to him again.

Seated in the bus, which was a particularly noisy, bumpy one, she faced what she had done. How was she ever going to tell Aaron about *this?*

Would she — should she — tell him why she had quit her job?

Now there would be a real worry to present to him along with his bowl of soup. And the poor guy already was carrying all the worry he could manage. Why should she burden him further? She was handling things from her end. Aaron was doing a long stretch of "time" at his precious hospital, which often, to Laurie, seemed a very hard jail.

Service in it had killed Tommy and perhaps was doing even worse things to Sam Miller.

So—

No. Laurie would not add another worry to Aaron's heap. She would find herself another job and then tell him. Not that it was going to be easy to find another good job. If she was pregnant, she would have to say so.

But she would find something! She'd contact some agencies tomorrow. Good secretaries with legal experience were always desired.

She went home, changed her clothes, and walked over to the hospital, glad that the day was a warmish spring one. Because she wanted to talk to Aaron, and because he especially wanted to talk to her, of course they were given no chance to talk at all. They got a small table, but the people close by, or who came along, all had things to say.

It was frustrating, but this sort of thing often happened. Aaron did get to walk her to the door.

"You look tired," she told him.

"I am tired. I did surgery today."

"*You* did?"

"Yes. I'm supposed to be trained for that,

324

you know. But I'm still young enough at it that I make too big a deal of removing a rib."

Laurie tied her filmy blue scarf around her head. "Well, I should think so!"

He grinned. "How about you? Are *you* all right?"

She nodded, her face serene. "I'm fine."

"Really?"

"Yes, really."

"I'll try to get a few hours tomorrow."

"You do that."

"Well, be careful. And get home safely."

It always worried him, that block-and-a-half walk to the apartment. But tonight she made it without any incident. She bought a paper and spent an hour checking the wanted columns. She furbished her clothes, doing things she had not been able to do with Aaron at home over the weekend. She was successful in not giving one thought to Mark. She went to bed at nine-thirty and slept like one exhausted. Which she evidently was.

Something woke her early — the sky was just beginning to lighten. A fire engine, or an ambulance for the hospital — a siren screamed beneath her windows. Laurie shivered and turned over, then she sat straight up in bed.

She was *not* pregnant. She was not! And *now* what was she going to do?

325

Half laughing, half crying at her own question, Laurie hugged her arms across her breast. She felt odd. She was even a little disappointed. Yes, she really was. She had come to the place where she was beginning to consider the baby — a baby — as a reality of small hands, a round smooth head, tiny-boned shoulders . . .

But she was also tremendously relieved. Oh, enormously relieved! Now there wasn't a worry in the world for her and Aaron. She wanted to call him; she wanted to call her mother-in-law.

Of course she couldn't and didn't. Not at six in the morning! But — well, life certainly had taken on a new look. Completely! From here on, she determined, things would be a breeze! She just hadn't known when they were good!

She dressed and went to the office, her step springy, her smile quick.

"Did you inherit money?" asked Sally, the receptionist.

"Oh no," said Laurie. Then she stopped. "Well, maybe I did," she conceded. "Or just as good."

Boy, had she ever been down!

But now . . .

She extended her lunch hour and went to a couple of agencies; the results were promising. She would, she said, be free to change the middle of the month. Yes, she thought she could arrange an interview. Oh, she was sure Mr. Hulsey would recommend her. Her reason for leaving? Criminal defense work was pretty depressing, you know? She rounded her blue eyes and looked as empty-headed as she could.

This was her day. That evening she and Aaron managed to get a table alone and few people bothered them. She could bounce a little in her chair and tell him at once. . . .

He stared at her, unbelieving.

"It's true," she said.

His hands reached out for hers. "Oh, Laurie," he cried. Then he leaned toward her. "Are you sorry?"

"Well, a little. If it had been a baby — and I had lost it — but this wasn't that. Was it?"

He smiled gently. "I don't think so, dear. Probably just a matter of nerves, tension."

She stared at him. "But why should I have nerves like that?" she demanded.

He was being so nice to her! As loving and kind as the time and place would permit.

She had every reason for nerves and tension, he told her. And she did have, but he didn't know. Oh, she was glad she hadn't told him. . . .

"I'll have to watch myself, won't I?" she

asked. "These barrel rides are rough!"

He laughed and shrugged. She laughed, too, but she was shaken and showed it. "It's like being given a second chance," she told him solemnly.

"Yes, it is. Eat your dinner, Laurie."

"I will. But — I've been thinking. What we are doing can seem so wrong, Aaron. And yet — it isn't, is it?"

"You mean, living alone, and not daring to have children — "

"Yes, and your working too hard . . . "

"But it isn't wrong, Laurie. We must know that. We must look toward our purposes. If they can seem worth while, then we are doing the right thing. Look!" he said. "Our situation isn't too much like Sam's and Linda's, but if they think his becoming a great heart specialist is worth what they are willing to sacrifice for it, our working hard and being lonely for each other — "

Laurie picked up her fork. "Do I think that is worth while? Well, whether I do or not — and I don't, always — it does seem to be something we have to go through. Or I guess we do."

"I'm afraid we do," Aaron conceded. "And I am going to spend some time trying to show you that it will be worth while."

"I think of you as being in jail," Laurie told him.

"Except that I want to be where I am, doing what I am doing."

"Then I guess we're both crazy."

He laughed and shook his head.

Laurie ate the last of her roast pork. "It would seem," she said, a note of desperation in her voice, "that there could be some better solution to a problem like ours, Aaron. We're not the only ones who face it. If doctors must be trained, there just must be a way to do it without turning him and his whole family into old men and women — "

"Hey, hey!" he cried. "We've been given that second chance. Remember?"

"Yes, I remember. But — will you get a raise next year?" Yes, she was desperate.

"A hundred dollars. I'll be paid a hundred dollars a month instead of seventy-five."

She tapped her fingers on the table, counting. "That will help," she conceded. "I can go to the dentist, and — well, yes, it will help." Then her attention focused on him. "But when I think," she cried, "that all over the country young doctors are going through what we are — "

"Enough are," he told her. "And they must think it worth while. Though, to be honest with you, some residents are better paid."

"Why not you?"

"Because I am a resident here at University,

one of the really great teaching hospitals. I work under Gage and Barr, the absolutely very best in their field. This hospital takes in a big percentage of non-pay patients in order to teach its residents. We get a wide spectrum of cases, and we consider the experience we get, the teaching we get, to be a part of our pay."

"You can't tell that to the dentist," she said bluntly.

He smiled. "Nor to the barber."

"And isn't there any way . . . ?"

"I have heard that better pay for residents — all residents — is a problem which should be argued publicly, because the most likely source of increase would be from health insurance. Then if people knew they could get better care by paying more, they might be ready to have their contributions increased."

"Oh, that sounds wonderful!" cried Laurie.

Aaron smiled at her. "There is talk of the doctor shortage, you know?" he asked her.

"Well — is there one?"

"Yes. And much is said about more and bigger medical schools."

She waited.

"I feel that some consideration should be given to preventing so many unfulfilled internships and residencies."

She thought about that, and he watched her. He always enjoyed watching Laurie, the way her lashes made dark, velvety crescents on her cheeks. The sweet line of her lips . . .

"I think I understand," she said. "You almost had to stop your training because I could have been pregnant. And Tommy — "

"That's it. Being just as careful as ever about allotting residencies, some effort should be made to help the best schools pay their residents a living wage."

"So that a doctor will be on hand when a person is sick — "

"Mhmmmn. We have to sell it to the public that, when one is well, he must forget the irritation there is behind his paying higher insurance premiums and remember what a fearful threat the missing doctor, the missing skill, is to someone who is sick."

Laurie reached for his hand. "Oh, Aaron!" she cried. "You are wonderful!"

He laughed. "That makes two of us."

Five minutes later the enunciator called him away, and Laurie went home, only mildly disappointed. She was too busy trying to remember the things he had said. It came out pretty well that doing what seemed wrong could be analyzed into seeming very right indeed.

But then, she thought, as she unlocked her front door, what she had done to Mark by resigning could seem wrong too. Today he had been really sweet to her — and the job as his

331

secretary was certainly a good one. Maybe she should have tried harder to convince him that she was ready only to be his secretary.

She could try again. Tomorrow she could tell him that she would try again. . . .

But — no! She would not! She knew what she should do, and the trick was to do it!

That evening Aaron had been called upstairs to examine a newly admitted patient. This was a return case. The man had been with them before and refused surgery; now his condition was such that the intern had wanted the resident's help with the examination.

Aaron, in turn, having checked the man in and given orders, went down the hall to talk to Sam about the case.

Sam listened, went to look at their man, and walked back with Aaron. "Thoracoplasty," he said gruffly. "It's his only chance."

This was radical surgery — permanently to collapse a man's lung.

"You must first check on the good lung," said Sam.

"Yes."

"Do that tomorrow, and schedule the surgery as soon as possible afterward. How about your doing it, Battle?"

Aaron shut his eyes against the thought. Swiftly his mind went over the surgery needed.

A section of the protective ribs would be removed. The operation — Aaron had watched, and assisted with, several. He knew how the white flesh would look against the incision, which would curve down the back, starting at mid-shoulder, and parallel the spine, as far as between the eighth and ninth rib, then forward until the tenth was reached — the white ribs, the parted fascia . . .

It would take a delicate touch to slit the membrane just enough, to lift each rib, and cut it —

"I can't do it!" he said loudly.

Sam grinned at him. "Of course you can do it."

"I'd have to have someone standing by."

"There will be someone. Come on in here. I've some anti-shock coffee on tap."

Aaron followed him into the chief resident's office, a small, neat room. Books on the shelves, papers in neat piles, a comfortable desk chair, a couch where a man could stretch out or Aaron now could sit. Gratefully he accepted the coffee. "This has been a day," he announced.

"Oh?"

"Yes. You see — " And he told about Laurie's "pregnancy."

"It gave us plenty to worry about, Sam," he admitted. "But the real shock came when we realized that we felt our only joy when we found it wasn't true. And — both of us — we decided that was pretty damn wrong!"

Sam nodded.

"It didn't take us five more minutes, either," said Aaron, "to decide that the whole damn system was wrong."

Sam drank his coffee. "It can seem that way," he said mildly.

"I should think you'd know about that!" Aaron cried angrily.

"I do," Sam agreed. "I've gone the course. I decided against taking a girl through it."

"But —"

"I didn't say I made the right decision there, Battle. I've made some gaudy mistakes in the last half-dozen years."

Aaron could think of no comment.

"It's a little like looking at a case, you know," said Dr. Miller. "You have a child, maybe, with a serious heart defect. Venous block, or some such. You operate, perhaps several times. There's a lot of trauma — just the stripping down of a vein can do things to the kid — and you have bleak moments of wondering if hands-off would not have been kinder. The kids cry, you know. They want to play baseball, and — they can't even be allowed to be naughty, to throw a tantrum. And you wonder. Then — you think. We brought that boy in here to make him well. We've known it would take time. And it has taken time. But after a couple of years, or three — and all the trauma — the kid is well. You can give him a baseball when he leaves the hospital. And when you look at the beginning and at the end — it does seem worth while."

Aaron nodded. He liked the chief resident. From his first time of meeting Sam, a raw medical student, and again as a frightened, grass-green intern, Sam had shown real interest in Aaron Battle.

He was interested in him now. He would hand-lead him through his first thoracoplasty, and Aaron would never forget him. If Dr. Battle ever became a good surgeon, the training of Sam Miller had been worth while.

He tried to say something of this, so clumsily that he embarrassed Sam in doing it. "But," Aaron blurted in conclusion, "I like Linda too. She is a really fine person!"

Sam nodded. His own face was grave, but all protest had been rubbed away. "We love each other, very deeply," he said quietly. "So much that we have had to accept the fact that nothing can come of our love. I would be willing to make any sacrifice — and I am sure she would. Except the one sacrifice she says we cannot make."

Aaron looked up questioningly. "What . . . ?"

"The destruction of our love for each

335

other," said Sam. He got up and refilled his cup. "You see, she argues this way. She says my career is a part of me."

Aaron nodded.

"She says that my being a good heart surgeon is part of the man she loves."

It was. "But," asked Aaron, "wouldn't she love you still if you lost a part of that career — say, if you had to give up working here with Gage, or doing the surgery he now does? The things you can have by not marrying her?"

"Your question is, would she love me as much, or still? Say, if I lost all chance of some day being head of the Heart Surgery project here at University. Well, that's a somewhat trite question, you know."

Aaron frowned.

"Sure it is," said Sam. "It's like asking should a girl stay by a man who has lost his leg. And the answer is trite too. Yes, she would still love me. Which sounds like the complete answer, doesn't it?"

Aaron waited.

"But Linda thinks — Linda is *sure* — that, after time went by, *I* would not love *her*. Because of what she had cost me, you see."

"Wouldn't you?" asked Aaron.

"I don't know."

Aaron shook his head. "It seems like a tremendous sacrifice. And it is. But you've come to accept it, haven't you?"

Sam shrugged. "I have no choice."

"Mhmmmn." Aaron looked up. "Is medicine worth that much?" he asked keenly.

"I guess it could be," said Sam.

Aaron stood up, dropped his cup into the wastebasket. "I guess it has to be," he said grimly.

CHAPTER 12

Laurie herself laughed at the strange way in which life's current could be changed.

She had on Tuesday evening, after coming home from eating dinner with Aaron, decided she should call her mother-in-law and tell her the news, that they'd not be needing the booties she supposed Margaret Battle had already begun to turn out.

Margaret was a little hurt that she had not heard from Laurie before this. Hadn't Aaron had a free weekend?

Well, not really. Only Saturday night and Sunday . . .

But the thing she called about . . .

"Well!" said Mrs. Battle. "I know you are relieved."

"I have to be relieved," said Laurie. "We can't afford a baby just now."

"No, I don't suppose you can. Though I imagine you would have found a way."

"Yes. But this way is better."

"I suppose. And now you can devote all

your time to helping Aaron, can't you?"

Laurie had thought she already was so devoting her time. But maybe not.

She hung up, repeating the words. It didn't make a bad slogan. She would devote all her time — to helping — Aaron. And work at the decision, make it a full-time project.

Though she hated the source of it. Only she must *not* go hating things her mother-in-law did and said — and —

Well.

She sat thinking. Idly her hand reached for a pencil, and she wrote the words on the memo pad beside the phone. "Take care of Aaron."

Again she sought to defend herself. Hadn't she been doing just that?

Well, not really. She had, it was true, taken care of herself so that he could do his "time" at the hospital, but there were ways and instances when she had thought first of Laurie — and scarcely at all of Aaron.

From where she sat she could see the light-blue suit hanging against the bathroom door. She must put it back into the dress bag. She should never have bought that suit. It was much too expensive, and she had not needed it, except for the times she would be with Mark and wanted to look well.

There! She should never have let those times crop up. She had worked in offices long enough to know dallying when she saw it. And when she did it too. There were sweet, and firm, ways to refuse the luncheon invitations, the offered drinks.

Probably, now that she was leaving, Mark wished she had employed those ways. It was going to be a nuisance for him to break in a new girl. If she had controlled things, Laurie would not now have to consider new job possibilities or need, herself, to break in to a new office's ways.

Even Aaron had been hurt — or he would have been, had he known what was going on. He would have known, too, or guessed, if he had not been so busy and so tired.

Though maybe he had guessed. Or even known. Tommy had seen her with Mark, and if he had spoken of that to Aaron . . . But Aaron had concealed this knowledge from her, thinking that she would realize what she was doing and stop, thinking that the thing could be better stopped if he would seem to ignore it. Because Aaron trusted her —

Well, O.K.! He *could* trust her! She had acted foolishly but not dishonestly. Though she had come close enough to the edge to recognize reprieve when she saw it. If she needed to wear that blue suit every day to remind her, she would never again give Aaron any chance to wonder about trusting her. As of the next day she would get another job. Already she knew of a couple — a legal secretary was in demand; she would take a job and go into it as fresh and interested as, last year, she had started to work for Mark Hulsey.

Last summer, when she had been a bride . . . Well, she could feel like a bride again. Start fresh, a new year for Aaron, a new job for Laurie — she would do everything she had done last summer. She would plan her clothes and her budget — she would be that eager "bride" again. Could she? Wiser as she was, with a bruise or two still able to make her wince? But, yes, she could start anew and feel for Aaron all she had felt for him last June, then perhaps build her feeling into more. She loved the man; now that she knew him better — how kind he was, how trusting, how grateful to Laurie — she understood his work better than she had a year ago. Tonight he had really talked to her. She could try to get him to talk to her again. And again.

For a week she ate dinner with Aaron every night, not changing into something old after she got home from work; sometimes she even put on a clean blouse with her suit, and she always burnished her hair and freshened her makeup, endeavoring to shine her spirit to match. One evening he was free for a few

341

hours; he came home tired, and she let him doze on the couch all evening. Though she had selected a movie, should he have seemed ready for diversion.

He was grateful for the unwinding, and she was glad she had done it. It was what she wanted too. She found that it was really no effort to think of him first. His second free night, when he brought home a stack of case histories to read, she listened when he talked about the particular case he was studying. And she was, she found, really interested in why people would delay an operation they knew they must have.

She and Aaron spent an interesting, and amusing, hour talking about the fears people were subject to and the pretenses with which they sought to cover those fears.

"So you have to diagnose this patient's fears as well as decide what is wrong with his lung," said Laurie acutely.

Aaron looked at her. "Hey!" he said. "You're catching on."

She shrugged. "Just throw me a line now and then — "

"I'll do it," promised Aaron. "I've decided that I've got me a smart wife, as well as a pretty one, and a cuddly one, and a — "

Well, love-making was definitely a part of it too. And that, she had always known, was easy when the man was Aaron.

The next morning she was up before the alarm went off, cute as a button, Aaron told her, in her white pajamas, with a red bandanna tied around her hair. When he came out of the bathroom she had coffee and orange juice waiting for him. And the information that she was, that day, changing to her new job.

He choked on the orange juice. "What new job?" he asked.

"I surely told you — "

"Not me."

"It must have been two other guys. Why, Aaron, I decided last month. This office is on Grand Drive. That's much closer than downtown. The pay is about the same.

Aaron came to stand in front of her. "Why?" he asked.

"I'm telling you. I like this job better."

"I always thought you liked Hulsey fine."

"I did. But — well, I'll like this job better. It's a big office — there are five partners. They do estate law. I'm to be secretary to an older man. Well — really, I'm hired to take the load off his secretary. She's getting old." Laurie giggled. "She's called Old Faithful in the office. But she's really a marvelous old girl."

Aaron watched her. When Laurie chattered, she always, sooner or later, said what she wanted to say. He had fifteen minutes to wait.

"She knows everything," said Laurie. "She can do anything. She has so much seniority, Aaron, that the other girls stand aside for her when she comes into the washroom. And in a pinch the boss man relies on her judgment more than he does on that of the next senior partner. The firm simply could not operate without her."

"What part of the load will you take off this woman?"

"I'll be the boss man's secretary too. Take dictation, you know. I'm going to like working with an older man."

Aaron reached for his black tie. "Why?" he asked. "Did you have trouble with the younger one?"

Laurie's cheeks flamed, and she was angry at the betrayal.

"Laurie?" he persisted gently.

"I didn't let it be trouble!" she said defiantly.

"Oh, Laurie, Laurie." He came closer to her and held her in the circle of his arm. "To think that I'd put you in danger of wolves and things."

"There wasn't any danger," she told him spiritedly. "Not the way I love you."

He kissed her, and she responded warmly. Then he put her away from him to look into her eyes. "Is the wolf to blame for your loving me more lately?" he asked.

"I've always loved you, Aaron."

"Yeah." But there had been a difference lately. Just lately. A week or so. Though he had better shut up about that. "I like it," he said, reaching for his jacket. "You just keep looking out for me and my needs — spoil me rotten — "

"I'm not spoiling you. I — well, don't you think it's time I began to understand a little about your work and what it takes out of you."

"Maybe you're right," he teased. "And I like that too. He picked up his thick folder of histories.

"I know I haven't been much help to you this past year, not understanding, you know . . ."

He pulled at the corner of the bandanna. "*That* wasn't in our contract. For you to know medicine."

"No-o. But it does make it easier for me to understand when your back aches if you'll tell me a little bit why."

He thought that over. "I guess it would," he admitted. "I'll try to remember about that. Though you may get tired of lungs and ribs and hearts and stuff.

"Do you get tired of 'em?"

"That's different."

"But no, it isn't, Aaron. Not really. If you can make them seem as important to me as they are to you — "

"I'll try," he said again. "Did you write your new telephone number down?"

She gave him a slip of paper, and he put it in his wallet, keeping one eye on the histories which he had had to set down. He must not leave them behind.

"Not that you ever call me," she said.

"I hope I don't ever need to. But look — maybe I should tell you that I'll be making a change, too, next week."

"You're going to Eads?"

He stared at her. "What do you know about Eads?"

She shrugged. "You mentioned it last fall. You said you would be going there this spring. I've been expecting to hear you *were* there."

"Oh, Laurie! I would have told you!" His sense of guilt made his tone sharp.

"I hope. How long will you be there?"

Until the end of June."

"Will you like it?"

He laughed. She could ask the most un-expected questions. "No," he conceded, "I don't think I will like it. But I have to do it. If next year I want to be first assistant on Thoracic, this year I have to do my full assignment as second in general surgery."

"There isn't any *if* about your wanting to be a first assistant, is there, Aaron? I thought that was something we both wanted."

"*We*," he said softly. "We." He kissed her, and she clung to him.

"I'll worry about you at Eads," she told him.

"Because of the inmates?"

"Why not? Crazy people?"

"Let's call them disturbed."

"I know about Eads. They even put the criminally insane there. And you'll be in an operating room with them, and knives —"

"And a good strong anesthesia," he added. "I'll have another doctor with me, too, you know. Nurses and trained attendants — Besides, I won't do a lot of surgery. Maybe."

"Maybe?"

"Well, other chaps who have done this tour tell me that some surgery comes up, of course. But it's more apt to be a broken bone or a cut — from a fall, honey. A *fall!* Of course, there are emergencies, among the personnel as well as the patients. Appendectomies, I suppose. Strangulated hernia —"

"Can you do those things, Aaron?" Laurie asked, genuinely concerned.

He stared at her. "Of course I can do them!"

"Well, I didn't know —"

"Look. Last June you thought I was ready to practice medicine on my own, didn't you?

Her face brightened. "Oh yes!" she cried. "I did! And that's what you'll be doing at this big institution, won't you?"

"That's what I'll be doing."

"Can I come down there when you have a free weekend?"

"Once a month. Your coming down will save me the time the trip takes, though it will be rough on you, Laurie."

"Pooh!" she said. "You and I — we get all sorts of roughness, don't we?"

He could not smile about it. "Yes," he said ruefully, "we do." He glanced at his watch. "Look. Grab your coat and walk a way with me — we'll go the back way."

While she got her coat, he took a piece of bread from the kitchen. He might not make breakfast until midmorning.

Laurie came back wearing her raincoat, with her keys jingling in her hand. They started out, going down the stairs and out to the almost empty sidewalk, damp from last night's rain. The day was going to be a warm one.

"There's quite a lot of roughness to the full

training of a surgeon," Aaron told her, biting off a corner of the bread slice. "Or the training of any doctor, I guess. I was talking to Miller one night this past week about that. You know, Linda has decided that they must break up because, if they don't, some day Sam will look back and regret giving up the things he would have to give up to marry her."

"Would he?"

"As they get older? Maybe yes."

"The way you'd have regretted my having a baby — if I'd had one."

"Oh, Laurie!"

"Well, *I* would have regretted it. And I know how much Sam and Linda — and we — are willing to give up for medicine." Laurie spoke sadly.

"But Sam, dear — "

"And you."

"All right. And me. Once men like us get into it, — once we know we're the sort of man who has to be a doctor if he wants to live at all — yes, that kind of man is ready, or compelled, to make any sort of sacrifice."

Laurie nodded. "I guess you both have to think it's a bit more than worth while," she said soberly, "or you wouldn't stay with it at all."

Aaron glanced down at her. She looked so

young in her red bandanna, loose tan coat, and the white pajama trousers. "He couldn't stay with it," he said firmly. But there was regret in his face.

Laurie saw it. And she took a little skipping step. "Things are going to be all right for us now, Aaron," she said comfortably. "Because we never did go into this for the money in it, did we?"

He laughed. "I don't see how we could have." Then his face became stern again. His hand touched her arm, to restrain her step. They would wait for the corner light.

"Look, Laurie," he said, so seriously that she turned to gaze at him in wonder. "Take this as a rule. None of the doctors — old ones or new ones — who take five or six years of residencies have had the money motive behind their studying medicine."

Laurie pulled the red kerchief from her head and smoothed her fingers through her hair. It was like corn silk, pale and shining in the early light.

"Those years," said Aaron, "I see it in Miller. I see it in Dr. Barr — "

"And that awful Gage?"

"Gage is not an awful man, Laurie. He is a charming person and a simply perfect surgeon. But, yes, it's in him too. Those years of hard work, of sacrifice — of staying with the thing — they become like a scar that stays with a man."

Laurie nodded. She had already seen the beginning of that scar in Aaron. The terror about her pregnancy, the relief that they would not have a child — even last winter's coat . . . "It's too bad," she said, stepping into the street with him. They had come to the edge of the hospital compound. Before them, above them, rose the great buff brick buildings, like torches in the morning sunlight, their windows flashing.

"It's not really too bad," Aaron was telling her. "But it does stay with a man. It's *there!*"

Laurie took five steps, ten. "What about Linda now?" she asked. "Now that she's convinced Sam he must give her up."

"They both have agreed that it will be worth while, you know."

Laurie flipped this away with a wave of the red bandanna. "Your wonderful Dr. Gage should marry her," she said firmly.

"I think he will," said Aaron. "Or I believe I can promise their old relationship will never be renewed."

Laurie frowned. "I don't know, Aaron. Even if she used to be attracted to him — and all — it won't be the same as marrying Sam."

"No," Aaron agreed, "it won't be."

Laurie put her hand on his arm. "You

351

know what?" she said. "I'm glad you and I got married exactly when we did, Aaron Battle."

He laughed. "Now what does that mean?"

"Well, sure. Because we can go through all this turmoil together — earn His and Her scars, in a sense."

"Oh, Laurie! You can't be *glad* of a thing like that! Unless, of course, you like scars."

"They're all right, when they come in sets."

He chuckled. "You're a nut. And I just hope you continue to think the one you'll get will be worth what it takes to get it."

"Oh, I know these next years aren't going to be easy," she told him lightly. "But don't you suppose the wife of any resident has to know that an end will come to these years?"

He could not speak. She was so young — and so wise.

"And that it will be worth while?" she persisted.

"Will it be, Laurie?" he asked her tensely. "*Will* it be?"

"Oh, sure," she said. "It will be. Well — 'by now . . . " With a quick toss of her head she flipped her yellow hair back from her face. Tommy had used to do that. His too-long hair . . .

Aaron reached out his hand and pulled Laurie close to him. "Take care of yourself, honey," he said gruffly. "And — be happy."

She gazed at him. "You didn't get any coffee," she said regretfully. "And I made some — "

He laughed then. "I'm sorry," he told her. "This morning I would have loved your coffee!" He turned to run up the drive.

And she turned, poised to run down the street. "Who's a nut?" she called after him.